Praise for Lindsay McKenna

"Captivating. . . . The ever-present sensuality is a magnetic force that propels the novel forward amid simmering suspense."—*Publishers Weekly* on *Wind River Wrangler*, a Publishers Marketplace Buzz Books 2016 Selection

"Moving and real . . . impossible to put down."—*Publishers Weekly* on *Wind River Rancher* (starred review)

"Cowboy who is also a former Special Forces operator? Check. Woman on the run from her past? Check. This contemporary Western wraps together suspense and romance in a rugged Wyoming package."—Amazon.com's Omnivoracious, "9 Romances I Can't Wait to Read," on *Wind River Wrangler*

"Set against the stunning beauty of Wyoming's Grand Tetons, *Wind River Wrangler* is Lindsay McKenna at her finest! A *tour de force* of heart-stopping drama, gut-wrenching emotion, and the searing joy of two wounded souls learning to love again."—International bestselling author Merline Lovelace

"McKenna provides heartbreakingly tender romantic development that will move readers to tears. Her military background lends authenticity to this outstanding tale, and readers will fall in love with the upstanding hero and his fierce determination to save the woman he loves." —*Publishers Weekly* on *Never Surrender* (starred review)

"McKenna's dazzling eighth Shadow Warriors novel is a rip-roaring contemporary military romance novel with heart and heat."—*Booklist* on *Running Fire* (starred review)

"McKenna does a beautiful job of illustrating difficult topics through the development of well-formed, sympathetic characters."—*Publishers Weekly* on *Wolf Haven* (starred review)

Books by *New York Times* bestselling author
Lindsay McKenna

WIND RIVER WRANGLER

WIND RIVER RANCHER

WIND RIVER COWBOY

WRANGLER'S CHALLENGE

and coming in April 2018

LONE RIDER

Published by Kensington Publishing Corporation

WRANGLER'S CHALLENGE

LINDSAY McKENNA

ZEBRA BOOKS
KENSINGTON PUBLISHING CORP.
http://www.kensingtonbooks.com

ZEBRA BOOKS are published by

Kensington Publishing Corp.
119 West 40th Street
New York, NY 10018

First Printing: November 2017
ISBN-13: 978-1-4201-4534-2
ISBN-10: 1-4201-4534-7

eISBN-13: 978-1-4201-4537-3
eISBN-10: 1-4201-4537-1

10 9 8 7 6 5 4 3 2 1

Printed in the United States of America

To John Harrer,
whoapodcast.com,
who loves horses like I do!

Chapter One

A bad feeling snaked through Army Sergeant Dair Wilson. The late October Afghan night chilled her to the bone. Wind cut against her face where it was exposed. Zeus, her Belgian Malinois combat dog, strained at the leash she had double wrapped in her gloved fist. Without NVGs on, night vision goggles, she wouldn't see where the hell she was putting her booted feet as her dog plunged ahead.

Behind her, eleven men of her Army Special Forces A-team, were strung out with plenty of room in between them. It was ass-freezing cold, and she thinned her full lips, sensing Zeus as he sniffed ahead of her. They were on a rocky, icy slope above a valley where the Taliban were trying to take over an Afghan village. The CIA had picked up chatter that a Taliban HVA, high value target, was going to be meeting local soldiers and confer with them on assault strategy to take over the village.

Over my dead body. She and her A-team lived in that village two thousand feet below them. Dair knew the chief and his wife, and the two hundred villagers there.

They were simple farmers who had no guns or weapons to defend themselves. This A-team had taken up residence three years earlier and stopped the incursions from the bloodthirsty Taliban, who were now making a late autumn attack on the village before the snows fell hard and deep, stopping all such warfare.

Her boots slipped on the icy rocks. She mentally cursed. Zeus had his head down, his sides moving in and out like a bellows as he inhaled and exhaled the many scents. A path led up the six-thousand-foot slope filled with nothing but rocks and a few scraggly bushes hanging on, barely existing in this harsh environment.

They all knew that the Taliban would bury IEDs along the trail to kill the goats and young goat herders from the village below. Goats meant survival. Their skin and fur was used for warmth, their milk for the children, and their meat for food. The Taliban knew goats were the only survival, other than agricultural endeavors, for the people of this village. And they were trying to decimate the goat herds to force the village into starvation this coming winter. It would, from a strategy standpoint, make it easier for the Taliban to attack next spring and find little resistance among the starved populace.

Not on her watch. Their A-team was beloved by the unarmed Afghan farmers and their grateful families. They had lived for years in that village and become part of the everyday fabric of it. Her captain, Davis Ackerman, had brought a well-digging outfit from a global charity named Delos, and now the village had a clean water supply. Children stopped dying as a result.

The whole team had helped build a huge irrigation pattern in the agricultural fields where many types of vegetables were now being grown. The military team worked alongside the Afghan men every day with shovels, hoes, and pickaxes.

And tonight, they were going after the head of the snake. Dair was their specialist with a WMD dog. Zeus was intrinsic to their team because every morning, Dair went out around the walled village, and her dog sniffed and often found IEDs planted overnight by the Taliban, who had sneaked close beneath the cover of darkness. Zeus had saved countless lives and she fiercely loved her six-year-old Belgian Malinois.

The wind was erratic. A cold front was coming through. Dair worried about such times. If the wind blew away from Zeus's sensitive IED-trained nose, he would not pick up the scent of the deadly explosive buried just beneath the ground. If the wind blew toward his nose, he would pick up the scent.

She felt her spinal column crawling with danger. Dair thought it was because they were going to try and capture the HVT on the other side of this ridge at a small mud and stone house that Taliban often used as a stopover and meeting place.

She'd like nothing better than to get this bastard who was responsible for the repeated attacks on the Afghan village. No one wanted him more than she and Zeus did. The villagers knew the team was armed, and as they watched them troop out beyond the huge wooden gates, shutting them behind them at dusk, they knew something deadly was up. Dair had seen the worry in many of the men's eyes. They relied on their A-team for medical services, for extra food, clothing, and shoes for their children given by U.S. charities. They did not want the team being killed by the Taliban. Dair had seen it written silently in their expressions.

She wore a level three Kevlar vest, the weight of the ceramic plates making her breathing harder as they continued the steep climb toward the ridge line. It weighed thirty extra pounds upon her frame. Her M-4 carbine was hanging across her chest. Her drop holster with a .45 pistol was strapped to her right thigh.

Her friends, the rest of the A-team, moved like silent ghosts behind her. They trusted that Zeus would find any IEDs buried on the only path up this slope, before one of them stepped on it.

She loved her black-faced, fawn-colored dog. They were a tight team. Zeus slept with her in her small mud-and-rock hut. He kept her warm in the winter with his seventy-five-pound body curled tightly next to hers. He was a guard dog and would send up a warning growl when Taliban were lurking outside the seven-foot, mud-and-rock wall that kept the village safe. Often, she and some of the other sergeants would get up, armed, and with their NVGs on, let Zeus lead them to where he heard the enemy outside the wall.

Over time, the Taliban lost too many soldiers skulking around, looking for a way to infiltrate the village at night. They knew there was a WMD dog within the walls. And, after losing twenty-five soldiers at night to the sharp-eared dog, they stopped coming.

This was her fourth deployment with her team. They were all like big, doting brothers to her. And she was like a little sister to all of them. Dair earned her position on the black ops team because she was very good at what she did. She was five-foot-ten inches tall, and at a distance, most people thought she was a man. Until they got closer and saw her half-Comanche face, the black braids she always wore, and her cinnamon-brown eyes. Then they were surprised, because the villagers hadn't seen many women soldiers before. She was an anomaly in their world.

The wind slapped at her back, and Dair slowed Zeus.

The scent would be gone and he wouldn't find it. The dog halted, the leash taut between his collar and her gloved hand. Her mic was resting against her lips. "Take five. Wind is the wrong direction."

"Copy that," Davis said.

Dair knew the team would be glad for the momentary rest. They were all carrying at least fifty pounds of gear and ammo on them. They knew what it meant when the wind was cooperating, at the right angle for Zeus to properly scent the area. Because of the dog, they'd gone four years as a team without any IED injuries. Dair wanted to keep it that way.

She keyed her hearing, the edges of her ears freezing and numb. The tip of her nose was also numb. It was below freezing on this miserable slope. The sky was thick with clouds, promising snow at some point. She hated the white stuff because IEDs became even more troublesome to locate. Watching Zeus through her NVGs, the dog's ears were up and he was panting heavily, his ribs bowing in and out.

The wind shifted again, this time coming directly at Dair. She gave Zeus the unspoken order to start sniffing again. Instantly, the dog lunged against the leash, nose just above the surface, moving it from side to side, trying to pick up the scent of a buried IED.

Dair's whole focus, her whole world, relied on her brave dog. They were the point of the spear. If Zeus found an IED, he'd instantly sit down, a signal that one was nearby. Then, Dair would have to halt the column and the two explosives-trained sergeants from their team would come up and locate it and defuse it. Then, they'd move forward once more. Her mouth was dry and she pulled the tube to her CamelBak, sucking deeply. Staying hydrated was important. Soon, she'd have to stop and give Zeus water as well.

The wind shifted, slapping her on the right side of her face. Dropping the tube that was held in her shoulder epaulet, Dair tugged on the leash to stop Zeus. The wind was taking away the scents he needed to pick up.

Suddenly, there was a flash of red and yellow light. Dair heard Zeus yelp. Burning heat swept across her as she was flung off her feet, tumbling through the night air. A thousand impressions assailed her as she felt her arms windmilling and she cartwheeled end over end. The sound of the explosion broke both her eardrums. Simultaneously, a sharp pain assailed her left foot and ankle. And then, she lost consciousness.

Dair heard herself moaning and it pulled her out of her unconscious state. Burning pain was ripping up her left leg. Even through her shut eyes, the light hurt. Trying to move, she felt weighted, weak and incapable of moving a finger.

"Just be still, Sergeant Wilson. We're taking you on board a C-5 for Landstuhl Medical Center in Germany in about ten minutes. I'm going to give you a shot that will knock you out for the duration of our flight."

Dair frowned, not recognizing the male voice. Her mind was spinning. Fragments of memory assailing her. Zeus crying out. And someone had screamed. Had it been her? The scents entering her flared nostrils were of alcohol, bleach, and other nose-wrinkling medical odors. Where was she? What was happening? Where was Zeus? And then, she felt herself spinning down, down, down, and that's the last thing she remembered.

The next time Dair regained consciousness, she was in a bed, her left leg slightly suspended above where she lay. There were voices. Men's voices, nearby, so low she couldn't tell what they were saying. Her hearing came and went. She was so thirsty and her mouth felt like it was going to crack because it was so dry. Barely opening her eyes, she tried to take in where she was. There was a gnawing ache from her foot and ankle that were bandaged and in that sling. Staring at it, her vision would blur and then slowly sharpen once more. Her mind was offline as she lay there. Was she alive? She felt heavy, like ten thousand pounds of weight were pressing her down into the bed.

"Hey," a man called, "get the nurse. She's awake."

Dair didn't recognize the man's voice. It sounded so far away. Was she dreaming? In a nightmare? It took so much effort to lift her eyelids a bit more. A light blue wall stared back at her. She heard a door open and close.

"Welcome back, Sergeant Wilson."

Blinking, Dair was barely able to turn her head. A blond-haired woman, dressed in Army fatigues, her hair up on her head, stood next to her, a frown on her face. She looked to be in her thirties.

"Where . . ." she croaked.

"I'm Nurse Mills. You're presently at Landstuhl Medical Center, Sergeant." She checked the two IVs, one on each side of the bed. "You were injured when an IED went off in front of you," she said briskly, returning to her side. "You've sustained injury to your left foot and ankle." Her voice dropped and she reached out, her hand on Dair's blue-gowned shoulder. "I'm sorry, but your foot and ankle had to be amputated. That's why it's in a sling right now. You're going to live. The orthopedic surgeon created a way for you to wear a prosthesis, Sergeant. You'll be able to walk again, eventually. We'll be transferring you to

Bethesda Medical Center back in Washington, D.C., for rehabilitation and any further surgery you might need." She patted her arm. "You're alive, Sergeant. That's the best news."

Dair stared up at her, shock rolling through her, reeling from the tersely delivered information. Her emotions were muddled to begin with, but now, she felt as if that nurse had taken her fist and slammed it as hard as she could into her jaw, stunning her nearly semiconscious. Her mind barely grasped all of what she'd said. She'd spoken so fast that she missed some of the words. What she didn't miss was that her left foot and ankle had been amputated.

"I-I need water," she croaked.

"Yes," the nurse said, walking over to the rolling table. She poured her some. Coming back, she pushed a button, half the bed coming up into a gentle sitting position for Dair. The nurse pressed the straw between Dair's cracked lips. "Drink all you want. I'll get your physician to get you off IVs and onto fluids and light food such as Jell-O."

Dair drained the glass, wanting more. The nurse placed the tray in front of her. There was a pitcher of ice water and the glass. She poured her more, holding the glass while she drank. She was so weak she couldn't have poured it for herself.

"Are you in pain, Sergeant?"

Hell, yes! All she could focus on was that her foot and ankle had been amputated. "Just . . . ache in my left leg," she managed hoarsely.

The nurse filled the glass and set it on the tray. "I'll get your pain meds increased in that one IV," she said. Giving Dair a sympathetic look, her hand on her shoulder once more, she said, "I know this is a huge shock, Sergeant, but you're alive. There's hope for you. You'll be able to walk again someday. They have the best orthopedic people in the world at Bethesda. You're in good hands."

"Wait," Dair called, her voice rasping. "Where's Zeus?"

"What?" she asked, turning toward her. "Who's Zeus?"

"M-my dog. I'm a dog handler."

"I don't know," she said with a shrug, and left.

Dair sat there in turmoil. She recalled only pieces of the past, of standing on that cold-ass ridge in the dark of the night, Zeus sitting in front of her. That's all she could recall as she ruthlessly tried to force her brain to work and remember.

Tears jammed into her eyes. Frustration flowed like acid through her. She looked to her right. There were six other beds in the ward, occupied by injured men in blue pajamas. Like her, they had a leg or an arm suspended. Did that mean they were amputees like her? Dair didn't know, spinning internally, feeling lost, abandoned, and in need of someone . . . her team . . . to tell her what had happened to her. She felt movement nearby and opened her eyes.

"Davis!" she cried, her voice barely above a whisper. She looked at her captain, who had just entered the ward and come to her bed.

"Hey, Dair," he rasped unevenly, reaching out, sliding his hand into hers, giving it a small squeeze. "I'm sorry I couldn't get here sooner. Red tape." He searched her face. "How are you doing?"

Gulping, tears flowed into her eyes as she clung to his large, rough hand. "I-I don't know. What happened? No one will tell me anything. Where's Zeus?" She saw him wince, his dark brown eyes narrowing upon her, a wave of sadness around him. Davis was a great officer, treated her and all the rest of her team like friends, not officer over enlisted.

"No one's told you anything?" he demanded, voice filled with disbelief.

"I-I don't remember much," she said. "What happened?"

"God, I'm sorry," he said, his voice thick with emotion. "Do you remember we were out on that ridge at night? Hunting an HVT?"

"Yes . . . the only thing I remember is being cold on that ridge and Zeus sitting down in front of me because the wind changed again." She searched his gaze, saw the tiredness and regret in his expression. His hand tightened around hers.

"After you waited for the wind to change direction, you took off with Zeus on the leash. The team was a hundred feet behind you. The winds were erratic, Dair. Zeus stepped on an IED. I'm sorry . . ."

Stunned, she stared at him openmouthed. "NO!" she cried, sitting up. The movement caused immediate pain in her left leg. Gritting her teeth, she fell back against the bed, breathing raggedly, the fiery agony racing up her leg and into her abdomen. She felt Davis's hand on her shoulder, as if to steady her.

"I'm so sorry, Dair," he whispered brokenly, his fingers moving in calming strokes across her shoulder. "Zeus died instantly. The blast went sideways because your dog was in front of you. We saw the explosion and saw you being hurled out of it. When you landed on the ground, we raced up to where you were."

She tried to get ahold of her emotions. Zeus was dead. Her good friend of four years . . . gone. Open and closing her mouth, trying not to cry, she felt hot, warm tears trailing down her cheeks. She saw so much regret in Davis's eyes. She gulped several times. "W-was anyone else hurt?"

Shaking his head, he said, "No. We were all fine. Beat up by the pressure waves, a few bruises, but that's all. You were our focus, Dair." He looked at her bandaged left leg. "Our two medics worked on you immediately. Your left foot and boot were mostly destroyed. You were bleeding out. They placed a tourniquet around your lower leg, just below your knee, to stop you from dying." He wiped his mouth, his voice lowering. "We knew then that no one could save your foot or part of your lower leg, Dair. Ted and John flew back with you to Bagram, aboard the medevac we called. The rest of the team got back down that ridge and to the village. Later, Ted called me on the radio and you were already in your first surgery there at Bagram's hospital. He said they were amputating your foot and ankle, that there was no possible way to save it. I ordered Ted to remain with you, and ordered John back to us at the village. I was trying to get to Bagram to be with you myself, but the next morning, the Taliban attacked us. We repulsed it and we had no casualties of villagers or ourselves. Ted remained with you, even though the docs put you into a medical coma. He tried to persuade them to allow him to escort you when they flew you to Landstuhl two days later, but it was a no go. We hated leaving you alone in Germany. I figured these people here wouldn't know the story surrounding your injury, or what happened to Zeus." He gave her a sad look. "Before we went down the slope, I had the men look for any remains of Zeus. But the explosion vaporized him."

"Oh, God . . ." Dair cried softly. She pressed her hand against her eyes, trying not to sob.

"Jason found this." He pulled something from the pocket of his uniform, handing it toward her.

Opening her eyes, she saw it was the twisted, partly melted piece of metal that had Zeus's name and his military number as a WMD dog.

"And this." He dug into his other pocket. It was half of Zeus's leather collar, burned and twisted. "That's all that we could find, Dair." He placed them on the table in front of her and pulled a ziplock bag from his shirt pocket. "We thought you might want to keep these things. You can keep them in this bag, if you want."

Her heart tore wide open as she picked up Zeus's partly melted metal identification tag. Tears blurred her vision. She sniffed.

Davis reached over and found a tissue box, setting it on the table before her. Pulling one out, he said roughly, "Here, wipe your eyes."

Dabbing them, Dair dropped the tissue on the tray, picking up what was left of her dog's working collar. Wanting to scream, fighting not to, she clutched the two items in her hands as she rested them on the tray. Bowing her head, tears dribbled off her chin.

"Damn, I wish I could do more for you," Davis said, patting her shoulder gently. "Zeus was a great dog. You two were tight."

She heard the tears in Davis's lowered voice, felt his pain as well as her own. Looking up at him, tears awash her eyes, she quavered, "At least you found these. Thank you, Davis . . . These mean so much to me." Her voice cracked.

"I wish . . . I wish we could do more for you, Dair. I ran down your ortho surgeon earlier and pinned him to the wall on what was going to happen to you now." He made a weak gesture toward her left leg. "He said you'd probably go through one more surgery after you arrive at Bethesda. And then, as soon as you are healed up to a certain point, they are going to fit you for an orthotic leg and foot." His voice turned more hopeful. "He said you'd walk again, Dair. That's important. He said it would take a year or year and a half after surgery and fitting your new leg, learning how to use it and all, and then you will be released from the Army."

"A medical discharge?"

"An honorable medical discharge," Davis told her proudly.

"What then?" she asked hollowly, wanting to have made twenty years in the Army to get a pension.

"Well," he said, more brightness in his tone, "the doc said that you'd need to go home and then register with the nearest VA hospital for ongoing orthotic treatment, learning how to walk again, and then getting on with your life."

Misery crawled through her as she clung to the pieces of Zeus. "The Army was my career, Davis."

"Yeah," he muttered, "I know that. Damn, I'm so sorry, Dair. I know I keep repeating that, and I feel pretty helpless right now. I wish I could help you a helluva lot more than just standing here telling you this."

She reached out after transferring the metal tag to her left hand, touching his arm. "I'm so grateful you came. No one here knows anything about me, or Zeus, or what happened to us."

"Yeah, they do the best they can, but they're really busy." He looked around, more sadness in his expression as he looked at the other soldiers in beds, all strung and trussed up.

Dair pushed her own suffering aside. She reached for Davis's hand resting on the side of her bed, covering it. "Thank you *so much* for coming. It couldn't have been easy cutting through red tape to get up here." She saw him grin sourly, his eyes glinting.

"I wasn't taking no for an answer, Dair. Let's just leave it at that."

"Well, we're black ops. You know how to manipulate the system."

"Yeah." He chuckled. "Are you thirsty? Can I pour you some water?"

Touched by his care, she swallowed hard, forcing back the tears. "Y-yes, I'd like that." She opened her hands. "I'm still feeling pretty weak and worthless," she joked.

Pouring water for her, he said, "I can stay another hour, and then I have to catch a flight back to Bagram. They're putting me on a medical C-5 returning there."

"To pick up another load of wounded like me?"

"'Fraid so, Dair. Are you hungry? Is there anything I can get you before I have to leave?"

Shaking her head, she whispered, "You're like a Christmas present to me, Davis. Just stay with me. Tell me how the rest of the guys are doing."

"Well, there wasn't a dry eye after we got you. Ted and John were on that medevac. At first, we weren't sure we could save your life at all. You lost five pints of blood, Dair. That's a helluva lot. But they stabilized you at Bagram. Ted kept calling on the sat phone and giving us updates. When we arrived back at the village, it was 0300, and everyone was asleep. I got the guys together at our makeshift HQ house." He looked up and away from her for a moment, his Adam's apple bobbing repeatedly. Finally, he turned, holding her gaze, and said hoarsely, "We all cried. We cried for the loss of Zeus and we cried for you because we knew your foot and ankle would be amputated. We were hurting for both of you."

She saw the tears threatening to fall from his eyes, saw him struggling to push them away. "I'm going to miss all of you so much," she quavered. Choking, she whispered, "I can't believe Zeus is gone . . . I just can't."

Breathing in roughly, Davis gripped her hand. "Look, you've been through so much in such a short amount of time, Dair. It's going to take you time to come out of the shock of it all. You've suddenly lost your Army career, and the dog you loved, and who loved you. Now you're an amputee. Aside from dying outright? I can't conceive of anything worse happening to you." His voice became low with undisguised emotion. "Whatever you do? Stay in touch with us. We don't want to lose you. None of us do. You already have my address in Afghanistan. Once you get to Bethesda and get settled into your new digs, let's Skype. Or at least email each other. The guys want to know how you are doing. We all love you like a sister, Dair. This is hurting us, too. So, whatever happens from here on out after you leave Landstuhl? Stay in touch with us?"

Chapter Two

February 1

Dair thinned her lips as she drove into Wind River Valley. It was a hundred miles in length, snow covered, flat, and prosperous looking from an agricultural standpoint. She'd done her homework, thanks to the employment team within the Pentagon. Because she'd been part of a special top-secret project of testing women in combat conditions, they were there to support her once she got released from the Army.

Her heart ached as she slowly drove down the wet asphalt road that had two feet of snow plowed onto either side of it. It was Saturday morning, February first, and the Wyoming sky was turbulent looking because of a weather front having passed through late yesterday. There wasn't much traffic and she was glad. Her hands gripped the steering wheel. She tapped her left foot, her prosthesis encased in a big, ugly-looking pink and white tennis shoe. Dair knew she shouldn't think of it like that. She was grateful to have it, as a matter of fact. A year and a half after that horrible, nightmarish IED explosion that killed her dog Zeus and left her without a foot and ankle, felt like one more battle she had to fight. Only this time, it was going through another operation, getting fitted with a prosthesis, and then learning how to walk with it again.

She missed her mother, Ruby, and her grandmother, Rainbow. Her mother lived just outside Laramie, Wyoming, and still had her ever popular day school for pre-kindergarten children. Her grandmother, now in her mid-eighties, no longer trained as many mustang horses, but she kept at it, only at a slower pace.

Dair had always wanted to be just like her grandmother, who was small, tough, and a full-blood Comanche. Her face was deeply lined, but her dark brown eyes glittered with fierce life within them. Dair frowned, pushing a few black strands off her brow. When she looked at herself in the mirror, she saw her light brown, cinnamon-colored eyes were flat looking. Inwardly, she felt hopeless. She'd had so many failures learning to use her wooden leg, as she referred to it. And maybe she shouldn't think of it in that light. As Rainbow had pointed out, at least she no longer needed a wheelchair and had to use crutches only occasionally, now. Things were looking up for her. Didn't Dair see that?

No, she didn't. Every time she tried to get a job near a VA hospital, she was never hired. It wasn't that she was stupid or uneducated. Her skills lay in training horses and dealing in combat with a WMD dog. Not much call for either of those out in the civilian world. How badly she wanted to stay with Rainbow and help her out. But Dair had no money to give her grandmother, who relied on social security, which was stretched to the max in order to feed the three horses she had in training. Her grandmother had always lived at the edge of poverty. To stay with her now would make one more mouth for her to feed, and Dair knew she couldn't afford it, so she'd left.

Luckily, Ruby gave Rainbow money every month from her preschool business. Without it, her grandmother would have died of starvation a long time ago. There was such poverty among the indigenous people. It was everywhere.

Her mother had made something more of herself, however. She put herself through college, held three jobs to pay for the tuition, never qualifying for a scholarship; and yet, Ruby graduated with a degree in social work. Coming home, Ruby took the money from her jobs to build a second house, which would eventually become her preschool center. Dair admired her mother greatly. She had Ruby's genes, that gut desire to succeed.

Blowing out a puff of air, Dair felt lost. Losing half her lower leg had totaled her in a way she could never have imagined. She simply wasn't mentally prepared for it. Would she get this job? She'd been turned down so many times in the past that she felt like she'd already lost this one. What was the use of trying one more time?

Now, Dair understood the depression that vets got after being wounded. The sheer sense of black hopelessness. On top of that, she had PTSD and nights were a special terror for her. She was terribly sleep-deprived. The job the Pentagon team had told her about, an assistant horse trainer at the Bar C, was a perfect fit for her. But what would the owner think of her not having two legs? She wiped a film of sweat off her upper lip, her stomach already knotting over the thought of the coming interview. There were twenty miles to go before she arrived at the ranch.

The Wind River Valley was coated in deep snow. Because Dair had been born in Laramie, Wyoming, she knew winters here were long and harsh. Growing season on the western side of Wyoming, around the Tetons, was only eighty days; not even long enough to allow a plant to mature to produce fruit or vegetables. Heaving another sigh, she pushed the dark glasses up on her nose, her gaze always roving from one side of the highway to the other. That came from being a combat dog handler. Even now, she could feel that nasty cortisol, part of the fight-or-flight hormones spewed out by the adrenal glands, leaking into her bloodstream. She felt like she was going into combat again. That is what job interviews were like for her since leaving the cocoon of the VA hospital. There, she'd been fed, clothed, and had a roof over her head.

The Pentagon team reassured her that this job interview would be different from the others they had sent her out on. Shay Crawford-Lockhart, owner of the Bar C, had been a military vet herself, seen combat, and had PTSD as a result. She'd come home to the ranch when her father, Ray Crawford, at age forty-nine, suffered a debilitating stroke that left him incapacitated and no longer able to take care of the huge, sprawling ranch.

Shay had been granted an Honorable Hardship Discharge upon her release from the service, and returned to take over the daily running of the big ranch. All that sounded hopeful to Dair, who had pretty much given up hope of ever getting a job. People looked at her lost leg and turned her down. Maybe Shay Lockhart would understand and be open to giving her the job. *Maybe.*

Her mind wandered as she drove. Dair never kept her cell phone on. She didn't want the distraction. At times like this, when she felt tension rising in her muscles, she turned to things that made her happy. She pictured her mother, Ruby, who was half-Comanche and half white, a woman who had come from desperate poverty. Dair was born the year she graduated from college at twenty-two, but never let it slow her down.

Her grandmother Rainbow cackled and said that she looked just like she had looked as a child: black, shining straight hair, golden-brown eyes that changed color when the sun struck them, and she grew to be tall and medium-boned. Her genes clearly favored her Comanche side of the family.

How she missed her family! Yet, as much as Dair tried, she'd never been able to get a job in Laramie. She'd had to widen her search, not wanting to leave Wyoming because she loved its wildness, its nature, and sparse human population. She'd never been in Wind River Valley before, nor the Tetons.

Picturing Zeus, his intelligent black face, those large brown eyes of his, pink tongue lolling out of the side of his mouth, she smiled. Her heart blossomed with such love for him. Even now, she grieved for him.

Rainbow had urged her to get a puppy, train it, and then have it as a companion, because she needed something in her life to love. Dair had resisted, her heart still given to Zeus. She understood the wisdom of her grandmother's words, but she still couldn't bring herself to do it. Like a good luck charm, she wore Zeus's twisted metal ID tag on a long silver chain that fell between her breasts beneath her bright red long-sleeved tee. She wore his tags today for good luck.

Her mind canted back to another episode. She met a man called Noah Mabry. Nine months earlier, she was on an outing to a horse farm fifty miles from Bethesda Medical Center. Dair remembered it with humiliation. She was still learning how to walk with her metal leg and that big, ugly-looking tennis shoe on her prosthetic foot.

Ten amputee vets had been invited to come for a two-day outing at the Danbury Horse Farm, a thoroughbred breeding facility tucked away in the rolling green hills of Maryland. She was the only woman in the group. The men's injuries ranged from the loss of one or both hands or arms to the loss of all or part of one or both legs. She felt lucky compared to her companions in that roomy hospital van that took them to the horse farm. The owner, Henry Danbury, had been in the Marine Corps, from what she understood. He was rich beyond imagination, and in the summer months, recovering military vets were invited, ten at a time, out to the facility. There, they'd get to rest, relax, experience farm life, and stay overnight in a specially built home just for them.

Dair was very excited for the opportunity, but she was far more inexperienced over rough, uneven ground with her prosthetic foot. She worried about making a fool of herself by tripping and falling. God knew, she'd done enough of that already. They'd been warned beforehand that the ground was uneven, especially around the huge, airy barns.

She had wandered off from the group because she spotted a huge oval corral behind one of the barns. In it were two men and an incredibly beautiful black thoroughbred stallion on a longe line, trotting around in a circle. Dair knew that the stallion was being trained on the thirty-foot nylon training rope. The silver-haired man who held the line in his gloved hand knew what he was doing. He was Henry Danbury, the owner of the farm.

As breathtaking as the stallion was, his ebony mane

flying and tail up like a banner as he leaped, kicked out with his hind legs, working off all that pent-up energy, her gaze was drawn to the man standing next to Danbury.

Leaning against the pipe-rail fence, her arms resting across it, Dair relaxed more than she had in a long time. Maybe just being out of the suffocating hospital, where there was no sunlight, no wind on her face, no way to move like she used to, made her feel a little bit more normal.

The stallion listened to verbal commands being spoken quietly but firmly by Danbury, but her gaze kept drifting back to the other man.

She didn't know the stranger, but he was easy on her eyes, from what Dair could see of his face. She almost laughed at the absurdity of the thought. Since being wounded, her sex drive had disappeared. Right now, she was interested in this good-looking younger cowboy who wore a straw hat, a blue plaid shirt with the sleeves rolled up to just below his elbows, and a threadbare pair of faded dungarees.

Glancing downward, Dair saw his cowboy boots were deeply scarred and scuffed, telling her this man worked hard every day. He was no armchair cowboy; he was the real deal. When he turned to the trainer, she saw his neatly cut, short hair was black, but she picked up red strands among them because the June summer sunlight was strong, highlighting them.

He took his straw hat off, and she smiled to herself when she heard his rich, deep laughter drifting her way. There was something strong and yet gentle about him, and she couldn't put her finger on why she felt that way about him. Memories of her father, Butch Wilson, nagged at her. When she was ten years old, he had jerked her from a kneeling position on the ground and broken one of the bones in her lower right arm. She didn't remember much about that day except that her mother had come flying out of the kitchen, shrieking and charging her abusive husband.

Shaking her head, Dair wanted to forget those painful, upsetting years. Life got much more peaceful and comforting after her mother divorced Butch. So why did this cowboy intrigue her just now? Dair didn't know and wished she could get closer to him and look into his eyes. From this distance, she couldn't tell the color of them. He was deeply tanned and his long legs were slightly bowed, telling her he'd probably been born in a saddle and rode a horse daily. She wondered what his name was. Was the man next to him his father? A relative? They seemed like good friends, always laughing, talking, and joking with one another. A good feeling slowly entwined her heart, the sensation so unexpected, yet warmed her soul. She leaned against the corral, content to watch them.

Near noon, lunch was served, and the vets all gathered at a one-story building that they called the dining room. Dair walked into it, still not truly steady on her prosthesis, so she used her cane to help maintain a sense of balance. She'd gotten rid of the hated wheelchair, progressed to crutches, and finally the walking bars, where she could practice how to walk with her new leg attached to her body. Now, the cane was the last tool in her arsenal to get well, and she was bound and determined to be rid of it sooner, not later. Today though, she absolutely needed it because they were walking around on mostly uneven lawn or graveled areas around the barns, corrals, and buildings.

The people from Danbury Farm had gone all out for them. A long table was covered with a white plastic tablecloth, real china, neatly laid flatware, and sparkling lead crystal glasses filled with ice water. One of the women who had brought them out to the farm showed them to their respective places; each one marked with a name on a placard. Vets in wheelchairs needed more room than others. A few sat opposite, leaning their crutches against the wooden wall behind them. Dair found herself at the end of the table, her back to the wall, able to look through the bank of large windows, out over the rolling green pastures and horses munching contentedly. It was a perfect day.

That memory flowed strongly through her, filling her heart, lifting her depression for a moment.

To her surprise, the handsome cowboy who had been in the arena was seated opposite her. Henry Danbury sat at the head of the table. A partial smile tugged at her mouth. She'd found out the eye-candy cowboy was called Noah Mabry. He said he was visiting his friend Henry. Dair had found herself suddenly choked up, nervous, and her mind went blank as she drowned in his warm gray gaze. Noah wasn't like other ego-busting wranglers she saw at the Laramie rodeo every year. No, this man was quiet, attentive, and sensitive to the vets around the table. She found out he'd been in the military, too.

That was nine months ago. And so much had happened to her while at the farm. Meeting Noah had made her feel more alive than she ever had in her entire life. There was no simple explanation as to why.

But he'd kissed her that evening, alone in the barn, and she'd melted in his arms. It had scared her for two reasons. Just before she boarded the bus to go back to the hospital the next afternoon, they'd traded email addresses and they promised to email one another. Dair chickened out and never sent Noah an email, too unsure of herself because she was handicapped; and secondly, she couldn't conceive of someone as handsome as he was, being interested in someone like her. She wasn't whole any longer. Dair never heard from him again. He was a good memory; one that reminded her she was a young woman of twenty-seven, who had a sex drive and who hadn't been kissed in nearly two years. He made her feel feminine when all she'd ever had was a man's job in the male-dominated military. She would never forget that afternoon.

Her brows fell as she realized twenty miles had gone by in a hurry. To the left were two huge twenty-foot-tall pine tree trunks, dug deep in the ground, that became the entrance to the ranch. The crossover log on top of them had black wrought-iron words across it: BAR C. This was the place. She braked, watching for traffic, and then made her turn down the muddy, rutted road. There was still snow on the road, but it was obvious trucks had been in and out of the ranch. The soil was slippery and she was glad she knew how to drive a three-quarter-ton truck in thawing conditions. Mud splattered the fenders and even smacked up against the windshield.

Craning her neck as she drove around the corner, she saw a huge three-story cedar ranch house. The logs glowed silver in the sunlight, telling her it was a very old structure weathered by brutal Wyoming winters. The white plaster was thick and even between each of those long cedar logs.

Her heart began to beat harder in her chest as she saw the oval parking area partially plowed, bits of dark, wet gravel peeking out here and there. There was a row of four houses off to the right and down below the mild slope. She saw a number of pipe corrals. Her eyes widened as she saw a green aluminum-roofed riding arena behind the main home. It was huge! She saw a number of pickup trucks parked down in the parking area and spotted a woman riding a bay quarter horse out of the open doors of the mammoth indoor arena. Next to it were two huge red barns, three stories high. The place was filled with activity for a Saturday, and she saw a number of wranglers here and there, all busy, all focused on their duties.

The training corrals, made of pipe, were painted bright red and caught her interest. She saw no horses in them and no one tending them. She wondered who the trainer was. The team at the Pentagon didn't know either, because she'd asked them. The only name they gave her was Shay Crawford-Lockhart, the owner.

Glancing at her watch, she noticed she was fifteen minutes early for the eleven a.m. interview. Mouth dry, heart thumping, Dair swung into the area where other trucks were at in front of the main home. She parked, turned off the engine, and sat there for a moment, absorbing the beautiful cedar wrap-around porch that curved around three of the four sides of the home. There was a cedar swing at one corner. She loved swings.

Dair had a keen, knowing eye. She grew up learning how to put a roof on a house, how to clean the siding, when to replace it, or when it needed to be painted once again. This cedar-log ranch house was lovingly cared for. She loved the bright red aluminum roof that was steep enough to shed the heavy snow load so it wouldn't collapse. The logs were clean and cared for. She could see the white plaster used between them, keeping the cold out, had been recently replaced.

It was a good sign these owners knew the benefits of upkeep on their property. A tiny trickle of hope spread through her. Dair tried to tell herself that once Shay Crawford-Lockhart saw that she had a prosthesis, she would doubt her ability to either train a horse or ride one. Climbing out of the truck, she pulled the bottom of her frayed Army jacket down into place. Her mother had knitted her a new muffler for the winter and it was bright red to match the long-sleeved tee she wore beneath it. It was the only thing she'd kept when her duffel had finally caught up with her. She'd sewn on the Army patches depicting her unit, an American flag on the upper left arm, and her name across the left breast pocket, stenciled in black, along with her enlisted rating.

Dair debated whether to keep her long hair in braids or allow it to fall freely. She decided to keep it in braids, knowing it would bring out her Indian looks. She knew some people held prejudice against Native Americans. And it could skew this interview, but she didn't care. She wasn't going to pretend to be someone that she wasn't. Shay would either accept her as is, or not at all.

Staring darkly at her cane sitting against the front seat, she decided at the last minute that she wasn't going to use it. She'd come a long way in the past nine months since meeting Noah Mabry. Still, as she moved carefully through the mud and snow to the white picket fence that surrounded the ranch house, Dair found herself already humming in synchronicity with the Bar C. It was full of life. It was clean. Updated. The people who lived here cared for their property. If they cared for the ranch house, she figured as she climbed the wooden stairs to the porch, then they would care about their animals and employees, too.

* * *

When Shay Crawford pulled open the huge cedar door, Dair saw her warm, welcoming smile. Instantly, some of her trepidation melted.

"Hi, I'm Dair Wilson."

"Shay Lockhart," she said, her smile widening. "Come on in, Dair. Nice to meet you!"

Dair was stunned by the woman's friendliness. She appeared to be around thirty years old, her face oval, bright blue eyes, and about two inches shorter than herself. Dair managed a slight, nervous smile as she crossed into the mudroom. "It's nice to meet you, too, Mrs. Lockhart."

"Oh, pooh," she called, shutting the door. "Call me Shay. No one stands on formality around here, Dair." She turned. "Just stomp your feet on the rug and hang your jacket on one of those pegs. I've made fresh coffee for us. Would you like some?"

Pulling off the jacket, Dair tried to keep her hopes tamped down. Shay was acting like a long lost friend. "Well . . . sure, I'd love some coffee. Thank you." She stomped her right foot a couple of times, not wanting to track snow or mud across that shining gold and red cedar floor that led into the huge main room of the log home. She was more gentle with her left foot. Hanging her jacket up, she double-checked the bottom of each of her tennis shoes.

"Oh, they're clean enough," Shay said. "Come on in and welcome to the Bar C."

Dair appreciated the owner's warmth. They moved into the open concept living room and kitchen. Already, she could smell bread baking, a hint of cinnamon in the air, as she followed Shay into the even larger kitchen. There was a twelve-foot-long heavy wooden trestle table located to one side of the area.

Shay gestured toward it. "Make yourself at home. I'll pour us coffee. What do you like in it?"

Angling off toward the table, Dair said, "Black, please." She decided to choose the chair at one end. The table was set with two small plates and a fork, knife, and napkin beside each one. "This is a beautiful kitchen, Shay," she said, sitting down. Deciding that Shay probably set the dinnerware for them, the owner had her sitting at the head of the table.

"Isn't it though? My family ranch is over a hundred years old." She quickly poured coffee, bringing it over. "Back in a minute. I baked us some homemade cinnamon rolls." And then she grinned. "And if I don't grab some for us, real quick when they come out of the oven? The rest of the vets will smell them and come running. You just have to get out of the way and let them feast. They're like a starving wolf pack. You'd think they had never had a cinnamon roll before." She chuckled.

Dair wrapped her hands around the bright pink mug. The coffee smelled good. "You bake these for them every day?"

Shay hurried to the kitchen, donned a pair of mitts, and opened the oven door. "Oh, no! I baked these for you and me. But the guys will smell them in the air and come snooping. They miss *nothing*." She pulled the huge pan of cinnamon rolls out of the oven, placing it on two metal trivets sitting next to the double sinks. "My husband, Reese, will be out of his office any second now. He knows the smell of cinnamon rolls when they are done." She laughed. "He also knows the guys will be coming in shortly, so he's going to make sure he gets his two rolls, or there won't be any left for him after they arrive en masse!"

Shay had no sooner brought over two cinnamon

rolls, oozing with melted brown sugar, when Dair saw a tall man emerge from a nearby hallway. He had to be Shay's husband, Reese. Because of her father's abuse, Dair always, to this day, went on internal guard over any male stranger. He was well over six feet tall, lean like a wrangler, with a square face, green eyes, and short black hair. The lines in his face told her he was a man who thought a lot, and that his gaze missed nothing. They settled on her for a moment. And then he smiled.

It was what Dair needed in order not to become even more guarded.

"You must be Dair Wilson," he said, halting for a moment at the entrance to the kitchen.

"Yes, sir, I am."

"I'm Reese Lockhart." He gestured to Shay, who was using a spatula to scoop two more bubbling, steaming cinnamon rolls onto a nearby plate. "And this is my lovely wife and partner who takes care of all of us. And call me Reese." He walked over to his wife, slid his hand across her waist, leaned down and kissed the top of her curly brown hair. When he released her, Shay smiled up at him.

"Okay, you get two for that kiss. Now shoo!" She handed him the plate of cinnamon rolls along with a fork, plus a paper napkin.

Dair smiled, liking the warmth between the couple. She felt a rock-solidness coming from Reese Lockhart. In comparison, Shay seemed like a busy bee, flitting here and there.

Reese walked over, extending his hand across the table to her. "How was your trip out here, Dair?"

She shook his roughened hand. "It was okay. No snow drifts to dodge."

He grinned and released her hand. "Well, you're a

Wyoming native, from what Shay told me earlier. You know how to drive in the wintertime in this state."

"Yes, my family lives in Laramie, and I do know how to drive in a Wyoming winter," she said, feeling his penetrating perusal, but few red flags were rising in her. Lockhart might be tall as hell, super confident, but he didn't threaten her. Most men did. He felt very calm, centered, and friendly.

"Well, we're glad you made it. I'll leave you two alone to talk." He looked toward the foyer and mudroom. "But you're probably going to get a lot of interruptions. I'm sure Garret and Harper will be in here any second now, to land like a pack of hungry wolves on what's left of those rolls." He chuckled, turning away, heading out of the kitchen and down the hallway once more.

"I'll be with you in just a sec," Shay called over her shoulder. "If I don't parcel these rolls out, Noah won't get any. He's in Jackson Hole, and he'll be really bummed out to hear the other vets got rolls and he lost out." She laughed.

Ears perking up at "Noah," Dair wondered about that. Could there be a wrangler here named Noah? She'd never found out where Noah Mabry had come from, except that he was with a ranch on the western side of Wyoming. What were the chances it was the same man? No. Impossible, Dair decided, sipping her coffee and appreciating it.

Just as Shay rushed over to sit down with her, Dair heard the front door swing open. There was a lot of stomping of boots.

"Uh-oh," Shay warned, giving her a merry look, "here comes the wolf pack . . ."

Interested, Dair watched two wranglers in sheepskin

coats, Stetsons, and Levi's, enter the kitchen. Their gazes were locked on the dessert sitting on the counter.

"Hey," Shay called to them as they both descended on the plates, "come and meet Dair Wilson."

Barely able not to smile, Dair saw the wranglers scoop up the plates with the rolls on them. They turned in unison, staring across the kitchen at her. Dair felt the same kind of energy from them as she did from Reese Lockhart, so relaxed and nonthreatening.

"Come over here," Shay said, gesturing. "Meet Dair Wilson. She's here to apply for the assistant horse training position. Dair? Meet Garret Fleming."

Garret was a huge, muscular man, an inch or two shorter than Reese. She saw his hazel eyes narrow slightly, taking her in. His sandy-colored hair was short and neat beneath that dark brown Stetson he wore.

"Nice to meet you, Dair. I'm Garret."

Garret's hand was huge and her hand was swallowed up within it. But he didn't break her bones or cause her pain when they shook hands.

"Hi, Garret, nice to meet you."

"I'm Harper Sutton," the other cowboy said, leaning over, smiling and shaking her hand heartily.

"Hi," Dair said, liking his wide smile and sparkling dark gray eyes. He too was lean, but below six feet tall, more in keeping with most wranglers she'd seen, around five-foot-ten inches tall.

Garret looked around. "Hey, you only gave me two rolls, Shay. I need one for Kira, my wife, who will kill me if I don't bring her one."

Shay snorted. "Then *share,* Fleming." She jabbed at the two rolls on the plate he held. "One for each of you."

Garret's face fell as he regarded the rolls. "Come on," he pleaded, "I know you got more squirreled away,

Shay. I'd like to eat these two. You know how good your rolls are when they're warm. Give me a third one for Kira?" and he gave her a wriggling eyebrows look.

Dair tucked her smile away, watching the drama. Shay was a tiny thing compared to her husband and this vet, but she held her own.

"No way, Fleming. I've got two saved for when Noah gets back sometime this afternoon from Jackson Hole."

Garret grimaced. "That pan holds fourteen rolls, and you've only accounted for ten of them. So there's gotta be more left over, Shay. Come on? One more for Kira?"

"Share, Fleming."

Harper snickered and hit Garret in the upper arm of his thick fleece jacket. "She's got your number, big guy."

A slow grin pulled at Garret's mouth. "Yeah, Shay's little but mighty."

"If you want a pan of cinnamon rolls," Shay said pertly, "why don't you make them for dessert tomorrow?" Shay turned to Dair. "Everyone on the ranch comes to our home for Sunday afternoon dinner with us. Garret is a real chef and he makes the meal for all of us. It's the best food in the world, not to mention his mouthwatering desserts."

"Sounds wonderful, Shay," she said, missing her own family, missing their Sunday dinner get-togethers.

Rubbing his chin, Garret rumbled, "I just might make all of us some more of those rolls."

"Oh, great!" Shay said, dropping her hands. "Maybe make two pans, hmmmmm?"

Garret gave her a fond look. "For you? I'd do it, Shay. Okay, dessert tomorrow afternoon is two pans of cinnamon rolls with my special white icing that everyone drools over."

"Yes!" Harper yipped, pumping his fist into the air.

Dair took the paper napkin and wrapped up one of the rolls and stood up, handing it toward Garret. "Tell you what. You're a big, strapping guy. How about I share one of mine with your wife, Kira?"

Chapter Three

Instantly, the kitchen grew silent.

Dair felt suddenly like a bug under a microscope, all three people staring at her. What was *that* all about? She was about to withdraw the roll she'd held out to Garret Fleming across the table, when he held up his hand. Then he looked over at Shay.

"I don't care who Noah wants for an assistant horse trainer, Shay. *Hire this woman.*" And then he turned to her. "Dair? You're my kind of wrangler. You're a team player, you know how to share, and you're unselfish. You keep your rolls, though. I'll make do and give Kira one of these. Thanks, though. Your offer means a lot to all of us."

She put the roll down next to her plate, shaken by Garret's rumbling words. Harper was enthusiastically nodding his head.

"Hey, Shay. You got a keeper here in Dair. Don't let her get away, okay?" He held up his plate of rolls. "And thanks for these. I'm gonna eat them now so Fleming doesn't try and steal one of 'em." He laughed and ambled out of the kitchen.

Shocked, Dair looked over at Shay, who had an amused look in her dancing blue eyes. "I . . . er . . ."

Holding up her hand, Shay said, "No apologies. Sit down, Dair. Enjoy the rolls while we talk."

"I guess," she admitted, sitting. "I'm not used to wranglers talking back to the boss."

Shay rolled her eyes. "We're not like other ranches, Dair. We're all military vets here. We've all been wounded, whether you can see our scars or not. And we all have PTSD. We see ourselves as a family. Garret fondly calls us 'the squad,' as in a squad comprises ten military people within a platoon. We see everything through the military lens because we were in the service." She opened her hands, becoming serious. "What you did just now? Well, it means a lot to all of us. I've interviewed two other vets for this position and they weren't right for it."

Frowning, Dair picked at the roll, delicately unwrapping it, the thick white frosting dripping over her fingers. "I thought I'd done something wrong."

"Oh, no," Shay reassured her, reaching out and patting her lower arm, "just the opposite. I started a program nearly two years ago here at the Bar C, with the intent of hiring only military vets who had been wounded in one way or another. I had my own PTSD to contend with and I knew I wanted to encircle myself with my own kind, military men and women. We were all hatched from the same egg. And while I do all the hiring, my vet wranglers, including my husband, Reese, all weigh in on the person. Between all of us, so far, we've chosen the right people who hold the same values and morals that we do." She pointed to the roll between Shay's long, delicate fingers. "When you offered Garret half your rolls? That was huge in their eyes because, believe me, they covet these things when either me or Garret makes them for everyone. We all share. And even though Garret was trying to hornswoggle me out of an extra one for his wife, Kira, he was just joking. You know how vets can unmercifully tease one another?"

Dair nodded, allowing the warm, doughy roll to melt sweetly in her mouth. "Yes, it's a take-no-prisoners kinda teasing. I'm very used to that."

"Right." Shay smiled warmly over at her. "You just became the darling of our ranch by offering Garret one of your rolls. That gesture meant everything to them. And to me." She sat back, sipping her coffee and assessing Dair. "Let me tell you about the job. And I'm hoping you think it's a fit. Noah, who runs the horse training program here, will have to interview you, too, but Garret will grab him as soon as he comes up the driveway and tell him what you did just now. Sharing goes a long way around here. And we share more than just food. We give one another support, too."

"That sounds really good," Dair said, wondering if she was making this all up. How long had she ached to have a second family instead of an employer-employee relationship? Garret was a wrangler, yet he cooked Sunday dinner for everyone. The two wranglers treated Shay like a beloved sister, and Dair saw the respect for her in their eyes. Reese was easygoing and didn't try to lord over her or use his power to control her. Instead, he'd walked in, introduced himself, and was not only respectful toward her, but kind.

"Okay," Shay said, placing her hands flat on the table, "here's your job in a nutshell. Noah is a military vet, too. Even though he was a WMD combat dog handler for the Army in Afghanistan, when he got out, he found us. His background was horses growing up. Matter of fact, his parents live in Driggs, Idaho, just across the Wyoming border. Noah has a way with animals, and I must say, with people, too. We hired him in response to the pleas from the valley folks to have a real horse trainer around. So, he stepped up to the call. He's been with us for less than a year, and he's contributed to our ranch not only monetarily, but in every other way. When we got the arena raised this last summer, he became the manager of it. We rented out horse box stalls to valley residents, teaching riding classes, plus training personal horses for people around the area. He's overly busy and can't do it all by himself any longer."

"So I would do all the above with him?"

"Well, I'm not sure. Noah needs a horse trainer more than anything else. He likes teaching riding classes. But besides all of that, Dair, we have a unique way of doing the finances around here. When I first got home to the ranch, my father, Ray Crawford, had had a stroke at forty-nine and he could no longer run the place." She frowned. "And he's an alcoholic to this day, and that didn't help his condition. Anyway, because of his alcoholism, and I was away in the military for many years, I didn't realize he was running the Bar C into the ground. Before, when he managed the ranch, most of our pastures were leased out to other cattlemen wanting to fatten their cows up over the summer months."

"I've never seen more beautiful, lush green grass than right here in Wyoming," Dair agreed.

"You're right. But my father's disease not only drove off all our wranglers who used to work here, but he lost the grazing leases as well, because he let the wood fences fall into disrepair. You can't have cattle in a fence that falls down by pushing it over with your index finger."

Grimacing, Dair said, "That bad?"

"Yes, that bad. I had to figure out a way to stop the

ranch from dropping into bank foreclosure, as well as start repairing the miles and miles of fences. I didn't have any money, the ranch was two months away from being lost. The bank was wanting it to fail so Marston, the valley banker, could sell it to a company that wanted to tear out everything, grade it flat, and build condominiums on it."

Dair made an unhappy sound. "That's enough to scare me to death. You said this ranch is over a hundred years old. Right?"

Giving an adamant nod of her head, Shay said, "Right. And I wasn't going to lose our family ranch to a greedy banker. I hired Garret first, and I made a deal with him. He had to give me fifteen percent of what he earned outside the ranch. All the wranglers have other skills and they are expected to have part-time work to bring money into the failing ranch. And for that fifteen percent, I provide three meals a day and a home for them. Their weekends are free. But they volunteer to work for the ranch on the weekends and usually it's post-hole digging, replacing the rotted ones, or putting up new barbed wire for a sagging fence line. Everyone around here ends up working about six days a week. I insist that on Sunday everyone get a rest and personal time for themselves."

"And you expect me to have an outside job off the ranch and give you fifteen percent of what I earn?" Dair asked.

"You'll earn your fifteen percent by training horses right here on ranch property. Noah has a set fee for all types of services, and you'll use that as your ruler to charge people bringing their horse in here for training."

"That's good," Dair said. "I can do that."

"We have four homes we built for the wranglers, two

employees assigned to each home. My father claimed one of them. I wanted you to be assigned to Noah's home. There are two bedrooms, two bathrooms, and we ask that you split the rent, which is two-hundred a month, between you. And we have a savings program on the ranch where we ask that you put ten percent of your monthly earnings into it. You won't make a lot, but you will have great food, a home, and a job you love with people who are like you, Dair. I'm not here to assess your skills in horsemanship. Noah will do that later today. And if you think you can get along with him and vice versa, then I'm hoping very much that you'll come and stay with us."

Dair nodded, mentally calculating the money going to the ranch. What she didn't know was the price that Noah charged for horse training, which sounded like that was where he needed the most support. "That's fair enough." She chewed on the cinnamon roll, loving the sweetness and spices.

Just then, the door opened and closed. Shay lifted her head. "Oh! That must be Noah!" She straightened, looking toward the kitchen entrance. "He's home early. Wait till you meet him! You'll love him!"

Dair barely had time to choke down the roll and turn her head when the wrangler entered. He was in his sheepskin coat, taking off his tan Stetson, when she gasped. It was Noah Mabry! Oh, my God! All she could do was stare at him when he jerked to a halt, his gaze flying and fixing on her.

For a moment, there was crackling silence in the kitchen.

"Dair?" he asked, disbelief in his voice. "Is that you?"

Shay frowned and halted by Noah. "Do you two know each other?"

Gulping, Dair whispered, "I didn't know you were here . . ."

Noah smiled a little, his hat dangling between his fingers. "Yeah, we do know each other, Shay. Met nine months earlier at the Danbury Farm in Maryland." He shook his head, giving Dair a questioning look. "You're here for the assistant horse trainer job?"

Her throat closed with terror. "Yes."

"Noah, come over here," Shay invited. "You're just in time. Go get rid of your coat and hat out in the mudroom. I saved two cinnamon rolls for you. Would you like some coffee, too?"

He managed a shy nod. "Yes, please, Shay." And then he looked at Dair. "I'll be right back. Don't go anywhere . . ."

Dair didn't know whether to be happy or sad about seeing Noah again. Why hadn't she put it together? He'd said he trained horses when they'd met in Danbury. But that burning, slow, hot kiss he'd shared with her, melting her into his arms, made her face burn with a blush. And he hadn't forgotten it either, if she was any judge of the look gleaming in his light gray eyes. Did he seem regretful that she was here? Dair wasn't sure of anything at the moment, feeling like an IED had just exploded next to her.

"I didn't know you two knew each other," Shay said, bringing the plate of cinnamon rolls to the table, setting it near where she sat.

"Well," Dair managed in a strangled voice, "I lost track of him. I didn't know he worked here, Shay. When you used his first name, I wondered, but you know. Coincidences happen." She saw understanding in Shay's eyes as she sat down.

"I think it's a great sign!" she said, excited. "And

you met at Danbury Farm. Noah is good friends with Henry Danbury."

"Yes, I saw them together in the training arena at that farm." Dair saw the amazement in Shay's eyes, a dreamy look. She wasn't sure what that meant, either. Nerves skittered through her and she was suddenly afraid she'd not get the job. She wasn't sure how Noah felt toward her, either. She'd not had the guts to email him after meeting him at Danbury. *Oh, God.*

Noah took his time wrestling out of the thick sheepskin coat. He'd already hung his Stetson on a nearby peg. Of all the people he never expected to meet again, it was Dair Wilson! Stunned by the turn of events, he ran his fingers through his hair, taking a deep breath, centering himself. He hadn't missed the surprised look in Dair's beautiful golden-cinnamon colored eyes, either. She looked like a deer paralyzed by a set of car headlights. And he'd kissed her in the tack room. Long, slow, deep, and forever . . .

Just thinking about that life-altering kiss he'd shared with her, anchored him to where he stood. His heart was flip-flopping in his chest because she'd never emailed him. And when she didn't, he had decided the attraction was just one way. On that weekend, he'd wanted to comfort her, but she was in rehab with the partial loss of a leg to an IED. And now, she was here. Asking for a job. How the hell had that happened?

Rubbing his brow, Noah knew he had to go face her. And Shay seemed giddy about having Dair apply for the job. Never mind that Garret had stopped him the minute he'd parked his truck and got out. He'd grabbed him by the shoulder and said, "Hire her. She's the right person to help you." And then, he'd walked away without any other explanation. What the hell!

What was worse? Noah couldn't justify the sudden sexual urge running through him. That was embarrassing. Dair was a beautiful woman. There wasn't anything to dislike about her; otherwise, he'd never have kissed her. Because he'd wanted more, much more from her. But it had come at the wrong damn moment in his life. He'd just gotten a job at the Bar C, and what could he offer her at that moment? *Nothing.* Besides, he knew she had at least another six months in rehab, stuck at Bethesda Medical Center.

Hell, he was in a fix and he didn't know what to do. Turning, Noah strode toward the kitchen. Entering, he saw Shay gesture for him to come over to the table. And he saw the stark uncertainty in Dair's darkening, worried-looking eyes.

Sitting down, he thanked Shay for the coffee she'd put in front of him. He figured he'd better start eating the rolls or she'd start poking at him and asking him why he wasn't hungry. Noah didn't want to go there with her. Lifting his gaze to Dair, he saw the concern and worry in her eyes as she moved her slender fingers slowly around the coffee mug in front of her.

"How did you two meet?" Shay demanded, all ears.

Noah cut her an uncomfortable glance and forced himself to eat. "I was at Danbury visiting Henry." He moved his gaze to Dair. "And the reason I didn't contact you by email after we met was because I had just gotten a job here at the Bar C."

"That's all right, Noah, I understand," Dair said.

"It wasn't like we had much time to talk," he apologized to her. No, they had been so damned drawn to one another, social conversation evaporated into that hot, melting kiss they'd shared.

She shrugged. "Life happens. I need a job since the medical center cut me loose and I'm finished with my therapy."

Noah was careful not to bring up her amputated leg. He didn't want to embarrass Dair in front of Shay. He knew that Shay and everyone probably already realized she was an amputee. It wasn't table talk, and he had no wish to make Dair feel any more uncomfortable than she looked right now. "I do need an assistant," he added quickly. "Since Shay and Reese had the arena raising, I've been overwhelmed."

"Shay said you are the manager of the arena, plus schooling horses," she ventured.

"Right." He smiled a little over at Shay, finishing off the first roll and wiping his fingers on the paper napkin. "We have snow here eight months out of every year, and Wind River Valley has a lot of quarter-horse people who show their animals around the nation. They need somewhere that's enclosed to continue to train their horses throughout the winter months. Our newly built arena has been a godsend to them and a financial windfall for the Bar C."

Shay glowed. "But the people are here because of you, Noah. You've made a name for yourself since you started working here."

Lifting a shoulder, Noah said, "In part, Shay. But the rest was your brilliant idea to build an arena in the first place." He glanced over at Dair, wanting her to feel a part of the conversation. "Shay is always looking for ways to make money for the Bar C because her father lost all the summer grass leases five years ago. Now, this place is getting rebuilt, literally, from the ground up. Me and the rest of the wranglers mend fences every week. We try to do it every day, if our schedule allows."

He thumbed toward a side window in the kitchen. "But when you have five feet of snow out there, it's impossible to do any fence mending."

Dair nodded. "That's true. So with the arena built, you can train horses all year around?"

"Yes." He took the second roll in his large hands, opening it up. "The problem is me. We've got a state-of-the-art facility for boarding, riding, and training, but too few personnel to run it. I'm looking for an assistant who does a lot of the training while I manage the place, giving riding lessons and ensuring the boarded horses get cleaned, fed, and watered daily."

"How many horses are boarded?"

"Twenty-five," Noah said.

"And by the time he's done watering, feeding, and cleaning their stalls, most of the day is gone." Shay gave him a worried look. "Actually, you could use two more hands plus a horse trainer."

"I can clean stalls," Dair said quickly.

"Well, what I'd like to do," Noah said between bites of the tasty roll and sips of coffee, "is take you out to the area and give you a sense of it all. And if you're up to it, I have a nice, well-mannered horse I'm training for a ten-year-old little girl, which I'd like to see you work with for a bit. I need to get an idea of how you are around a horse. That's not something that you can put on your résumé."

Dair knew Noah had refused to hire two earlier applicants for the position. "Sure, not a problem. I've brought my toolbox, my gloves and working gear. They're in the truck."

"Great," he murmured, licking the last of the frosting off his fingers. He looked over at Shay. "I'll drive her down to the arena and we'll finish the interview there."

"That's fine. But you need to know that everyone wants to hire her, Noah."

He managed to give her a sour look. "I'm listening, Shay."

"Good," she said, standing and patting his broad shoulder.

"It's gonna take a few hours, maybe until four p.m."

"That's fine," Shay said.

Noah was concerned about Dair's performance. He remembered nine months earlier she had been unsteady walking on uneven ground. Yet, when he studied her beneath his lashes, Dair looked confident. Maybe it was her high cheekbones, her burnished skin, those incredibly beautiful eyes that he could lose himself in. At the same time, he cautioned himself. Their kiss had meant something to him. He wasn't sure what it had meant to her. It had been a damned long time since he'd kissed a woman, and Dair's lips had felt like a soft welcome against his mouth as he'd tasted her fully.

He nodded to Dair and stood up. Trying not to stare at her as she rose, he wanted to assess her balance. Knowing she was nervous, he understood better than most. "This should be a piece of cake for you," he said, wanting to tamp down the sudden tension he saw in her body as she stood and squared her shoulders. Dair relaxed a bit, and that was good. He'd been around all ten of those military vets for a day and a half at Danbury Farm. And it struck him as never before how lucky he was to have his arms and legs.

Leading the way down the hall to the mudroom, he saw her old Army jacket and picked it up, handing it to her.

"Thanks," she murmured.

"It's warming up out there," he said. "But it's about fifty-five out in the arena, a good temperature."

She shrugged on her coat and buttoned it, pulling the red knit muffler around her shoulders and neck. "How many people are down there riding right now?"

If Noah didn't know she was an amputee, he'd never have guessed it. Dair wore Levi's and thick, rugged-looking sneakers. She walked with balance and with ease. "Probably five or six." He looked at his watch. "It's getting close to lunchtime, so most of them will be gone soon. We'll probably have the arena to ourselves for an hour or so." There was relief in her eyes. No one knew better than he that when some horses got around one another, territoriality ruled. Especially with stallions.

Opening the front door for her, he said, "Let's get your tack gear. We'll take it down to the arena in my truck."

"Okay," she said.

There were steps to go down, and Noah watched her from behind. She had a fine butt, of that there was no question. He watched her reach for the rail with her gloved hand, probably to balance herself. Otherwise, he'd never have suspected she didn't have two good legs. At the bottom, he gestured to his truck that was parked next to hers. "Why don't you climb in? Your gear on the seat of your truck?"

"Yes, in a cardboard box. Nothing fancy." She managed a half smile.

Noah opened up the door on his black Toyota truck. He started to cup her elbow, to help her climb in.

"No . . . I can do this by myself," she said.

Stepping back, he gave her room. Noah remembered their conversations when they were together. Dair had been working to appear not to be an amputee. That had been her goal. She didn't accept help or handouts, as he'd found out at Danbury. She hauled herself up, and although a bit awkward, she climbed into the truck just fine. He knew she had powerful upper-body strength in order to compensate for that leg that wouldn't always act like a real one would. He closed the door for her.

Walking over to her parked red Dodge Ram truck, he opened up the passenger-side door and pulled out the box that contained her gear. He set it in the back of his pickup and climbed in. The sky was getting less gray, with more blue spots opening up in the low cloud ceiling. The wind was brisk, off and on. But it smelled clean. Shutting the door, he started the engine, turning to her.

"What time did you get here?"

"At 0900," she said, falling into familiar military time.

He grinned. "Well, it's 1030 now. Let me get you to work with Thunder, a nice five-year-old gray mixed-breed mare. They want her trained for their ten-year-old daughter, who's horse crazy."

"What's the girl's name?"

Noah backed out and then turned down the muddy driveway, heading down a narrow gravel road between the wrangler housing area and a group of pipe corrals. "Lori. She's a cute little redheaded kid with huge freckles across her cheeks and nose. Her parents bought the mare and she named her Thunder."

"Oh? Is that because she is?"

Noah tried to quell his sensitivity toward Dair. He wondered if she even remembered their kiss. She was a damn fine-looking woman any man would be proud to have on his arm. He tucked that all away. "No. Lori loves storms. The mare is sweet, quiet, and she listens well. I don't think you'll have any problems with her."

"Where are you at within her training schedule?"

"I'm longeing her daily, using voice commands right now at the walk, trot, and canter. This is where I start the basic foundation work."

"It's a solid plan," Dair agreed.

"Here's the arena," he said, gesturing with his gloved hand in that direction.

"It's huge."

"Only one in Wind River Valley. Shay struck it rich on this idea. It's bringing in badly needed money for the ranch as a whole. It's going to allow her to probably hire two more wranglers before late spring. And we desperately need them."

He pulled into the asphalt parking lot next to the huge Quonset-hut-looking building made out of aluminum and glass. The green tin roof was shaped to make the arena look like a loaf of French bread. The curved roof forced the heavy snow to automatically slide off it so the structure remained sound and sturdy.

"Okay, here we are." He pointed to a red door on the side. "That's our office. We'll go in there first." And then he hesitated, realizing he'd used the word "our." It was probably just the team spirit that the Bar C wranglers had with one another, as well as with Shay and Reese. But maybe it wasn't. Maybe, Noah thought as he climbed out and pulled her cardboard box of gear into his arms, he'd already made up his mind to hire Dair, even though he'd not seen her work with a horse. That flummoxed him, because he was conservative and careful about people being around a horse he was training. Not all horse people knew everything they needed to know about a horse—how to ride it, how to care for it, or train it. He needed to see that Dair was at that pinnacle where she had enough experience. Walking around the truck, he opened the door for her, noticing she had a bit of a slip on the icy area. But anyone would, not just her.

In the next hour he would know whether he was going to hire Dair or not. And as much as he personally liked Dair, he wouldn't put his horses at risk with anyone who didn't know their horses a hundred percent. He hated having to be the teacher rating the student, but that is what this was all about. And judging from Dair's unreadable expression, she knew it, too.

How badly Noah wanted her to pass with flying colors. Because he wouldn't hire her if she couldn't do the job.

Chapter Four

Dair sat on her anxiety as Noah led her down a swept-clean concrete aisleway. On each side were roomy oak stalls and each contained a curious horse who had stretched its neck out of the half door, nickering a hello as they passed. There was only one rider in the arena at the moment; the rest had left because it was near lunchtime. The whinnies of several of the horses were welcoming.

Nostrils flaring, Dair inhaled the scent of sweet timothy grass.

"You have a friendly group," she said, walking down the aisle. She liked that Noah cut his stride for her sake. He had his game face on, and she wondered if he would ever relax so she could more or less tell what he was really feeling right now. Worried, Dair knew if she wasn't sufficiently agile or balanced due to her prosthetic limb, he would never hire her. Horses sometimes moved fast and unexpectedly. Even the best horseman at times couldn't get out of their way.

She was sure he was going to grade her severely on the fact she was an amputee. It only made her anxiety amp up more, but she kept it tightly closeted. Plus, if she got too tied into her fear of not getting the job, the horse would feel it and act out anyway. Dair put all her control into tamping down her emotions. She'd done it as a WMD handler. She'd do it now. Never had she wanted a job more than this one. The fact that there was warmth and camaraderie between the owners and the wranglers, was heaven to her.

"Yeah, most of the horses here are owned by our renters." Noah gestured down the aisle toward a set of box stalls. "I have six horses in training right now, and they're all down at the end, on the right-hand side. You can see Thunder, she's watching us coming." He smiled a little at the small, alert mare.

Thunder was the only gray that Dair could see in this section of the stall area. "She's got a pretty head. Maybe some Arabian blood in her? She's got a slightly dished face."

Giving her a pleased look, he said, "Good call. Thunder is half Arabian and she's got mustang blood in the rest of her. She was caught and captured by the BLM in the Nevada desert a year ago. Lori wanted a small horse because she's small. The girl has tamed her with love and gentleness, so she's not spooky and flighty like most mustangs are, coming off the range. But she's super alert, which all mustangs have learned to become."

A little relief flooded through Dair. "That's pretty much all I broke and trained for my grandmother Rainbow," she shared. "She took mustangs from the BLM because they were cheap to buy, spent a year breaking them with love and training them. Then she could get a couple thousand dollars for them by selling a safe horse to a deserving family."

"Interesting," Noah said, slowing as they approached

Thunder's stall. "How long did you train at your grandmother's place?"

"I started at nine and did it through age eighteen. After I joined the military, I didn't work with horses anymore, just WMD dogs."

"I remember when we met, you told me that you'd been a combat dog handler."

Pleased, she saw some of his game face slip. "Yes, we shared that in common," she murmured, coming to a halt near Thunder's stall. The mare had a perfect Arabian head with small ears, large, dark brown liquid eyes, a slight dish in her face, and a small muzzle with wide, flared nostrils as she leaned forward to avidly sniff at Dair.

"I'm going to stand back and let you handle her," Noah said. "Training these six horses is something you'd do five days a week." He gestured toward the other stalls. All the horses looked out their open stall doors, watching and listening to them. "The longe line is on a hook on her door." He pointed toward the long red nylon rope neatly coiled up on the oak wall.

Dair nodded and moved forward, offering the mare the back of her hand so Thunder could sniff and acquaint herself with her. The mare was pretty, compact, and had a short back, which was typical of both bloodlines. Thunder licked her hand and Dair laughed, moving to one side, sliding her fingers along the mare's jaw and across her gray-and-black streaked mane. "She's really sweet."

Leaning against the other stall, arms across his chest, Noah said, "Lori did a really nice job of getting her trust with love."

"That's the only way to do it," Dair murmured, watching Thunder as she continued to stroke her neck.

Wanting to find out if the mare had any issues, she slowly moved her hand to first one ear, and then another. Many horses had issues due to a past trauma and didn't want that part of their body touched by human hands or brushed with a halter, bridle, or saddle. Thunder half closed her eyes as Dair gently massaged each of her ears. "I'm going to work with her from the start to see if she's got any issues with touch on a particular part of her body," she told him, keeping her focus solely on the mare.

"That's a good first step."

She heard the low, pleased sound from Noah, who stood behind her. A lot of her trepidation dissolved because when she got around animals, she relaxed. It was just a natural reaction. And Thunder was probably the most reliable, steady horse of the six. Noah was giving her a break of a sort, and Dair knew it. He could have probably handed her off to a nasty horse that had been abused, suffered at a human's hand, and been tough to deal with. But he hadn't.

How badly she wanted this job. She'd already kissed her boss. What would happen because of that, if anything? As Dair stroked the mare's elegant neck, speaking to her in low tones, she reminded herself they'd never emailed one another afterward. That was a good sign in her book, because it meant he wasn't interested in her, man-to-woman. He'd let bygones be just that, and it lifted her worry about the awkward situation.

Dair placed the red nylon halter on Thunder and led her out to the nearby cross-ties. Noah said nothing, just watching. Pretty soon, she forgot that he was standing there as she critically examined the mare, running her hands over her entire sleek, well-fed body. Dair missed nothing, noting an old barbed wire scar on the mare's right rear pastern. She picked up each of

Thunder's hooves, examining each one for cracks or other potential issues. With the hoof pick, she cleaned out each one. When she was done with her inspection, she turned to Noah while keeping her hand on the mare's rump.

"Are you doing anything about that old scar on her rear pastern? Has it affected her gait at all?"

He eased away from the stall and walked up to the mare. "Good catch. When Lori's parents bought Thunder from the BLM, it was already there. They said it had pink scar tissue on it at the time, meaning to me that she'd probably got caught in a rancher's barbed wire fence with her herd. They will often break down a fence to get to the grass on the other side of it."

"That's pretty common," Dair agreed. "Herds will try to get through wire to get to grass, wheat, or anything else that's edible."

"Right. Lori didn't ride Thunder for three months because she was slowly breaking her to ride during that time frame. The mare was not favoring that leg at any time."

"What about now, though?" Dair asked, gesturing toward the horse. "Because when you longe a horse, it's a pretty tight circle and does put a lot more stress on their joints and legs as a result." She saw praise in his expression once again and it made her feel good.

"Right on. I've been longeing her every day for fifteen minutes at a time for the last thirty days now. I haven't seen her favoring it. But I'm not cantering her on a tight circle for five or ten minutes at a time, either. I'm concerned about it like you are, and I don't want to make the mare lame if it does start to act up. I'm taking Thunder slow and steady because of the injury."

"You've got that arena. Why couldn't you let her loose in there to let her run, trot, and walk?"

"I'm doing that now. Thunder is pretty much voice trained to move or change gait on my command. I just stand in the center of the arena, and she has her halter on, and I let her go. That way, it's not putting undue stress on that pastern."

"And how long have you been doing that?"

"About two weeks now. I want her to stretch out and really run when she feels like it. When she first gets loose, she bucks, twists, and runs like any horse will. After that, she'll settle down and listen to you."

Dair smiled a little, running her hand over the mare's short back. "Typical of any horse who's stall bound most of the day."

"Yes. But we also put all of them out in a large pasture daily, weather permitting."

"I've examined her and I don't see any other issues. Have I missed anything, Noah?" She held his game face expression once more.

"No, you did good. I'm happy to see you opened her mouth and examined her teeth, too."

"Well," she said, clipping the longe line to the bottom of Thunder's halter, "if her teeth need to be floated, they can interfere with the bit and cause a lot of pain and discomfort for the horse, so it can be a bad ride for the rider as well."

"The vet floated her teeth about three weeks ago," he said. "We keep a written schedule on each vet visit in a file in my office, plus an XLS spreadsheet."

Dair nodded. "That's good to know. Anything else I missed?" She wanted to show Noah that she wasn't the type of trainer coming in new, asking the old trainer about everything regarding each animal.

"She has no bad habits. Lori did a good job. She's an easy ride, too, but I'm not asking you to saddle and ride her as part of evaluation today."

Nodding, Dair released the ties from Thunder's halter. "Okay, let's go play out in the arena." She saw one corner of his mouth quirk into what she thought was a bit of a smile.

"After you. Just follow the aisle until you see the opening to the arena on the left at the other end. I'm going to continue to just watch. If you have questions though, ask."

"Right," Dair called over her shoulder, leading Thunder down the aisle. The *clip clop* of her shod hooves echoed the length of the passageway. More horses nickered. A few whinnied, wanting to go with her. Dair didn't blame them. She'd go crazy in a stall for twenty-three hours a day.

"Tell me something, Noah. Do you let all these horses in training out to stretch their legs daily during the winter?"

"When there's snow and ice on the ground, I let them out in the arena instead. Usually, I get them all out at the same time and they get about thirty minutes of slumming around."

"And they all get along with one another?" Because some horses would kick, fight, and bite one another.

"They're all geldings and mares. No studs among them."

"Well, that's good to know. But I bet there's still seniority among them?"

"Yeah, and everyone knows their place," he said, wryly.

Dair felt confident on a solid concrete surface with her prosthetic. She worried about the deep sand of the arena. What if she fell? Besides potentially hurting herself, she would look inept and Noah probably wouldn't hire her. Mouth tightening, she could do nothing about it. Her limb was state-of-the-art metal, but it didn't have near the flexibility of a real leg or foot. Training would take place on uneven ground, and that was the biggest obstacle staring her in the face. Dair had no worries about her horse-training abilities. But she had plenty of real-time concerns about surfaces.

She opened the gate that led to the huge, airy arena. No one was in it. There was a wide area between the oval pipe fence so that riders could ride outside it to take their horses to and from the stabling area. She saw a nice washing station at the other end, with thick rubber mats placed over the concrete floor so that horses being washed would not slip on the slick surface and harm themselves. Noah had thought of everything, from what she could see. It was a cool-ish fifty or so degrees, according to the digital thermometer hanging on one of the sturdy oak walls as she walked Thunder across the riding area toward the main gate.

She saw birds flying up in the rafter area, their cheeps and songs pleasant. Thunder looked up, ears forward, as she watched several gray mourning doves fly from one end of the arena to the other. A place like this would always have small birds in it. She knew from experience that mustangs were super alert to every little movement around them. Out in the wild, it could mean a cougar stalking them, or a pack of wolves. To horses, movement equated to potential danger, and as she opened the metal pipe gate, Thunder was looking around and checking things out just like she should.

"I'll close the gate behind you," Noah called.

"Thanks." She led Thunder into the center of the huge oval arena that had a sandy base, which was safe for a horse to move around in. The mare was relaxed, and one of her ears was always cocked toward Dair, as if waiting for a verbal command. Dair knew from long experience to never wrap any longe line or lead line of any type around her hand. If a horse ever bolted suddenly, that could tighten instantly and she'd be dragged, unable to unwrap the line from around her glove. Instead, she quickly put the rope into a safe position and held it in the middle with her hand. That way, if Thunder bolted or ran, all she had to do was drop it. Noah was watching her for such small but important things. Glancing up, Dair saw he'd lifted one boot up on the lowest rail midway down the arena so he could easily judge her work with the mare.

All her focus was on Thunder. Once she had the longe line safely in hand, she pushed the mare's shoulder lightly with her other hand and said, "Walk." The command was quiet but firm. Thunder obeyed. She went as far out on the longe line as possible and began to walk around Dair. One never trotted or ran a horse on a longe line right away. Their muscles weren't warmed up properly and they could pull a ligament or tendon in one of their slender legs, causing a lot of problems for weeks or months to come. So Dair allowed the mare to amble at a walk, look around, and take in all the sights and sounds around her. The mare relaxed and circled Dair calmly, one ear cocked toward her.

After five minutes of walking in both directions, Dair gave the command for Thunder to trot, and she did. It was a slow, easy gait, and again, it was about warming the horse up properly. Dair found the footing, the sand, deeper than she expected and it forced her to lift her amputated leg higher and be constantly aware of where she was turning her foot.

Time stood still around her and Thunder. Dair knew from long experience when she worked with a horse, all other noises and activity around her faded deep into the background. She forgot about Noah critically assessing her, as well. There was a magic that always occurred within her when she was working with any animal; it was a melding of heart and spirit with the horse, and they became one. Dair could feel Thunder's joy as she moved with her quickly as the horse cantered, enlarging the circle so the mare could really get a good workout without tight turning all the time.

When it was all over, and she'd cooled Thunder out after taking her both directions on the longe line, a twenty-minute workout all together, Dair broke the connection she had with the happy, complacent mare. Lifting her chin, she glanced to the left where Noah was leaning up against the rails. The expression on his face was very clear to read. This time, his game-face mask was gone. He wore a crooked grin, his light gray eyes sparkling. She couldn't help but ask, "What?"

"Turn Thunder loose. I want you to work with her off-line and use your verbal commands. Let's see how she responds."

Nodding, she called "whoa" to Thunder, who'd been trained to stop, then turn and come directly to the person. And as she did, Dair smiled, rubbed the horse's damp neck, smoothing her forelock between her ears into place once more. "Okay, girl, you get to run free." She unsnapped the line from the horse's halter.

For a moment Thunder stood there, looking at her, and Dair could swear the animal was mentally trying to connect with her. "Go counterclockwise." She turned the horse with her hands in the opposite direction and pushed. The mare walked away, her ears flicking, listening for a command from Dair.

Once Thunder was nearly to the rail, a good hundred feet away from Dair, she called, "Trot!"

Instantly, Thunder responded, lifting her tail and beginning to trot, moving along the rail. She lifted her head in a characteristic Arabian toss, nostrils flared, nose up in the air, her long black-and-gray streaked mane unfurling as she floated into an extended trot. Dair watched her, grinning. She knew Thunder had wanted off the longe line. Most horses would. But now she was free, and Dair watched the mare extend her legs, snapping them out from beneath her, straight out, all four feet off the ground for a moment, as she soared past her. Joy tunneled through Dair, because a horse freed her inwardly. Tears burned in her eyes, which she quickly squelched. Dair continued to face the mare as she seemed to float around the arena at that long, stylish extended trot for a good five minutes.

"Walk!" Dair called out to her.

Snorting, tossing her head, Thunder made her objection evident, but then she broke her gait and came down to a prancing, snappy walk, almost as if she were dancing. Dair laughed outright because that was such an Arabian way of walking. In the Middle East, they were known as the "dancing horse," precisely because of this genetic predisposition to perform such a flashy, romping, strutting walk that was really a trot in place. Dair allowed Thunder to express herself. Horses didn't do well mentally when always kept in a box stall. Fresh air, sunshine, movement, and plenty of room to run, were intrinsic to all of them, regardless of breed.

Finally, with a toss of her pretty head, Thunder walked sedately. Dair laughed again, her hands on her hips as she watched the perky mare remain close to the pipe rail. She turned toward Noah. "Is it okay to allow her to gallop free, or not?" Dair did not know the condition of Thunder's scarred pastern and she didn't want to risk injuring the horse.

"Yeah," he called. "Let 'er rip."

Smiling, Dair held his glinting stare. "Okay." And

she turned to Thunder. "Canter!" she called to the horse.

Well! Thunder took off like a shot! Dair watched her leap into the air, kick her rear legs upward, land with a flurry of sand veils flying up around her. Clouds of it flew up behind her back hooves as she dug in, hurling herself forward. This was no canter. It was an out-and-out hand gallop, as it was known in the trade. That meant the horse was going full throttle. And what a beautiful sight the gray mare with the black-and-gray mane and tail made for Dair.

Thunder's hooves hitting the deep, cushioning sand made it sound like thunder to Dair. Literally, the mare tore around the enclosed area, tail held like a proud flag waving behind her, that long, silky mane straight out from her neck, her nostrils flared, blood-red inside, telling Dair she was drinking in huge draughts of oxygen. The mare was dainty and small, but she was riveting to watch. Dair's experienced eye saw a lot of good work done by Lori, because the mare was collected and not strung out. She had tucked her head as she galloped, nose perpendicular to the ground. Thunder was breathtaking! Dair's heart lifted with unparalleled joy as the mare raced her heart out, and then skidded to a stop at Dair's command. When Dair pointed in the opposite direction with a hand signal, the highly intelligent mare spun around on her rear legs and leaped in the other direction, clockwise.

Finally, her coat glistening with sweat after a good, long gallop around the arena, Thunder returned on Dair's command. The mare halted in front of her and nuzzled her chest. Laughing, Dair hugged the happy horse, inhaling the scent of her sweat that she loved so much. It brought back so many happy memories with her grandmother and her mustangs. Placing her arms around the mare's neck, Dair hugged and then patted her. Thunder was breathing hard, head-butted her again, playful, letting Dair know she loved this as much as she did.

Later, after cooling the horse down, Dair took her back to the barn, put her in the cross-ties, and brushed her until her shaggy coat shined. She cleaned her hooves and finally placed her back into her large, airy stall.

"Here," Noah said, coming up to her, his hand extended, "she might be looking for this."

There was a big, bright red apple in the palm of his calloused hand. Dair smiled up at him and took it.

Thunder was already at the stall door, head sticking out, all her considerable attention on the apple in Dair's hand as she approached. Dair ruffled her forelock, then, hand open and flat, she gave Thunder her well-deserved apple. The loud crunching noises that followed made Dair's smile broaden. The horse was thoroughly enjoying her after-workout dessert.

Turning, Dair saw Noah studying her intently, his arms across his chest, mouth puckered. There was a sense that he was fighting something, but she wasn't sure what. Was he unhappy with her handling of Thunder? Dair didn't think so, because Noah would have instantly corrected her out there in the arena if she'd done something wrong. As it was? He'd not said a peep and she figured he knew that she was very good at what she did.

Thunder finished the apple, foam around her lips here and there, licking it all off with her long, pink tongue. Dair patted her and said goodbye to the small, stalwart horse. Walking to a bucket of water beside the stall, she leaned down, washing her sticky hands off. Drying them on her jeans, she approached Noah.

There was still a look of deliberateness on his face. "Do you have a critique for me?"

He allowed his hands to fall to his sides. "None. You did really well with her, Dair. The mare obviously likes you, wants to please you, because she followed your every verbal command."

"She's a dream to work with, believe me, compared to some of the mustangs I've worked with in the past."

"I could see a lot of muscle memory in everything you did," he said, walking slowly down the aisleway beside her. Outside, the sun was breaking through, with more blue sky showing. "You don't get to that level unless there's years of experience behind it. I felt you handled Thunder very well."

Preening inwardly, she remained humble. "Thanks, Noah."

He halted at the tack room, opening it up. "Come on in here."

Following, Dair loved the fragrance of the clean leather. The tack room was spotless, every bridle and saddle, martingale, and any other leather training aids, gleaming with recent oiling or soap, and constant, meticulous care. He gestured to her to sit down on one of the large tree stumps at one end. He seemed to be chewing on something.

Sitting, she faced him. The tops of the stumps had been smoothed off, sanded, and had many thick coats of varnish so they wouldn't snag and tear a person's clothing. "Something's bothering you," she said, placing her hands on her thighs. "What is it?"

Taking off his gloves, Noah stuffed them in his back pocket before sitting down. "I don't know how to go about this, Dair, and I don't want to upset or hurt you."

Her black brows fell. "What are you talking about?" Now, Noah looked truly uncomfortable.

Tipping up his hat, he admitted, "I've got no experience around an amputee and because of it, I don't know the extent of what you can or can't do as a horse trainer."

"Well? Try me," she ordered. "You're not going to hurt my feelings by asking me questions." Dair saw his shoulders drop a bit and realized, like most people, he felt uncomfortable around a person like herself.

Giving her a look of apology, he said, "I feel like a fool in some ways. I have such respect and admiration for anyone who has lost a limb and had to fight to come back from it." Opening his hands, Noah offered, "But I don't know the first thing about your limb, how you feel after a workout like that in the arena. Are you sore? Bruised? How's your back? Are you in pain anywhere?"

Wanting to smile but withholding her reaction, she stretched her left leg out, leaning over and pulling up the dusty edges of her trousers, folding them up to expose her metal leg replacement. Dair felt no embarrassment about it because she'd been surrounded by patients with artificial limbs, mostly men, at Bethesda. She looked up to see Noah staring at the prosthesis, a scowl forming on his face. "This is my replacement leg," she said, moving her fingers down the shining, sleek metal and joint at her ankle. "My real limb is tucked in here." She curved her hands around the long oval. "It's called a socket. There's a thick lining inside it that protects my residual limb. It's what is physically left of my leg. Down here below it? The round, smooth metal is called the skeletal component. My prosthetic foot is in this ugly pink and white tennis shoe, and if I took it off and showed it to you, you'd see a metal joint attached to it so I can move it."

"Okay," Noah said, giving her an apologetic look, "does this device weaken your residual leg if you use it too much?"

"Some people use a curved blade for a foot instead of the type I have, and they run in Olympic races." She pulled her jeans down over the device and straightened. "When we're on our feet for a long time"—she patted her socket hidden beneath the fabric—"any of us can feel that the residual leg is somewhat worn, or at worst, bruised."

"Does it feel that way now?"

Shaking her head, Dair said, "No. I've been working out for the last six months in the gym and at the track at Bethesda, getting my residual leg, as well as my whole body, in shape. The socket has to be snug enough so it isn't sliding up and down but not so snug that it cuts off circulation and causes other problems."

"Right now," Noah asked, "is there any discomfort in your real leg?"

Dair treated his hesitant questions seriously. She could tell he was embarrassed, his cheeks ruddy. "None."

"How many hours of this type of work you just did with Thunder would make it happen?"

"How many hours a day do you train?"

"Right now I have six horses. An hour apiece."

"Then, I don't see that as an issue here at all. I'm physically fit to work just as hard as any wrangler would around the ranch. I don't need special treatment, Noah."

He took off his hat. "What about riding a horse to train it, Dair?" He gave her a long, searching look.

"I was riding at Bethesda. I rode at Danbury Farm that day we met. You saw me ride."

"Yeah, I did. And I was impressed. But you know when you train a horse, you're using a lot of leg aids. Sometimes you're using your weight, your thighs, most often your calves or your heels. How does that leg stand up to that kind of demand and workout?"

That was the real issue, Dair realized. She'd passed ground training with flying colors, but Noah was clearly concerned and questioning her ability to use her metal leg and foot correctly for riding. "I've worked a lot, until the snow flew in Maryland, experimenting with my left leg in just such a condition." She touched that leg with her fingers. "All my strength must come from my knee and thigh, which aren't damaged and are completely well. Henry Danbury was very kind when I called him about three months after we met. He, too, has an indoor arena. I told him I wanted to get back into horse training and riding. I needed a dressage-trained horse to practice on. He had several and told me to come out on weekends. By that time, I had my own truck. I drove out every weekend and he was kind enough to allow me a bedroom in his guest house." She saw relief come to Noah's face.

"And what was the result?" he asked.

"I trained with a dressage instructor at Henry's breeding farm. She and I worked together on how to give signals with weight and leg aids. At the end of six months, I was able to achieve the same level of competency as someone who wasn't missing a leg." More relief showed in his clouded, troubled eyes. "I can prove it to you if you want."

He shook his head. "No, not necessary. Henry is an old family friend, and I know him to be generous. He has Olympic-qualified dressage instructors out at his farm, and if you pleased them, I'm sure you'll do just fine here." He sat up, rolling his shoulders, and then gave her a warm look. "I think you're just the person I need to help me here in the training arena, Dair. Would you consider a job with the Bar C?"

Chapter Five

Noah felt like a fool, embarrassed that he had put Dair through all those questions regarding her amputated leg. As much as he was drawn to her, he couldn't hire her if she couldn't keep up with the demands of horse training. It was that simple and that complicated. If Dair was bothered by his questions, she didn't seem to be as upset about it as he was. He knew from his own experience that sharing how he got PTSD wasn't comfortable. And yet, he'd had to ask her to bare it all about the loss of her lower leg. It bothered him.

As Dair sat there, considering his offer for the job as an assistant trainer, she seemed calm and centered compared to how he felt. His gut was twisted in a knot.

Yet, maybe it showed her under pressure, and she'd handled it with grace. Dair would be the same with a fractious horse, too, Noah was sure.

Her beautiful light brown eyes were narrowed as she thought over his offer, and never had he wanted anyone to say yes more than her. Noah knew she needed a job, but maybe his questions about being able to ride and train had upset her even though she wasn't showing it. Tension thrummed through him and he forced himself to sit there and try to relax. As a WMD dog handler, if he had communicated his tension or worry down the leash to his dog, the animal would have instantly picked it up, and that wouldn't have been good. Noah was glad he could hide his real feelings and present a quiet demeanor to Dair.

"You'll let me train from the saddle?" she asked.

Dipping his head, he said, "Absolutely." He saw some relief in her eyes.

"How many horses are you planning on bringing in for training? I know you said you have six already."

"If you look at saddle training on those six, that's six hours out of your day," he said. "I'm going to need your help elsewhere, so I can't have you training eight hours a day. From where I'm sitting, six is the max. Are you okay with that number?" Noah knew her income would be from horse training, and she had to have enough to pay herself as well as the ranch, on a monthly basis. At six horses a day, that would be doable. Noah could feel her thinking. He liked her questions; they showed she was engaged with the possibility of working under his direction.

Rubbing her palms down the sides of her jeans, she said, "Yes, I'd like to work with you, Noah. I think I can contribute in a lot of ways other than just training horses." She smiled a little and straightened, holding up her hands. "I'm pretty good at cleaning stalls, too."

Frowning, he said, "I'm hoping Shay will find another vet who can do that. Both of us need to be released from normal barn-cleaning duties to manage the arena and people coming to ride their horses in it. Never mind, we have training to do."

"It looks like a pretty big job," she agreed. "But I can help. When I was at Henry's farm, I would go down and help the guys clean out stalls." She patted her leg.

"This doesn't stop me from doing hard physical labor. So don't treat me like I'm fragile. Okay?"

Shrugging, Noah gave her an apologetic look. "I'm feeling pretty ignorant about amputees in general, Dair. I'm sorry I had to ask you those questions, but I just didn't know what you could or couldn't do with your leg."

"It's okay," she said, shrugging. "How could you know? Not many people have been around an amputee."

"I know." He sighed, slowly unwinding and standing, pulling his gloves from his back pocket. "But I didn't mean to make you feel uncomfortable or embarrassed."

She stood, dusting off her rear. "Don't ever be afraid to talk to me about my leg, okay?"

Nodding, he lifted his hat, pushed his fingers through his hair, and settled it back on his head. "I'll try. It's personal, you know? I wouldn't want anyone poking around in my combat issues, and that's what it is for you, too."

She walked with him out of the tack room and into the aisleway. "Listen, when you lose a limb, you get used to it. At the hospital, the personnel there treated people like me every day. I'm accustomed to talking about it. It's not an embarrassment. Okay?"

"Yeah," he grunted, pulling on his gloves. He glanced at his watch. "If you want, come with me to my house and I'll throw some sandwiches together for us. It's noon, and you've got to be as hungry as I am."

"Shay said if you hired me that I'd be assigned to your house?"

"Yes. I'll show you your bedroom after we eat. Come on."

* * *

Dair tried to hold on to the bubbling joy within her. She had a job! Her step felt lighter as they walked over to Noah's pickup. The sun was shining brightly, the sky clearing, becoming a light blue vault above them as she climbed into the passenger side of the vehicle.

This time, Noah didn't try to help her. She could see him struggling to treat her as if she weren't a bird with a broken wing, and she wasn't. Still, her heart cracked open a bit more because he cared. There was a lot of protectiveness in the man, but she didn't find that a minus, but a plus. Dair didn't want Noah to see her as injured and not whole. At least, not job-wise. He had to have a hundred percent belief she could do the jobs asked of her, regardless of whether she had two real legs under her or not. He seemed highly uncomfortable asking about it, but she hoped, over time, it would become a non-issue.

When Noah parked at the single-story home, she saw Garret heading into his house. He raised his hand in hello before disappearing inside. She followed Noah up the shoveled concrete sidewalk, and he opened the door for her. Knowing military men were taught to do such things for women, she nodded her thanks and moved past him. She wasn't going to make an issue out of it. And it was kind of nice, she had to admit. Inside the mudroom, she saw pegs to hang jackets and hats. She appreciated the wooden bench on one side of the red tiled floor. The walls were a pale beige, but the color brightened the area.

Noah sat down next to her, pulling off his muddy, wet cowboy boots. "When we get you moved in here, if you have another pair of dry shoes, you might want to put them over there where I keep mine."

"I've got a second pair," she assured him, "but I can't pull off the one on my prosthesis."

"Oh." He frowned. "Sorry . . . I didn't think about that."

She nodded and took a roll of paper towels, tearing off a few to wipe off the bottom of her sneakers. "I can't take off my right tennis shoe or I'll be out of balance, because the shoe on my prosthesis has to stay on."

"No problem," he muttered, embarrassed. Placing his boots aside, he leaned over, grabbed a clean, dry pair of boots, and tugged them on. "We'll make it work however it's best for you, Dair."

She could feel him scrambling again, feel him inwardly chastising himself for not thinking about her needs under the circumstances. "You couldn't know," she said softly, finishing cleaning the mud off the treads. Dropping the paper into a nearby wastebasket, she stood and smoothed her jeans.

Standing, he held her gaze. "I imagine this has caused you all kinds of changes in a routine I take for granted."

Touched by his sensitivity and the awareness of her issues, she smiled faintly. "Yes, it turned my world upside down. Having two legs, having an ankle that would turn and twist, or my foot bending and flexing as I walked, it never entered my mind that one day I wouldn't." She gestured to her left foot. "There's prosthetics out there that enable someone like me to be more adapted to uneven ground, but they cost a heck of a lot of money and it's not covered by my medical insurance."

"Your prosthetic foot doesn't bend or flex?"

She heard the concern in his voice and saw the care in his gray eyes. It did something warm to Dair, and she felt more emotional than normal. Noah was trying to be kind and aware of her situation, and she appreciated that. It wasn't that he was smothering her. He was grappling to understand her world. "No, not as much as I'd like. But I compensate for it."

Noah gestured for her to go into the kitchen. "How do you do that?"

"I pay attention to the uneven ground ahead of me, and my back and legs do the rest of the compensation." The kitchen was painted a light blue, with white and blue curtains at the end of a long row of windows at the sink and counter. The amount of light made the large, homey-looking kitchen bright and lively. Dair stood just inside it, appreciating its warmth and how comfortable it felt to her. Noah moved up to her shoulder.

"What do you think? Do you like it?"

She smiled a little. "Gas stove. That's great. I cook. Do you?" She lifted her chin, catching his mirthful gaze. His mouth was a wonderful part of him. and she felt something stir deep within her. Although Noah was quiet and appeared to be a type B sort of person, Dair knew he wasn't. She could feel that competitiveness within him, although it was well cloaked.

"I work at it," he said, chuckling. "Have a seat at the table. I have some leftover tuna in the fridge. You okay with a sandwich?"

"Sure, I like tuna sandwiches," she said, "but can I help?"

"Nah, sit down. We'll get all this sorted out in the coming weeks."

The rectangular table looked to be made out of golden-brown maple. She pulled out one of the chairs and sat down, watching him go to work in the kitchen. He wore an orange, blue, and white plaid flannel long-sleeved shirt, the fabric stretched across his broad shoulders. Noah was lean but built tight and hard, which was typical of wranglers she knew in the past.

She liked that he had slightly bowed legs, telling her he rode a lot.

"Want coffee?" he called over his shoulder.

"Yes, please."

He reached into the fridge. "I got sweet pickles."

"Always go good with tuna. Sure."

He pulled out the jar, setting it on the white marble counter that had black lines through it. "Chips?"

"Roger that." And she smiled when he did. Falling into military lingo was so much a part of her life. Their life.

"Isn't it nice to be able to talk in military speak?" Noah set the bowl of tuna on the counter.

"Sure is." She watched him quickly wash his hands in the sink and then cobble the sandwiches together. The ceramic plates were clean, bright colors, and soon he brought two of them over to the table. "It's nice to be waited on," she told him, taking her plate, their fingers briefly touching, "but I could have gotten mugs and poured our coffee for us." She liked the idea of living with this man. But another part of her wondered about it because she was so drawn to Noah. And that kiss . . .

"Let me spoil you a little today."

The look in his eyes was more than just kindness. There was something else behind it, but Dair couldn't discern what it might be. "I'm not used to being spoiled at all. Where I grew up, everyone worked hard seven days a week."

He poured coffee into the mugs and brought them to the table. After sliding one into her hands, he sat down at her right elbow. "I guess it's my upbringing," he admitted, pushing the open bag of Fritos her way. "My mother was insistent that I learn to be a gentleman toward a lady. And of course, in the military, that's ingrained in me, too."

"Military men are a throwback to an age where they were expected to open doors for women, treated them like they were fragile and needed to be protected," she agreed drily.

"I know the military is moving to women combat slots, but I'd have problems with it," he admitted between bites. "Not that the women who do it aren't capable. It's just what's ingrained in me from my family teaching me differently."

"We're in a time and place where women and their roles are changing pretty quickly," she agreed. "This is a good sandwich, Noah." She saw ruddiness come to his cheeks and he had an endearingly bashful expression. It occurred to Dair that Noah rarely received compliments.

"Thanks. I'm not a very good cook, and I'm limited to just a few dishes. If you want a chef, wait until tomorrow when Garret makes our Sunday afternoon supper. You'll come to look forward to his cooking every weekend, believe me. All of us do."

She smiled. "Well, I think for a guy, you're doing okay with tuna sandwiches." Dair saw color deepen in his cheeks. Almost like a terribly shy little boy who was told that he was wonderful. What kind of family did he have? She had a lot of questions about him, but tempered her curiosity.

"At least I won't kill you."

She laughed outright, seeing the sour grin hover on his mouth and the amusement dancing in his gray eyes. "That's good to know."

"Generally speaking, when there's two of us in the house, we split up everything, from cleaning to cooking and washing clothes."

"That's fair," she agreed. "How do you want to do it? Me cook for a week and then trade off with you?"

"Whatever works for you, Dair. When Kira first came here, she was assigned to Garret's home and they traded off weekly. That way, when groceries were bought, we had everything we needed for that week." He shrugged. "I'm open to whatever you're comfortable with." And then added, "I'm really looking forward to someone else doing the cooking. As I said, not much of a selection: hot dogs, hamburgers, and stuff like that. Garret makes an incredible dinner, and that's when I get something other than my own attempts at cooking."

She chuckled. "Okay, I get it. I've been in my mother's kitchen from the time my head reached the kitchen counter. Is there anything you don't like to eat?"

"I hate organ meats—liver, heart, and kidneys. My dad is a hunter and what he killed, we ate growing up. I liked the venison from the deer and rabbit, but I couldn't stomach the other parts."

She grinned. "I grew up on wild meat, too. But I love the organs. My mom used to make a stew out of them."

Groaning, Noah said, "If you want them, that's fine, but I'm not eating them. I can always throw together my perennial favorite: a peanut butter and jelly sandwich."

"Oh," she deadpanned, picking up a sweet pickle, "I think I can live without those things. I hope to drive to Laramie and visit my family from time to time, and I'm sure I'll get my fill over there." She saw relief come to his expression and appreciated that his game face had left the moment he was done interviewing her. Dair understood why. And she knew WMD dog handlers had to have the ability not to translate their real emotional state down the leash to their dog. In this case, he was dealing with her in a similar way, and that was fine with her. But here, in the house, it looked like he relaxed and showed his real self, warts and all.

"Good to know."

"What else don't you like to eat?"

"I'm pretty easy on everything else. Really."

Her lips twitched. "Okay. Guess I'll find out as I go along. I'm half Comanche and I was raised on wild foods, greens and herbs. My grandmother Rainbow would pick things such as dandelion greens and drive to my mom's home and leave a bunch on the drain board for us to steam for dinner at night. Stuff like that."

"Hmmm, I've never had dandelion greens."

"Or watercress in salads?" She saw him give her a wary look. "Nope, you've never tasted them, I guess?"

"No. My mom shopped at the Driggs grocery store."

She withheld her laugh. "Okay, you're a drugstore cowboy. I get it, Noah. And I'll make things you can eat. Fair enough?"

"Yeah . . . thanks. Limited palate and all, huh?"

"You have other nice qualities about you that more than make up for it," she murmured, meaning it. Again, that ruddiness in his cheeks deepened for a moment. Did he always blush like this? Dair didn't know and wasn't about to embarrass him further by asking.

"So," Noah said, "tell me about how your physical body adjusts to wearing that prosthesis. You said you compensated for it since it wouldn't move in the same way a real foot would."

Feeling his earnest desire to understand, she said, "When I'm doing heavy-duty physical work, by the end of the day, the bottom of my residual leg is aching. The socket is very well padded and custom built, but a lot of jarring downward on it causes soreness. Because my mechanical foot doesn't absorb shock the way a real one can, the energy moves up my prosthesis to my residual leg."

"What do you do about the soreness? Does it go away after a night's sleep?"

"Depends," she admitted, finishing off her sandwich. "I love baths, but it's tough for me to climb in and out of one without a frame to grab onto. So, in a shower, I just stand under hot water, lean back and let the water fall on that leg. The moist heat takes out the soreness pretty fast."

Nodding, he said, "I see."

Tilting her head, she felt him ruminating about something, but he wasn't saying what it was.

"Each bedroom has a bathroom," he said, "and there's a shower and a bathtub in each one; it's nice to have a choice."

"It is," she agreed. There was turbulence in his eyes. Beginning to realize Noah thought a lot but said little, she wondered if there would come a time when she could ask questions and get him to open up.

"Do you get a sore back?" Noah wondered.

Groaning, she said, "I don't know of anyone, man or woman, who has a leg prosthetic and doesn't have lower-back muscle soreness. The prosthesis just doesn't behave like a real leg would, and again, that energy is transferred upward to the hips and spinal column."

"When you were out at Henry's farm, did riding a horse make your back sore?"

"Never. Riding always helps because my legs are off the ground and the horse's legs are doing the work instead."

"That's good," Noah said, finishing his sandwich and closing the bag of Fritos. "So what does make your back sore?"

"Oh, sometimes when I'm not paying strict attention over uneven ground, I can trip, almost fall. Or"—she grimaced—"I'll fall. I've learned when that happens, how to roll and not injure my left leg in the process, because I could."

"What about cleaning out stalls?"

"I cleaned stalls at Henry's place because he refused to charge me for the training his dressage instructor gave me. I wanted to pay him back somehow, for his generosity to me. I would clean about ten stalls a day on the weekends. Then, I'd get some lower-back achiness if I did too many."

"Anyone would if they're shoveling horse manure and shavings or straw for that many stalls."

"Well," she said with a grin, "that's true. But again, my left knee and my leg in the socket, take brutal, constant stress."

"And that energy is again moved up to your lower spine and hips?"

"Right. Humans are built such that their spinal column is primary to everything they do. The hips become our balance point. I never realized just how much until I got wounded. But I do now."

Shaking his head, Noah muttered, "I'm really sorry this happened to you, Dair."

"Hey, don't pity me."

"I wasn't."

"It sounded like it, Noah. Treat me as if I don't have a prosthesis, okay? Pity is something I can't handle." She saw him move uncomfortably and then he grabbed the Fritos and the empty plates, heading for the kitchen. Okay, she sounded a bit defensive about it. *Dammit.* And there was no way to fix this. He was going to have to adjust to her condition whether either of them liked it or not.

Dair wondered if he saw her as weaker than the normal human being. Most people did if they saw someone with a prosthesis. Saw them as less than whole. Mouth tightening, she decided to sit on her thoughts. Noah was trying to understand, was all. Nothing more, her gut told her.

He came back over with the coffeepot and refilled their mugs. "I've got a lot to learn, Dair. Keep teaching me, okay?" He lifted his head, holding her stare.

"I'm sorry," she said, "I got defensive. I can't stand people feeling sorry for me. I've worked damned hard to be able to do what everyone else does. And I can."

"Yeah, I get it," he said. "Want some dessert? I made brownies a couple of nights ago."

She brightened. "You made brownies?"

"Well," he hedged with a grimace, "it's a box mix, nothing fancy."

"That counts," she said. "Sure, I'd love one." She saw him lose that darkness in his eyes. Dair wanted to get around this uncomfortable moment with him, too. "Do they have nuts in them?" she asked, hopeful.

"Yeah, I put black walnuts in them. Shay has three trees and she picks them every fall. They weren't in the mix, but I decided to add them because she said she always did. She's helped me expand the list of foods I can prepare."

"Sounds great." All the upset she saw in Noah's face over their previous discussion was gone. Dair was learning a lot about him just through his body language, voice tone, and his facial expressions. She'd been trained to do this because as a dog handler, she had to be excruciatingly aware of her dog's slightest change. And dogs didn't speak English. If she translated her worry, tension, or anger in other ways to her dog, it would distract him. Now, she was glad she had that training because reading Noah's face was helpful to her. He seemed happy now, and she felt the brownies were a peace offering he wanted to share with her. It spoke to his wanting her to be a part of his team and that was a good sign, too.

Bringing the pan of brownies over, he set a small plate in front of her. "I think I overbaked these. They're a little hard. Bite carefully. I don't want you to break a tooth on one of them." He sat down.

Taking one large square, Dair could feel how hard it was. At least the guy was trying. "Did your mom ever force you into the kitchen to learn to cook?" She nibbled on the hard brownie. It was going to take some work to soften it up in order to eat it, but it tasted fine. Maybe dunk it for thirty seconds in some hot coffee? She didn't want to embarrass him like that.

"Can you tell she didn't?" He took one of the brownies and clunked it on the napkin. "They're hard as rocks."

"But they're edible, Noah. That's all that counts and they aren't burned. You know you can soften them in a glass of milk, tea, or coffee." She could see he was apologizing for them, but he didn't need to. "I don't know about you, but my mom would send me a tin of cookies over to Afghanistan. And they were always hard as rocks by the time they arrived because they took so long to get there, and it was so damned hot in the summer. I dipped them in a tin cup of hot coffee and ate every one of them." She smiled fondly. "And I always gave Zeus, my WMD dog, one of them, too, if it didn't have chocolate in it. He never got brownies. But she'd send me over sugar cookies and blondies, which he loved as much as I did."

"Bet he thought it was a bone like this one." Noah

grinned, holding up his pitiful looking, hardened brownie.

Laughing a little, Dair nodded. "Yeah, he probably thought it was a chew toy or something. My mom knew Zeus couldn't have chocolate brownies, and she'd always add a rawhide bone for him to chew on instead, and he loved it. I'm used to rock-hard cookies, so don't worry about your brownies here. I'll eat whatever you give me. They're good."

"Are you always this easy to please?"

She raised a brow. "Pretty much. Why?"

"That's a good trait to have." Gesturing, he said, "Soon enough, unfortunately, you're going to meet Shay's father, Ray Crawford. And he's anything but easygoing. Shay did warn you about him?"

"Only that he is an alcoholic and he lives in the last house on this row of houses. Why?"

"Well, he had a stroke two years ago. In the will he wrote—and this was when Shay was in the military, so she had no idea he'd written one—it said that if he became incapacitated for any reason, that she would become the legal owner of the Bar C. Actually, she was already the legal owner of the Bar C because her mother willed it to her, not him. He always said he owned it, but he didn't."

"Maybe male pride? She mentioned her father had a stroke, and she got an honorable hardship discharge and came home and took over."

"Right." Noah's dark brows fell as he nibbled on the brownie. "What you may not know is that Crawford is working hard to overcome his stroke condition, which has partially paralyzed his left side. He was wheelchair bound, but then when Shay had the arena built, along with these four homes, he wanted to leave the nursing home in Jackson Hole and live on the ranch. He made it known he wanted to pick up the reins of the ranch once more if he got strong once again."

"But," Dair said, "Shay said he's an alcoholic."

"Yeah, a really nasty drunk," Noah muttered, shaking his head. He searched her eyes. "He's a hateful, angry, abusive bastard. And you need to stay as far away from him as you can, Dair. He's not nice to anyone. Kira, Garret's wife, took care of him for a while, making him food to eat, cleaning his house, and stuff like that. But he got so nasty, she refused to work for him. That was when Ray had a screaming match with Shay and Reese. He told both of them that he was going to take the Bar C back because he didn't like the way she was running it."

"Oh, no," Dair whispered. "I didn't know this."

"Well, I'm sure Shay was waiting to see if I was going to hire you before she aired any dirty laundry or the skeletons in her family closet. It's none of anyone's business, but Shay has always treated the wranglers like her real family, and she's honest and open about the issue. Plus, Reese, who married her, is now the shield protecting poor Shay from her rabid father."

"There's bad blood in every family, I guess," Dair said quietly, holding his turbulent stare. She felt a sense of protectiveness emanating strongly from Noah. "Has Ray taken legal action yet?"

"Not yet. Reese has a lawyer, though. There was a blow-up with Kira a while ago and Reese had had enough of Crawford going after everyone. Garret and him took him to a condo in town, rented it for him and told him not to come back to the ranch. But Ray got a lawyer and without going into a major legal battle with him, he's returned back to his house here on the ranch. It's not a happy situation for anyone and Crawford refuses to leave. Reese is working at mounting a defense because they know Crawford won't stand down. The guy can walk pretty well, now. He's still weak on his left side, but he's at the gym every day, has hired a trainer, and he's getting better and better. What he wants to do is sue Shay and Reese to get the Bar C back. Crawford wants to be able to walk into court looking fully healed from his stroke, no longer needing a wheelchair, crutches, or a walker in order to get around. That would prove to the judge sitting on the case, that he's fully capable of running his ranch."

Dair's stomach went into free fall. "And if he did such a thing and won? What would he do with Shay and Reese?"

Snorting, Noah muttered, "Crawford has already told them he'd permanently kick them off the ranch. But the deal is that Shay's mother's will entitles Shay to win any case that Crawford tries to mount against them. It's a lot of time, money, and stress for Reese and her."

Sorrow flowed through Dair. "Poor Shay . . ."

Noah reached out, tapping her forearm. "Crawford has made it his business to hunt down every wrangler on this ranch and tell them to his or her face that when he gets the Bar C back, they're fired. He hates military vets. He thinks we're the dirt of the earth, and he'll call you other names if he gets within earshot of you, Dair. You need to avoid him at all costs." His voice deepening with concern, his fingers resting on her arm, he said, "He's going to go after you because you have a prosthesis. I worry about that, Dair. Everyone else around here is wounded just as much as you, only it's not so physically obvious. We all have PTSD pretty bad. But those are what I call internal, invisible wounds, not like yours." He forced himself to remove his hand from her arm. "I'll try to protect you from Ray, but a situation may come up in the future when I'm not around to take him on. And you'll have to defend yourself."

"He's that bad?" Dair wanted Noah's roughened hand to remain on her arm. His touch was welcome, and her flesh beneath her tee tingled pleasantly. Not fooling herself, she knew he'd done it out of worry and concern for her. It wasn't about lust or anything else, judging from the concern in his gaze.

"That bad. If he does find and corner you? Leave. Don't speak to the bastard. Talking to him only enflames him, and he might lose his control. Reese is this close"—he held up two fingers with a quarter inch of daylight between them—"to kicking him off the Bar C for good. He's already spoken to the lawyer about having a restraining order issued to keep Ray off the property, but Shay is against it. She's the daughter caught in the middle. But she doesn't want to see us flayed alive under Crawford's anger and filthy mouth, either. She's being torn in half by her father."

"Whew," Dair murmured, "that's stressful for everyone. I feel sorry for Shay and Reese, though."

"I wanted to clue you in because you need to know this before you take this job, Dair. Crawford is a burr under everyone's saddle around here. If there was a legal suit, it would take more than two or three years to get to court, but still, you need to know that your job isn't as secure as you might want. Okay?"

Chapter Six

February 12

Dair was feeling lucky. She'd been at the ranch for a full month and never had a run-in with Ray Crawford. It was a quiet Monday morning, and she rode a black quarter-horse gelding named Poke around the indoor arena at a slow trot. She felt bad because Noah was cleaning horse stalls while she was out here enjoying herself riding and training.

The covered arena was empty at nine a.m. All the horse owners who had their charges stabled at the Bar C were at work. It got busy in the evenings around six, she'd found out. But she now had eight horses in training, and Dair had been up since five a.m. sharp, starting work at six.

Poke was a registered quarter horse and his owner wanted to put him into Western classes at state-level shows. The only problem was that Poke would often, at a canter, change leads the wrong way in an arena. And in judging, the horses had to be on the correct lead to win or qualify for a ribbon. She kept her calves against the barrel of the chunky quarter horse, who snorted with each beat of the canter. It was a slow canter, one designed to bring Poke into a collected balance. When she and Noah had seen the owner ride Poke for the first time, the horse was strung out, his nose leading, and he wasn't properly gathered up and collected, as it was called in the training industry. If a horse was collected, it meant he was in balance. But when a horse was strung out, they often switched leads back and forth when they shouldn't.

She'd had Poke for a month, and the horse was stubborn by nature. Most quarter horses she'd worked with were friendly, open, and trusting. But Poke wasn't. He wanted control and constantly tried to wrest it from whoever was riding him. To stop this bad habit, he had to learn to become collected.

So, after discussing him with Noah, who was very knowledgeable, they switched him to a snaffle bit with a running martingale and she kept her hands on both reins. In Western riding, the reins were held in one hand. But for training purposes, she had her hands down by the horse's withers, keeping them quiet and asking him to keep his head properly tucked. When Poke found out he couldn't tear the reins out of her hands, that she had the control, he sulked. But every time Dair started to loosen those reins even an inch, he'd jerk his head forward, yanking them away. He was a work in progress. Sooner or later, Dair would gain his trust.

Outside the windows, the sun was shining brightly, gold patches here and there along the thick, sandy ground within the arena. She wore her denim jacket, a red muffler, her hands encased in warm gloves, and denim jeans. Dair loved what she was doing. Everything was perfect here at the Bar C for her. She loved the Sunday dinners Garret cooked for everyone over at

Reese and Shay's home. There was so much laughter and good times on that special day for all of them. Ray Crawford always had an invite to join them, but he refused to eat with the vets. That was fine by her, because the vet wranglers were tight with one another.

She'd made good friends with Kira, Garret's military vet wife, and Shay. The three of them often got together and had a good time. Her mother and grandmother were happy for her, as well. Things couldn't be much better, and Dair thanked Shay and Reese for embracing her and giving her a job at the ranch. It was a dream come true.

Her heart stirred as it always did when she thought of quiet, serious Noah. It was getting tougher for Dair to keep her distance from him. She was tempted to reach out and touch him from time to time. Not a flirt, Dair felt a need to be close to him in an emotional sense. A lot closer than she had with any other man in her life. That threw her, more than falling off a horse or getting bucked off by one. Her relationships with men were few and had turned out to be certified disasters.

Dair heard the door at one end of the arena open up. Twisting her head in that direction, she saw Shay and Kira come in. They smiled and waved at her. Dair smiled back. As she cantered around to their end of the arena, she pulled Poke to a stop where the women had hung their arms over the top rail. "What are you two up to?" Dair asked, patting Poke's damp, black neck.

Shay grinned. "Hey, we were going to go into Kassie's Café for lunch." She gestured around. "Kira and I need a break from the ranch and the winter. We'd love to have you join us. Can you come with us, Dair?"

Looking at her wristwatch, Dair said, "Well, I can take an hour at noon. Would that work?"

Shay nodded, giving Kira a happy look. "Absolutely! How about we pick you up here and we'll drive into town and have a girls-only lunch?"

"Sounds great," Dair said. "You two stay out of trouble. You've got that look in your eyes."

Kira laughed. "Hey, I'm climbing walls. I'm not used to eight months of snow. Feels like I live in Alaska. I need to get out and about for a while."

Dair knew that Kira made her living by translating Arabic documents to English and vice versa, for global clientele, and contributed financially to the Bar C. "You weren't born in Wyoming, that's why," she teased.

Wrinkling her nose, Kira laughed. "Got that right! If I didn't love Garret so much and being here at the Bar C, I'd find warmer digs elsewhere, for sure."

"I hear you," Dair called, turning Poke around. "See you two girls at noon."

"So?" Kira prompted, sitting opposite Dair and Shay in a bright red vinyl booth in Kassie's Café. "How are you and Noah getting along?"

Dair smiled over at the black-haired woman. She, too, had gray eyes like Noah, but they were pewter colored compared to his lighter ones. Kira had been in a Special Forces Army A-team with Garret Fleming. Their story was one of pain, loss, and heartbreaking separation. It did her heart good to hear that Kira had wandered into the Bar C, looking for work, not knowing Garret was already there. It was a swoon-worthy love story with a happy ending for both of them. "Now, Kira, there you go again, playing matchmaker, as usual."

Kira tittered, pushing her large platter of sweet-potato fries into the middle of the table so they could all share them. "Noah's single, terribly good-looking, and he has no bad habits that I can see."

Shay chuckled. "Unlike most guys who have bad habits you could drive a truck through, Noah's almost perfect in comparison."

Dair gave Shay a wry look as she sank her teeth into the delicious Angus beef hamburger. Kassie's Café was the most popular eatery in the small town of Wind River. The place was packed, noisy, and she loved the laughter she'd hear from time to time from the patrons. Kassie was cooking in the kitchen today because one of her cook's called in sick. She, too, hired women vets as waitstaff because she'd been in the military herself. It made Dair feel far more loyal to Kassie as a result. Dair always came here to eat because she was taking care of other women vets. "No one's perfect," she agreed between bites.

"Actually, I don't know if Noah told you this yet or not," Shay said, licking the ketchup off her fingers, "but he was married to a woman named Chandra a long time ago. But that was when he was in the military. He's never said much about it, except that they got a divorce when he was twenty-three."

"Sorry to hear that," Dair said. "He's twenty-eight now."

"Yeah," Kira said, waving a fry at them. "Noah's really sensitive underneath that skin of his and I think the divorce broke him in a lot of ways."

"That's because he's like us," Shay said. "I haven't met a military vet yet who wasn't loyal to death. It's just part of who military people are: They're team oriented, love unity, and are loyal to a fault."

Dair took one of the proffered sweet-potato fries. "I didn't know that about him."

"Noah's slow to warm up to people, but eventually,"

Shay told her, "he does. I think he's been hurt very badly by his divorce. He blames himself for it, not his ex-wife."

"Well," Kira added, "he's never had a girlfriend since he joined the Bar C, Dair. You should know that."

Lips twitching, Dair saw the glint and devilry in Kira's gray eyes. "Don't you feel guilty at all?"

Laughing, Kira said, "Not in the least! From what Garret's said, he thinks Noah's lonely as hell and he was glad to see Shay assign you to his home. We're all hoping you two might get together on a personal basis."

Rolling her eyes, Dair mumbled, "Hey, I'm not the pick of the litter, believe me. I don't do men well at all."

"Why is that, Dair?" Shay asked gently, tilting her head and holding her gaze. "You've never talked about your family. Are there skeletons in your closet, like I have in mine?"

Wiping her fingers on the napkin, Dair felt enough trust with these two women vets to open up. "My father, Butch, was a mean abuser. My mother, Ruby, didn't know it until later, about a year into their marriage. He changed a lot at that time, I guess, from what she said. He became mentally and emotionally abusive toward her, always trying to control her."

"Ouch," Kira murmured, giving her a sad look. "What happened after you were born? Did he get worse?"

"He did," Dair said, sitting back after pushing her empty platter aside. "I don't want this intel to get around, okay?" She saw them become serious and nod their heads. "When I was nine, my dad got angry at me. I was down on my hands and knees in our garden. He'd yelled at me to get over there to him. I guess I didn't move fast enough for him and he came roaring down the garden, grabbed me by this arm"—she held up her right one—"and jerked me up, hard. It broke one of the two bones in my lower arm."

Both women gasped.

Dair grimaced. "My mother heard my screams of pain and came running out of the house. She lit into Butch, beating him with her fist and the rolling pin she was using to make pie dough. She forced him to let go of me. Long story short? She picked me up, ran to the car, and drove me to the hospital ER. On the way, she called the police, charged him with assault, and they threw his ass in jail. She immediately got a restraining order against him. In the meantime, she hired a lawyer and divorced him. He got four years in prison for breaking my arm." Shrugging, Dair added, "I was glad my mother divorced him. After he was gone, we were both a lot better off."

"That's just awful!" Shay whispered, pressing her hand to Dair's upper arm. "I'm so sorry that happened to you."

"Bastard," Kira snarled under her breath. "I have no patience with abusers in general. I lose it if I see a child being beat on by a parent. I won't tolerate it. I immediately get involved."

Dair gave her a look. "Yeah, so do I. It's a real hot button issue for me, too."

"Is your arm okay now?" Shay asked.

"It's fine."

"What happened to your father?" Kira asked.

"After he got out of prison, he left for California and we lost track of him. My mother was fine with that, and so was I. He's probably out abusing some other poor woman in that state or beating up on her kids."

"They should put him away for good," Shay muttered, anger in her low tone.

"Well, your father," Kira pointed out, "was abusive toward you and your mom. He's still that way."

Glumly, Shay whispered, "I know. It's a messy, complicated situation with Ray now."

"I've barely seen him since coming here," Dair told them. "I sometimes see him getting in his truck to go into town, but that's all. He doesn't seem to do much around the ranch. I heard he spends most of his time in town, at that condo Reese rented for him. He seems to slide between it and the house here on the ranch."

"Oh," Kira warned, "he's going to be around. It's just a matter of time. Garret saw him over at the arena the other day, checking out the horses we board for folks. He ran into him because he was going to help Noah clean the stalls. Ray told him he was going to take one of the Bar C horses for his own. Garret asked him if he'd talked to Reese and Shay about it first." Wrinkling her nose, Kira said, "Ray cursed him out and said he didn't need anyone's permission to take one of his *own* horses to ride."

"Oh dear," Dair said. "Noah said nothing about this to me."

"Garret came to me," Shay said. "Reese was in Jackson Hole with our lawyer at the time, and I told him when he got home last night."

"I'll bet Reese isn't happy about this," Dair said. "I sure wouldn't be."

"No," Shay said, "he's not."

"What a FUBAR," Kira muttered, finishing off her burger. "Your father's a mean, abusive man. I know because I had to take care of him the first couple of months I came here. And he still drinks to this day, defying his doc's orders to stop. He's a selfish, self-centered bastard."

Dair gave Shay a sad look. "This has to be really

tough on you, Shay." She saw the woman's blue eyes grow cloudy and she could feel a lot of unspoken emotion around her.

"I'm so glad Reese is in the breach with me in this situation," Shay told them. "He's not emotionally involved with Ray like I am. We've got a good lawyer and he's giving us sound legal advice about how to deal with Ray. One day, we think he'll go over that legal line and then? We can get a restraining order against him that will stick. Until then . . . we wait."

"You are looking to get him kicked off the ranch?" Dair wondered. To her, that would be a wise move. As long as Ray stayed at the Bar C, he was going to continue creating upset and friction among everyone who lived there.

"We're working toward that goal," Shay admitted. She pushed her half-eaten burger away, folding her hands on the table. "But we have to do things within the law. Otherwise, Ray could use our actions against us in court, and it could go against us." Shaking her head, she whispered, "It's such a stress on us. Every morning when I wake up, I wonder if we'll have the ranch or not when it's all over. It's a terrible feeling to know your own father is plotting and planning to hit us with a civil law suit to take this ranch back at some point, regardless that my mom willed the Bar C to me."

"Smells good in here. How'd your day go?" Noah asked, coming in from the mud porch at six that night.

It was Dair's turn to cook for the week, and she was at the sink, washing her hands. "Good. We're having roast beef, gravy, mashed potatoes, and fresh green beans."

"You're a great cook," he said, giving her a warm look

of approval. "I hear through the pipeline that you three girls went out for lunch today at Kassie's." He came over to the counter, looking at the bowl of salad she'd just made, picking out a sliced carrot and popping it in his mouth.

"Yeah, it was a good mental health outing, Noah. I needed a break." She glanced over at him. Her lower body tightened and she tried to ignore the pull that always leaped between them when he was nearby. She wiped her hands dry on a towel. "How was your day?"

"Better now that I'm home here with you," he admitted wryly. He picked up a couple more slices of carrot. "Can I set the table for you?"

"No, thanks. Why don't you go get cleaned up? I'll take care of things around here. We're eating in half an hour."

"Okay, sounds good. I'll be out here by then."

As he ambled off, Dair stood there watching him walk. Noah was boneless and that came from being in terrific athletic shape. Her heart thumped once to underscore her joy over seeing him. Usually, during the day, they saw little of one another because of their different duties. He was so handsome. More than anything, she liked his quiet, sensitive demeanor. He bestowed it on humans and animals alike, but then, he'd been a WMD dog handler and it took great sensitivity to do that very special job. Dair had it herself.

Every night, it was getting tougher to ignore him on a man-to-woman level. Her body wanted him. Her heart yearned for him. But her memory, and it was a long one, put up a big red stop sign.

She quickly set the table and made the thick, brown, fragrant gravy. Cooking was something she could do without thinking, and her mind, plus her heart, were centered on Noah.

The days flew by and she always looked forward to the nights with him in their home. And it *was* a home, she realized. He was a tower of strength to her, unlike the other men she'd been drawn to in her youth. Noah's constancy, stability, and quiet way of moving through life appealed so strongly to her. How many times had she lain awake at night throughout the years, wishing for a man just like him? Dair honestly thought she'd never meet someone like Noah, that it was all her idealistic imagination. But it wasn't. Noah Mabry was as real as they got. And that had thrown Dair out of her bitter promise to never get into a relationship with a man. *Ever.* She'd been hurt too badly, too often. Her heart was wounded and suffering. Somehow, Noah eased that dull pain and reminder. He drew her, and that scared the hell out of her.

"Need any help?" Noah called as he reentered the kitchen later, rolling up his sleeves to his elbows.

She turned, seeing he'd changed into a dark gray long-sleeved tee that brought out the lighter shade of his eyes. "You can take the roast and set it on the platter," she said, gesturing to it sitting on the drain board. Now, in the evenings, he changed into a pair of gray flannel gym pants and traded his cowboy boots for a set of sneakers. His black hair gleamed from the recent shower, but the dark stubble below his high cheekbones gave him a dangerous kind of look. Not a bad one, but one that made Dair very aware of how masculine Noah was. Her body glowed with desire, making her frown.

She brought over the salads and vinaigrette dressing, setting them down. Dair knew it was supposed to be first soup, then salad, and then the entrée, but ranch life wasn't Miss Manners. She brought over the bowl of piping hot green beans, sprinkled with slivered almonds with pats of butter melting across them. Noah retrieved a steaming bowl of mashed potatoes after finding a big spoon to stick into them. Butter melted from the center of it, spreading golden tentacles outward. She had added pepper and a bit of crushed basil over the top of it. In no time, they were sitting down and eating.

"So?" he prodded, cutting into the succulent roast beef, "how was your girls' lunch out? Hear any gossip?" He grinned a little, teasing her.

"Nothing new," she said, and told him about Ray.

"He's a burr under everyone's saddle." Pouring thick gravy over his mound of mashed potatoes, he said, "I'm just glad you haven't crashed into him yet."

"I don't want to, believe me," Dair said between bites. She saw the satisfaction on Noah's face as he ate slowly, savoring every bite, as if it were sacred or something. He always did that when it was her turn to cook. When he did his week of cooking, which was made up of pretty basic foods and food groups, he never had an expression on his face as he did when he consumed the meals she made for them.

"He was out in the barn while you girls were at Kassie's getting lunch," he warned her. "I was over in the other part of the green barn, where we keep our ranch horses and ran into him over there. He was checking them all out."

Groaning, Dair said, "Did you have a run-in with him?"

"No," he said, wiping his mouth on the white linen napkin. "I generally find if I'm respectful and keep my distance, it doesn't set him off as much. He asked me about Poncho, the bay quarter horse we just added to our string."

"That's the one you worked on because he was a kicker?"

"Yes. Reese had assigned Poncho to Garret because the horse is twelve hundred pounds, and he's the biggest wrangler we have. The two are a good fit."

"Does Garret know Ray was over there today? And has an interest in Poncho?"

Mouth quirking, Noah said, "No . . . not yet."

"Did you tell Reese about it?"

"Yes. It's his job to tell Garret. Reese is the foreman, and all these types of issues go to him first."

"What do you think Garret will do?"

"Oh, he won't be happy. Poncho was a notorious kicker and I finally got it worked out of him with two months of intense training. He and Garret have this understanding. Poncho knows if he lifts a leg to strike out at Garret that the horse sees him as bigger than himself. And Garret's six-foot-three, and two hundred and twenty pounds, so that horse is smart enough to put two and two together and not try to raise a rear leg to kick him. I'm not so sure he would do it with someone as short and thin as Crawford. Poncho respects size and that's about it. As a matter of fact? His previous owner who raised and broke him, has Crawford's size and weight. I'm afraid Poncho might put it together and kick the hell out of him. I did warn him that he's a kicker. Crawford shrugged and said nothing, so it's on him. I warned him."

"Horses aren't dumb," she agreed. "Well, what else did Ray do?"

"He's not that strong yet to deal with taking a horse out of a stall and putting him in cross-ties. But he asked me to bring Poncho out so he could take a closer look at him, and I did that for him. I'm not interested in having a battle with the man unless it's necessary."

"I like your peaceful live-and-let-live attitude." She saw him grimace. "What happened next?"

"Well, Poncho was good in the ties as Ray walked around and inspected him. He didn't say anything. And then, he just walked away without a word."

"You mean he didn't even thank you for your help?"

Noah gave her a droll look. "Ray, thank anyone for anything? You're kidding me, right?"

Shaking her head, Dair muttered, "He reminds me so much of my father that I hope I *never* have to deal with him personally." She stabbed at a bunch of green beans with her fork, brows drawn downward. She glanced up and Noah was studying her, an odd look in his expression.

"What?" she demanded.

"You've never spoken much about your family," he began. "Was your father like Ray Crawford?"

There was an edge of concern in his tone, and she saw him grappling to not allow it to show, but she could hear it in his voice. Even more surprising? Dair felt an incredible sense of protection pouring off Noah. Frowning, she couldn't understand his reaction except that no one liked an abuser, which is probably why she sensed his guardian-like energy surrounding her right now. "Worse," she muttered. "It's not dinner-table talk, Noah."

"Yeah, I get it." He scowled deeply. "Sorry . . ."

The silence cloaked them, the clink of flatware against their plates the only sound for a good five minutes. Dair swore she could feel Noah thinking. There were times when he went into that deep thought process, and she could always feel that shift within him. His gray eyes would darken a bit and he wouldn't talk for a while, as if digesting some huge invisible issue only he knew about. It wasn't that he was ignoring her, but something she'd said had triggered something within him. Reminding her of a dog gnawing on a bone, he just seemed to go away for a bit, as if chewing over something very important.

Sometimes Dair wished she could hear what was inside his head. Noah was a deep thinker. He usually spoke little, thought a lot, but when he did speak, it was always important and she always paid attention. He wasn't one of these guys to pop off, went ballistic, or get the cart before the horse. Just the opposite of her abusive, knee-jerk father.

She was cutting her roast beef when he said, "Do me a favor, if you can."

Dair's fork and knife poised over the meat. "Sure. What is it?" There was a turbulent darkness in his eyes and she'd come to know that when they were that color, Noah was upset about something.

"Would you, when it feels right to you, tell me more about your family and your father?"

For a split second, Dair froze, but then went about cutting her meat. "It's not a happy episode in my life, Noah."

"I got that. But I want to know." His gaze burrowed into hers.

If Dair hadn't felt that protective warmth of his enveloping her in that moment, she'd have said no. Instead, she murmured, "I'll think about it . . ."

Chapter Seven

Her residual leg was aching, and Dair removed her prosthesis, rubbing her flesh gently as she sat on the edge of her bed. The door was closed and she had removed the artificial limb after pulling off her boots and jeans. It was nearly nine p.m., and she felt tiredness lapping at her. A hot shower earlier had helped.

Today she'd dealt with a fractious two-year-old who needed to be broke to ride. Dair didn't believe in scaring a horse while introducing it to a saddle. The young sorrel gelding had been mishandled by the owner out of ignorance, but it didn't make her job any easier. The horse had knocked her sideways and she'd fallen backward, twisting her leg in the socket.

She massaged her left limb below her knee, and it felt better after a few minutes. Leaning over, she grabbed her light cotton nightgown, which fell to her knees. She didn't feel comfortable moving around in the house without her prosthesis. Noah had tried very hard not to pamper her, but she decided being protective was just his nature. Most people who hadn't been around an amputee wanted to smother them with help, when just the opposite was needed.

As she sat there adjusting her soft cotton gown over her shoulders, she couldn't ignore her growing feelings for Noah. There was nothing to dislike about him. At least that she could see, so far. He was far from perfect, but his imperfections matched her own and they gave each other a lot of breathing room as a result. She was so damned lonely, and he filled that space in her with his quiet, strong, gentle presence. Brows dipping, she smoothed the gown over her knees. Why had she been testy with him at dinner a week ago, over his request about her father? It had pushed a button in Dair and she didn't like the way she'd backed up on him.

To Noah's credit, he didn't take her reaction personally. Instead, he'd just given her a warm look, as if he understood. Dair knew he didn't. And she knew that Kira and Shay, although they knew about her father, would not gossip about it around the ranch. It was something terribly private and something she was ashamed of.

Running her fingers down her residual leg, she continued to massage it gently. She wasn't whole anymore. Noah made her question her confidence in herself as a woman. What man would want a woman with half of one of her legs missing? Although the surgeons had done a good job on what remained of her left calf, it still looked odd and, to her, ugly. Dair knew that wasn't fair to the doctors who had done incredible work to save her limb. Still, she didn't feel beautiful. Not even pretty. And she wasn't like other women who had two legs.

Dair decided maybe it was time to push out of her comfort zone. She cared enough about Noah to open herself up to him. There was something in him that gave her the courage to try. What she didn't want as she walked around on her crutches when she wasn't wearing her prosthetic, was for him to feel sorry for her. She didn't want him reacting to protect her like he had in the beginning. Her heart yearned for Noah, and she wanted an equal partner when that intimacy sprung so strongly and wonderfully between them.

Unsure, she unbraided her hair and reached for her brush and comb, which she'd set on her pillow. Just brushing her thick, long hair soothed some of her worry. What would Noah think if she came hobbling out on her crutches, wearing the knee-length gown? He'd see what was left of her lost leg. And it wasn't pretty like a woman's lower leg should be. Had he ever seen someone who had such an injury? Dair didn't think so.

The loneliness ate at her like acid. Waffling, Dair placed her comb and brush aside and picked up the aluminum crutches lying next to her on the bed. She could hear the TV was on, the sound barely drifting down the hall to her bedroom. Noah would often watch some of his favorite shows at night. Sometimes she'd join him, but not always.

Well, it was now or never. Standing on her one leg, she placed the crutches beneath her arms. Taking a deep breath, Dair moved to the door, reached out and opened it.

Noah was half asleep, resting in the corner of the flowery couch, when he heard a noise in the hallway. Sitting up, he twisted around, looking in that direction. His heart dropped for a split second as he saw Dair on crutches, wearing a pink nightgown, part of her lower left leg visible beneath the hem. Swallowing hard, he anchored. He knew she didn't want to be pampered. Or suffocated, as she wryly referred to it. Feeling helpless, he saw her lift her chin, their gazes meeting as she came into the living room. How badly he wanted to get up and go help her. But the expression on Dair's face was set, her beautiful gold-brown eyes looking anxious. She was nervous about him seeing her injured leg for the first time.

"Hey," he called, "I just made a bowl of popcorn. Want to come and join me while I watch *Hawaii Five-O*?" Instantly, he saw relief on her face as she slowly made her way across the gleaming cedar floor.

"Yes. The popcorn smells really good."

There were so many emotions twisting inside him. Noah sat there, watching her progress. "Come on over," he invited. Other than the lamps on either end of the couch, it was dark. The light caught her gown for a moment and he could see her naked body silhouetted within it. Noah wasn't going to say anything. He could see Dair was nervous, because she licked her lower lip as she came around the couch. What to say? He shouldn't stare at her odd, narrow-shaped residual leg, so he forced himself to stay still and wait for her to sit down. He'd never seen Dair in her nightgown before, nor had he seen her with her hair down. She looked incredibly beautiful, that shining black mass framing her face.

Picking up the large red plastic bowl filled with popcorn, he placed it in his lap as she sat down, smoothing her gown over her knees and placing her crutches to one side. Feeling her anxiety, he wanted to do something about soothing her but was flummoxed as to what. "Here," he said, setting the bowl within her reach, "have at it."

"Thanks," she said, barely meeting his eyes.

Noah sat back, crossed one ankle over his other knee, trying to appear relaxed. "You okay with *Five-O*?"

He slanted a glance in her direction, his voice teasing. He saw her smile nervously.

"Yes . . . sure . . . the popcorn is great."

"I put lots of butter and salt on it. I'm glad you like it."

Nodding, she said, "I do. It's a good nighttime snack."

He began to relax. She leaned into the other corner of the couch and began to settle against the cushions. Noah felt like they'd just passed a test with one another. "Your hair is beautiful," he said, meaning it. He caught her reaction, her glance of surprise.

Dair touched the strands curled across her shoulder. "Oh . . . thanks . . ." She managed a faint, hesitant smile.

"I always see you in braids. It's nice to see your hair down." Noah saw pleasure come to her expression this time, a tinge of pink spreading across her high cheekbones. She was blushing. Wasn't she used to men giving her compliments? That endeared Dair to him even more. He picked up the remote, un-muting it. "Okay, let's see if our heroes can solve the next case."

Dair nodded, smiling, her hands in her lap, watching the large wall-mounted TV.

Noah felt his gut relaxing as the time passed during the one-hour TV show. Dair kept nibbling delicately at the popcorn from the bowl. He'd take a huge handful and eat out of his hand. He saw the stump of her left leg that couldn't be hidden by the gown. It was shaped and narrowed, and he supposed it was done purposely by the surgeons so it would fit snugly into the prosthetic socket. There were so many questions he had for her, but he wasn't sure if it was appropriate to ask them right now or not.

The shadowy light brought out Dair's classic features, those full, soft lips of hers, how large and beautiful her intelligent eyes really were. There was nothing not to like about this woman. Noah couldn't care less if she'd lost part of her leg. She was attractive to him in every possible way, and he sat there mulling it over, not really listening to the TV show at all.

When the episode ended, it was time for the news. He muted the TV and asked, "Do you want to watch the news?"

Wrinkling her nose, Dair said with distaste, "God, no. All they do is present the latest police report, who killed who, and the dregs of humanity are paraded before me. Neither the local or national news ever has good things to say about people. Only the darkest of the dark are considered newsworthy." She flourished a hand toward the TV. "If you want to watch it, go ahead. I'll leave."

"No . . . stay, I don't watch it either, for the same reasons." He flipped the TV off and set the remote on the lamp stand beside the couch. Noah didn't want her to go. He enjoyed her company even if they sat at opposite ends of the couch. When she lifted her fingers, pushing that thick, ebony mass across one of her shoulders, an ache centered in his lower body. It didn't surprise him. How many torrid dreams had visited him, of making love to this woman? If Dair knew that, he was sure she'd blush bright red. Nudging the popcorn bowl between them, he said, "There's a little left. Why don't you finish it off?"

"No." She met his gaze, "I don't want to go to bed on a full stomach. I have enough trouble sleeping as it is."

"Yeah." He sighed, sitting back. "I know that one. But I never hear you up at night."

Shrugging, she said, "I always have my iPad with over a hundred books on it. When I can't sleep, I read."

"Oh . . . good idea."

"Why? What do you do?"

"I get up, come out to the kitchen, make myself some

hot chocolate." He flashed her a boyish grin. "My mom taught me that hot milk at bedtime puts you to sleep."

"Does it work?"

"Yeah," he said, scratching his head, "it seems to."

"Maybe I'll join you some night. Hot chocolate might put me back to sleep faster than reading one of my books."

"I'd be more than happy to make up a second cup of hot chocolate for you, so come out, okay?" Because he would. Noah *wanted* to do things for Dair. Little things, but nice things. She deserved some sweetness in her life as far as he was concerned.

"Thanks . . . that's really nice of you." She cleared her throat, her fingers moving nervously in her lap. "Last week at dinner?"

"Yes?"

"You asked about my family?"

Noah saw the anxiety in her eyes again, the uncertainty. "I was out of line, Dair. That's none of my business."

"No . . . it's okay . . . it's just that"—she opened her hands—"I'm ashamed of my past . . . my father. It's a sad story. Most people aren't interested in sad stories or police reports, anyway."

"Well, I am." Noah turned, facing her. He saw her expression become confused. "Were you an only child?" he wondered.

"Yes. You?"

"Yep. The one and only." He smiled a little.

"What kind of family do you have?"

Noah sensed she wanted to share about her father, but he felt her holding back, maybe wanting a comparison, for whatever reason. Why, he didn't know. But if it made Dair feel better, he'd share some of his personal history with her. Intuitively, he felt that there was something in her past that made her skittish and distrusting of men. It was just a hunch, and he'd need a lot more than that to prove out his instinct.

"My dad, Blake Mabry, owns a small construction company over in Driggs, Idaho. It's just across the border from Jackson Hole. My mother, Bess, is a rancher's daughter and they married when they were twenty years old. I came along when she was twenty-one."

"So? You grew up on a ranch?"

"Yes, my dad has about a hundred-acre ranch, nothing big, more hobby than anything else, because he's into earth-moving equipment and construction. My mother is a real cowgirl, and together they raised a small herd of quarter horses. I grew up being taught by her how to handle foals, breeding, breaking, training, and such. She's won national championships in Western riding. I'm not as good a rider as her, and I didn't like showing horses because I was happier cleaning stalls, rubbing the horses down, and riding them out on trails." He saw Dair relax, drawn into his narrative.

"Do you see your folks often?"

"I try to get over there about four times a year. I talk to them by phone a couple times a month. They're pretty busy and so am I."

"That's nice," she murmured, folding her hands, staring down at them. "A nice, happy family. You're really lucky."

Noah could feel her tiptoeing around telling him about her family. "Well, maybe sometime, if you wanted, you could drive over with me. I normally stay for a Sunday dinner with them and then I drive back here that night. You'd like my mother's breeding stock of quarter horses. She's got some good lines and some beautiful animals over there. I'm sure you two would get along famously." He smiled a little.

"Yes . . . I'd like that. I like happy endings, I guess." Dair shrugged, looking out into the grayness of the room for a moment.

"There aren't many happy moments in life," he agreed, feeling pain around her. She chewed on her lower lip for a moment and he could feel how badly she wanted to say something. "I always try to look for happy moments in every day. It makes up for the other stuff we all have to deal with," he admitted.

Turning, Dair studied him, the easy silence strung between them. "That's just another thing I like about you, Noah. You're an optimistic person. I guess I'm not. Maybe it's because of how we were raised . . . the stuff that happens in a family . . ."

"My mother, Bess, is always positive, always sees the silver lining in everything that happens," Noah said. "My dad is a brutal realist. I guess I got my mother's optimistic gene," he admitted with a grin, watching her respond, some of the sadness he saw for a moment in her expression, dissolving. "Life is never easy, Dair, and we know that better than most because we were in the military."

"Yeah, I guess it compounded my dark outlook on life after leaving for the military at eighteen."

Noah held her tentative gaze. "What made you feel that way, Dair? I watch you working with the horses and you're upbeat with them, you praise them, and pat them often with affection."

Squirming, she looked down at her hands again. "My father. You asked earlier about him?"

"Yes." Noah felt as if Dair had suddenly become fragile. That shocked him, because she always seemed so low key—confident and quiet, but not broken. An ugly feeling moved through him. Something very bad had happened to her. "What about him?" he coaxed her quietly.

"I'm not proud of it . . . or him. He was abusive to my mom, Ruby, before I was born. And then after I came along, he became much worse. He was always impatient, angry, blew up and did stuff like that."

Noah tempered his reaction, remaining calm. "What was his problem?"

"He was bipolar. I found that out much later, after he was sent to prison. My mother knew of his issues and tried to support him, but he was out of control most of the time. He refused to take his meds and took recreational drugs, instead. He was fired from jobs constantly, and then he'd come home and blame it on her. Or on me."

"Sounds rough."

"I never knew what he'd be like when I arrived home from school. It got so I ran out the door of our house to the bus in the morning, glad to get out of there and away from him. And I hated coming home at night. I used to get stomachaches on the bus as it brought me closer and closer to my house to drop me off. Sometimes, I wanted to throw up . . . sometimes . . . I did . . ."

Noah said nothing, clearly seeing the pain in her eyes. He heard the terror in her husky, hesitant voice. The words were being pulled out of her and she was fighting to share them with him. More than anything else, that told him how deeply her father had wounded her. "Did he ever seek medical help?"

She snorted softly. "No. He said he was fine. And it was our fault he reacted the way he did. We were the ones who made him angry and impatient."

"You lived in a war zone, twenty-four seven, three sixty-five."

She snapped her head up, eyes widening as she held his somber gaze. Noah could feel the release within her as he recognized how she really felt but probably had never put it quite that way into words. "Yes . . . a good way to put it, Noah."

"I'm sorry, Dair. You shouldn't have had to live through that kind of ongoing battle." He wanted to do more. So much more. The moment he'd fully connected with how she felt about those years, for a split second he saw the frightened little girl who lived inside her. She'd started out life wounded by her mentally ill, drug-addicted father. And probably no one ever explained his condition to Dair so that she could comprehend his actions. She only realized it after she'd left home and matured.

"Things came to a head when my father broke my right arm in a rage one day," she told him quietly. "My mother came out of the house and saved me from further injury. She called the police on my father, got me to the hospital, where my arm was put into a cast."

Noah drew in a ragged breath, rage flowing through him. He knew to show it would only impact her adversely. "You had to be in shock over all of that."

"Just a little. The cops took my father away and threw him in jail because my mother pressed charges against him. Then she took out a restraining order when he made bail. A year later, he went to trial, my mother and I gave our testimony before the jury, and he was found guilty and given a number of years in prison."

"What did he do when he got out?" Noah wondered, frowning.

"Left for California, never to be seen or heard from

again." She shrugged. "I was glad. I was so damned scared of him. I had horrible dreams of him coming back to the house and killing us with one of those guns he kept in his bedroom."

"So from that age onward, until you left for the Army, it was quiet and peaceful? You and your mom lived alone?"

Nodding, she lifted her hands. "It was calm for the first time in my life. I loved it. My mom put herself through college, got a degree, and opened a center for preschoolers. I stopped having stomachaches and looked forward to coming home. Life got a lot better for both of us."

"I'm glad."

"My grandmother, Rainbow, is a full blood Comanche. She broke and trained mustangs that she bought from the BLM. She tried to rescue as many of them as she could. So many of them were bought up by dog food factories and they were killed and ground up. Awful," she muttered, shaking her head and looking away.

"You stayed with her sometimes?"

Dair met his hooded gaze. "Yes. Usually I spent weekends with her. I loved being with my grandmother. She taught me everything I know about breaking and training horses with love and respect."

"I was wondering who gave you that nice touch you have with the horses," he said, smiling a little. Noah could see the darkness in the depths of her eyes, that shattered childhood of hers still haunting her to this day.

"She's my rock," Dair admitted. "When my father was still around, my mom would send me to my grandmother as often as she could, just to get me away from him and out of the house. She was trying to protect me."

"Yeah, I understand. Your mother sounds like a good person."

"She didn't realize when she married Butch that he was a monster. He hid it from her. She admitted to me just last year that she'd wanted to divorce him a lot sooner, but he kept promising he'd change." Her mouth compressed. "But he never did. He lied to her all the time."

"Well," Noah said gently, "if she loved him, she probably wanted to believe him and help him get better."

Nodding, Dair said, "That was it, but he killed her love just as he killed mine for him. I feared and hated him in the end. I still do."

Noah reached out, giving her hands in her lap a squeeze. "You were in a war zone, Dair. You have a right to how you feel about it." Noah forced himself to lift his hand away from hers. He hadn't expected the reaction he got from Dair. Her eyes had been sad and dark, but as soon as he'd grazed her folded hands, he saw such hope and a burst of something wonderful that he couldn't interpret. All he sensed and saw was that she seemed to truly relax and somewhat melt at his contact. He needed time to replay it later when he wasn't with her, because she stirred up his need. Was it lust? Yes. But it was much more than that. "You know? You're a pretty courageous woman. Did you realize that, Dair?"

Shaking her head, she gave him a wry look. "Not even. I don't see myself that way at all. If you're saying that because of my family background, I'd use the word 'survivor' instead."

"Okay," he said, settling back against the couch, "there's no question you're all of that."

"I always thought of myself as emotionally crippled," she whispered, unable to look at him, speaking into the grayness. "And what was so ironic when that IED blew up on me and Zeus? Then I really was crippled." She shook her head and turned, holding his stare.

Sitting up, Noah rasped, "You've *never* been a cripple, Dair. Not in my eyes or heart. People here at the ranch don't see you like that, either." Taking a huge risk, he reached out, taking one of her hands from her lap and holding it for a moment. "I see you as a whole, vibrant, beautiful woman. And so do they. I don't see your prosthesis, either. I know it exists for you, but that metal leg doesn't even begin to define who you are." If he didn't let go of her hand, he was going to move closer and draw her into the fold of his arms, because Noah could see how badly she needed to hear those words he'd just spoken.

"So," he said lightly, releasing her hand, "don't keep thinking that way. Okay? Everyone around here admires the hell out of you, Dair. They think you're so damned strong and brave. So do I. If anything, your rough childhood, and then getting wounded in Afghanistan, has done nothing but bring out the best in you. You're more than just a survivor, you're a winner."

Chapter Eight

Dair woke up feeling incredibly lighter, even happy. As she got ready for her day, she could hear Noah puttering around in the kitchen, making them breakfast. Oddly, she felt that happiness so profoundly that it chased away the dark cloud that always hung above her since she'd been wounded. She pulled on a cotton camisole in lieu of a bra, and then a favorite cranberry-red flannel long-sleeved shirt, and quickly buttoned it up.

Earlier, after she'd washed and dried her hair, she'd hesitated a moment, looking at herself in the steamy mirror. She never studied herself in the mirror any more than she had to. Wondering what Noah liked about her thick, black hair framing her face and falling to her breasts, she was perplexed. In the military, she had always worn braids. Her hair was never down, except to wash it. His compliment last night had warmed her in wonderful ways and this morning, her lower body still simmered, reminding her she had needs. Groaning softly, Dair quickly braided her hair, avoiding her reflection in the mirror.

The smell of waffles scented the air as Dair made her way down the hall to the kitchen. It lifted her spirit to see Noah at the sink. She smiled because he always wore an apron to stop from getting his clean jeans and shirt dirty. Never mind all the dusty, dirty work he'd be doing all day long in the arena. Her heart warmed. "Hey," she called, letting him know she was in the vicinity, "those waffles smell wonderful."

He twisted a look in her direction, filling a pitcher with maple syrup. "I got creative this morning. I put pecans and dried cranberries in them."

She came to the refrigerator and pulled out the butter. "I'll eat them."

He grinned. "How many?"

"Three?"

"I'm making myself four."

"Yeah, well you're a growing boy," she teased, walking to the kitchen table and setting the butter dish on it. He'd already set the table. "Orange juice?"

"Yes, please."

Dair loved their morning routine. They never got in one another's way and they were a good team. It was his week to cook now, and that meant morning, noon, and night. The partner filled in where needed, too. She hummed quietly to herself as she came over to the counter, bringing a plate with her so Noah could open up the waffle iron and put one on it.

"Ladies first," he said, taking it off the iron and dropping it onto her plate.

"Thanks," she said, and set his plate nearby.

"How did you sleep last night?" Noah asked over his shoulder as he poured more of the waffle batter onto the hot griddle.

Sitting down, she said, "Surprisingly, I slept all night through. That's a new record for me."

He nodded. "I slept deep, too. Nice not to wake up in the middle of the night."

"Musta been the popcorn?" she teased, grinning as she slathered the waffle with butter and then a thick coat of maple syrup.

He chuckled. "Could have been, Dair."

Her heart swelled every time he said her name. It always rolled off Noah's tongue, and she could hear emotions behind it as well. "I don't know," she murmured, cutting up her waffle. "I've had popcorn before and it never made me sleep like this."

"Hmmm," he said, turning, resting his hips on the counter as he waited for his waffle to get done. "Maybe being able to talk to someone about your family life took the burden off you? My mom is always telling me to spill what's happened to me or whatever feelings I'm holding on to."

The tender look in Noah's eyes made her melt inwardly as she met his inquiring gaze. He was sensitive in ways most men she'd known never were. "You're probably right. Do you off-load to your mom?"

He shrugged a little. "Sometimes," he hedged. "I mean, there's things that have happened to me over in Afghanistan I would never tell my parents. It would be just too upsetting for them to hear it."

"Yeah, for sure," Dair agreed quietly. Her fork hovered over the waffle. "But it was relief of sorts to be able to tell you about my father and what he did to us. I woke up this morning feeling so much lighter that it caught me by surprise." She saw satisfaction come to his expression before he turned to retrieve his waffle. Noah placed it on his plate and walked over to the table and sat down.

"That's really good you feel lighter," he said, buttering the waffle. "Have you been able to tell anyone about your family war?"

Shaking her head, she muttered, "Just Shay and Kira. I'm ashamed of it, to be honest, Noah."

"Shouldn't be," he chided gently, cutting his waffle up. "You were a child. What happened in your family will never be your fault even though your father tried to hold you and your mother accountable for his mood changes."

"I know you're right. It's just damned hard to put it all behind me, Noah. I try all the time, but things happen in my present world and it instantly reminds me of something he said or did to me or to my mom."

"What do you mean?"

"Oh," she said, "about two weeks ago I saw Ray Crawford. He was yelling at Garret, and I was just close enough to see his face and hear the rage in his raised voice. Garret was unruffled by it, took it in stride, but it triggered so much in me, I was really upset for hours afterward." She gave him an apologetic look. "That's why on that day I didn't start training my horses until I'd calmed down. I didn't want them picking up on me being upset."

"I was wondering why you were late coming in for dinner that night." He frowned. "Why didn't you tell me about this?"

Sighing, Dair admitted, "Because I'm ashamed that I can't control some of how I feel. I try to bury it, but not anymore. I used to be able to, but for whatever reason, now I can't."

He tapped her arm on the table. "From now on, if that ever happens again, will you come hunt me up? We can take the time and you can off-load it. I'll listen. I won't judge you, Dair. This is about having a witness to how you're feeling. And I think if you have someone you can share this with, you'll feel better, maybe lighter, like you do this morning." He searched her gaze.

Dair felt his gentleness. "I really appreciate you not judging me, Noah. I hate that. People don't understand and they automatically think they know why you're behaving in such a way." Her lips flattened. "And they don't."

"Lots of those folks out there," he agreed, amiably eating. "But look, you hunt me up next time you're upset, okay? I'll just listen." He gave her a boyish smile. "Then you can be on time for dinner."

Managing a short laugh, Dair nodded. "Okay, I got it. Thanks for being there." She saw a pleased expression come to his face and they ate in companionable silence. Noah made several more trips for her third and his fourth waffle. By the time they were done, it was six a.m. It was still dark outside, although Dair could see a bare, gray ribbon beginning to form in the east along the Salt River mountain range.

They quickly cleaned up the table, placed the dirty dishes in the dishwasher, and moved to the mudroom to don their winter clothing.

"Hey, I have to go to Jackson Hole about ten a.m. today," he told her. "I'll be back about four, in time to make us dinner, so don't worry."

"Oh . . . okay." Dair saw something, maybe amusement, in his light gray eyes as he buttoned his coat and settled the Stetson on his head. "I'll make myself some lunch, no worries."

"Great," he said, opening the door, the cold February air rushing in.

Dair was walking back from the horse barn, boots crunching in the gravel, when she saw Reese, Shay, Garret, and Kira. The women were all dressed up and pretty. The guys were in suits. What was going on?

Shrugging to herself, she didn't know. It was four p.m. and the sky was clear, but the winter darkness was looming and would be here in another hour. She'd seen Harper earlier because he was giving the horses their nightly hay and sweet feed. She moved to the walk that was now dry and clear of ice. With her prosthesis, ice was a particular danger to her. Hustling up the walk to their house, she quickly moved inside, the temperature around twenty degrees Fahrenheit.

She smelled something cooking, and frowned. Had Noah returned from Jackson Hole earlier? Whatever it was, the food smelled darned good. Sitting down, she cleaned off her muddy sneakers. In a few more moments, her coat and hat were hung up. Tugging her shirt down around her hips, she walked into the brightly lit kitchen.

"Happy Valentine's Day, Dair."

Stopping, she blinked once and stared. Noah was standing there with a bouquet of red roses in one arm. In the other, he had a heart-shaped box of chocolates with a big red ribbon across it. And he was giving her a bashful grin, as if unsure she would take his offerings.

"Oh," she stumbled, at a loss for words.

"I—uh, well, I wasn't sure you knew it was Valentine's Day, but I wanted to surprise you." He extended the bouquet toward her. "I hope you like roses. They smell pretty good."

Dumbly, she took the dozen red roses, pressing the blooms to her nose and inhaling. "They smell wonderful," she admitted, tucking them into the crook of her left arm. "This is such a surprise, Noah. You didn't have to do this for me." But she loved it, giddy with the surprise. Noah looked relieved and pleased.

"I wanted to do it, Dair. I wanted to make you happy. Here's chocolates. You do like chocolates, don't you?"

She laughed a little and took the proffered candy. "What woman doesn't like chocolates? Thanks."

"I had to drive into Jackson Hole because we don't have a florist here in Wind River." He wriggled his finger toward the box of candy. "And that's See's chocolates. They're the best. They have a store up there, so it was easy to pick up some nice roses and candy for you. One-stop shopping."

Heat fled up into her cheeks as she stood there with her bounty. Noah looked shy. He'd stuck his hands in his pockets, rocking back on the heels of his boots. There was a ruddiness to his cheeks as well. "Gosh . . . this is so sweet of you. I love See's candy. How did you know?"

"Well," he hedged, moving from one foot to the other, "Shay told me. I asked her about a week ago. She told me you loved it. I got the idea to go to Jackson Hole and surprise you. Guess I did?" He cocked his head, giving her a crooked grin.

"You sure did," she whispered, touched. "I didn't even realize it was February fourteenth."

"I was hoping you didn't." He put a thumb over his shoulder toward the kitchen. "I also ordered us a nice Valentine's dinner to go, from one of the best restaurants up there. It's prime rib with all the fixings."

"That's what I smelled!" she said. "Let's go put these roses in water."

"Yeah," he said, turning, "I'll get a vase from under the sink for you."

For the next few minutes, as Dair unwrapped the fresh red roses and cut the stems, placing them in the vase filled with water, she watched Noah work around the kitchen. He'd already set the table. Everything warming up in the oven smelled mouthwateringly delicious, and her stomach growled.

"You probably saw Reese, Shay, Garret, and Kira leaving?" he asked, pulling out the au gratin potatoes slathered with melted cheddar cheese.

"Yes, I did. They were all dressed up. Now I know why." Dair carried the cut-glass vase to one end of the table and set the roses there so they could both appreciate their beauty and smell their heavy fragrance.

"They were driving into Jackson Hole to go to that same restaurant I got these dinners from."

"That makes sense," Dair said, coming to the drain board. "Shay and Kira looked really pretty all dressed up." She looked down at her jeans.

"Well," he said, handing her the bowl of au gratin potatoes to set on the table, "they'd asked me a few weeks ago if we'd like to go with them, Dair. I didn't feel at that time that we'd bonded enough, but I thanked them. I hope that was okay with you?"

"I don't even own a dress, Noah, so it was the right answer." A little thrill zinged through her as she set the bowl on the table. Up until last night when she'd unloaded her past on Noah, there had always been a certain detachment between them. But this morning? The feeling she had toward Noah was warm, strong, and it made her feel good. She'd never felt like this toward any man before, and she liked that sensation. Was Noah aware of it? Something told her that he was. He was far too sensitive not to feel subtle shifts and changes between them.

"Well," he murmured, bringing over a platter with the two huge medium-well-cooked prime ribs, "that's going to have to change."

She smiled a little, drowning in the heated look he gave her. And there was no mistaking that look. He desired her. But it was mutual, even though Dair wouldn't admit it to him right now. "This is the perfect dinner for us tonight," she said, choking up. "No one's ever done this for me before, Noah." She reached out, touching his broad shoulder momentarily as he set the platter between their plates.

Straightening, he held Dair's tearful gaze, seeing her struggle not to let the tears fall. "Come on, let's enjoy this dinner together. We've earned it."

For a moment, Dair felt as if Noah were going to reach out and haul her into his arms and hold her against him. Her heart leaped at the thought. So did her lower body. She was befuddled by all the lovely, unexpected surprises, and he came around and pulled out the chair for her to sit down on. She thanked him, once more touched by his being a gentleman. None of the men she'd had a relationship with ever thought to pull out a chair for her. She watched Noah sit down at her right elbow. He rubbed his hands, smiling.

"This is going to be a very nice meal. Dig in."

Dair was hungry. The food from this particular restaurant was mouth-melting delicious. There were baby carrots slathered in honey, a European-greens salad with walnuts, beets, and feta cheese. The au gratin potatoes with the sharp cheddar cheese made her groan with pleasure. And the prime rib was so tender it dissolved in her mouth. Everything was perfect. Just perfect.

When she was finished, Noah took the empty plates and asked her to remain sitting. Usually, she got up to help him clear and clean up. Puzzled, Dair saw him pull something from the oven. He had a proud look on his face as he brought it over, two dishes sitting on his oven mitts.

"This restaurant is known worldwide for their famous coconut bread pudding," he said, placing her bowl with a flourish before her. "I found out from Shay that you love bread pudding, so I thought you might enjoy this."

It was a huge rectangular piece, drizzled with heavy whipped cream and garnished with three mandarin orange slices. She could see caramel sauce had been added to it, as well as the coconut sprinkled over the top of it. "Wow," she murmured, grinning up at him, "you really know how to spoil me." For a moment, there was a flicker of something in his amused gray gaze that told her he wanted her. And then it was gone as swiftly as it had appeared. She watched Noah's mouth draw into a grin to match her own as he placed the second bowl in front of himself and sat down.

"Like I said, Dair, it's time something nice happened for you. I like when you smile, and it does my heart good to hear your laughter. You have a beautiful, husky laugh. Dig in, huh? This is too good to waste."

"I feel like the heavens just opened up and I won the lottery," she teased, spooning the warm concoction into her mouth. She saw Noah take a taste, closing his eyes as he slowly savored it. He hid nothing from her, and Dair appreciated that even more than this wonderful meal.

"Manna from Heaven." He gave her a meaningful look between bites. "Expect more to fall out of the sky for you."

She laughed, feeling giddy, like she was a teenage girl who had a crush on a boy. Dair knew that feeling because she once had a crush on red-haired Bobby Spencer in the ninth grade. Being immature, she hadn't understood all those happy, wild, wonderful feelings she experienced when Bobby was around her. That puppy love waned as school let out in June and his parents moved to another state. Dair remembered how brokenhearted she was to learn that. Now, that same feeling was embracing her heart, and she knew it was because she liked Noah. He was a kind, thoughtful person.

Noah was worried. He tried not to voice it to Dair. She'd just agreed to train a chestnut thoroughbred-and-Arabian-mix stallion named Champ, who had a lot of bad habits. The horse was nearly fifteen hands tall, built for running. The owner, a girl of fourteen from Jackson Hole, with very rich parents, had brought the animal for Dair to train. The only problem was that none of those people knew anything about horses. The animal had been in an auction and the girl, Joy, had fallen in love with his bright chestnut coloring with four flashy white lower legs, a wide blaze on his face, and sporting a showy, creamy-colored flaxen tail and mane. The horse was colorful and beautiful in that sense, but Noah would never have bought him for Joy. In fact, no teen should be handling a stallion. In his personal opinion, the animal should be gelded, far more safe for a girl of her age. Stallions were pure testosterone and could not be trusted if a mare was around. They would bite in a heartbeat and anyone who had ever been bitten by a stud never forgot it. Further, they would run over the rider or trainer if leading them on the ground to get to a mare in heat. Stallions were not afraid of humans in the least. And Joy had never had a horse before. He worried a lot about the situation.

Noah watched from the pipe-rail fence around the arena at seven in the morning as Dair brought Champ out on a longe line for the first time. She carried a buggy whip in her other hand, because they both agreed that the horse was mean and looked for ways to hurt a human. He'd already, when being loaded into a trailer at the auction, lashed out and caught one of the men doing it, in the leg. He'd gone to the hospital. Further, Champ snapped and bit at any and everyone within reach of his long, snaking neck. And that was why Champ was here: to get rid of his desire to bite and kick at any human who approached him. Noah had tried to talk the parents into selling the horse, and even offered to go look at more suitable horses for sale for their daughter. But Joy cried, begging her parents to keep the animal. And so they did.

Mouth thinning, he watched Dair intently. The stud had dainty ears and they were constantly flicking between her and the rest of the arena. What Noah didn't like was that the horse had small, close-set eyes; a sign of pigheadedness, outright meanness and stubbornness all mixed in. He didn't know why Dair agreed to try and work out Champ's bad habits. Maybe it was the money.

He looked up at the windows at the top of the arena that brought so much mid-March sunlight down into the huge, quiet building. The sky was blue, with a few scudding white clouds here and there. Like Dair, he was in a goose-down vest over his long-sleeved flannel shirt. It was warming up, a pre-spring thaw he supposed, and it was nice to get out of the heavy work jacket.

Dair and he had checked Champ's teeth in cross-ties earlier, being alert to not getting close enough to his hind end to get the shit kicked out of either one of them. Galvayne's groove was found on the upper corner incisor tooth of any breed of horse. The groove was a dark brown vertical phenomenon. It was barely visible at the top of Champ's incisor tooth, meaning he was probably around ten years old. The groove didn't start forming until that age.

Dair had told Joy's parents that since Champ was that old, his habits were ingrained and it was going to take a miracle to work them out of him, if ever. The horse needed to be gelded, too. No young girl should be working around a stallion like this. Noah agreed, and he had warned the parents, too. But tearful Joy convinced them to keep the dangerous animal.

Noah had a bad feeling about it, but said nothing because Dair had more than proven herself able to train and handle all the horses they had right now. But Champ didn't like humans and he was sure that the horse had been mistreated a lot at an earlier age. He felt bad for the horse, but a thirteen hundred-pound animal could kill Dair. And he'd put nothing past this stud.

Dair had already told the parents that she'd give Champ a try for a week, and if he didn't start coming around, she was not going to work with him any further. Noah more than agreed with her evaluation. He knew Dair had a soft spot in her heart for underdogs because she saw herself as one. But she was smart enough to know when a horse was intractable and putting her into danger. They'd discuss this at length. Still, Noah didn't even want Dair around this animal.

This was one stud that he would never have agreed to even try to work with. There, he and Dair were different, but he respected her decision. He just didn't trust Champ at all. The horse was smart and he'd been abused. The stud could wait until just the right moment and then strike like lightning, catching the rider or trainer completely off guard. He curved his gloved hands into fists, and then forced himself to relax as he watched Champ trotting around in a circle on the longe line.

* * *

Dair clucked softly to Champ, who had one ear aimed toward her, which told her he was listening to her. He was kicking and bucking, hating being controlled by the longe line. She was using quite a bit of strength, keeping him moving in a large circle, not allowing him to call the shots. The stallion would trot a few paces, then rear, leap into the air, and come down, bucking and trying to brush close enough to her to bite or kick her. She was on to his tactics and lightly flicked the buggy whip, stinging his rump to remind him to stop edging toward her. Instantly, Champ snorted violently and leaped forward, nearly jerking the longe line out of her gloved hand. There was no question the stud was testing her in every possible way. And he knew he weighed a helluva lot more than she did.

Dair couldn't imagine little Joy ever riding this horse. Thank God the parents had had the good sense to first contact Noah and get the stud trailered here for evaluation. Champ could kick Joy in the head and kill her outright, or give her a TBI, traumatic brain injury, ruining the rest of her life.

Mouth tightening, Dair watched Champ suddenly lunge forward, galloping just as fast as he could, the dirt flying upward from his hind hooves. She was aware Noah was nearby, leaning casually on the pipe-rail fence, watching them intently, but saying nothing.

Glad that he was there, she kept her full focus on Champ. She'd seen mustang stallions who were wild and reckless, usually at a younger age, but this one was dangerous, no matter what his age or breeding. She'd already made up her mind that there was no way she was going to train Champ, because the horse was looking for an opening to kill her. She saw it in his small, close-set pig eyes. That is what they called a horse like this. And they were always trouble of the worst kind. She'd handled a pig-eyed mustang when she was seventeen. Rainbow had warned her about horses with close-set eyes in a narrow face. The grulla colored animal had already tried twice to brush her off on a barbed wire fence. He'd caught her off guard and kicked her in the thigh two weeks earlier. She still had a purple lump where he'd nailed her in the leg. In the end? Rainbow said enough and she sent the grulla off to the dog food factory, saying he wasn't worth her being killed by the animal. Sometimes, her grandmother had told her, arm around her shoulders as the horse was trailered off the property, there was no saving a mean horse. Dair had cried, having the hope of the world in her heart for any animal. But it was an abject lesson because her grandmother rarely gave up on a mustang.

A mourning dove that had a nest high in the rafters of the arena sailed downward past her head and in front of where Champ was galloping. Dair's neck hair stood up. Before she could react, the horse used the bird flying near him as an excuse. Champ wheeled sharply on his hind legs, lifting his front legs. Teeth bared, he bore down on Dair.

The horse turned so swiftly that Dair took a step backward in case he bolted. She knew all horses were super sensitive to any movement and would react violently to a perceived threat. Champ spooked, but he used the situation to come after her.

The seconds slowed down. She saw the stallion turn, spin around, and then deliberately lunge directly at her. He curled his upper lip, exposing his teeth, ears laid flat against his neck, pig-eyes focused solely on her.

Her whole world felt like it had suddenly halted as she lifted the whip in her right hand, tightening her grip on the longe line in her left one. The animal's eyes were ringed white, a crazed look in them as he bore down upon her. His long neck snaked out, his teeth opening to bite her.

Dair had no time to think. Everything she did was instinctive to save herself from being run over by the angry stallion.

She heard Noah shout a warning.

She smelled Champ's breath as he opened his mouth wide. Stepping back, Dair crossed her feet because her left one wouldn't flex fast enough. Just as Champ lunged, she felt him bite down hard on her left shoulder muscles. In an instant, the horse grabbed her and tossed her like a rag doll up into the air. She was tumbling. Her shoulder hurt. Closing her eyes, Dair tried to relax on impact with the sand floor.

Noah's shout broke through her shock as she slammed into the arena sand. Striking her head first, stunned, Dair lay there for a second, feeling her left leg being repeatedly struck by the horse's sharp front hooves. But it was striking metal, not her residual leg. Trying to roll over, she lifted her hands and arms over her face to protect it. Champ came at her again, feet striking out, going for her head this time.

And that was all Dair remembered. Her world turned black.

Chapter Nine

Pain ripped up Dair's left knee, bringing her out of unconsciousness. She was moving. Forcing open her eyes, she felt the cold March air against her face. Recognizing Garret Fleming's back in front of her, Reese on the other side, Dair realized she was being carried on a litter. Her gaze shifted and she saw Noah walking beside her, his hand on her shoulder. In the background, she heard Harper shouting something to someone.

Noah looked down at her. "Just rest, Dair. We called the fire department. The paramedics have arrived and they're taking you to the Jackson Hole hospital. How are you doing?"

She saw the terror banked in Noah's eyes, heard the tightness in his voice.

"W-what happened?"

"That damned stallion turned and charged you." His hand tightened for a moment and then smoothed her shirt across her shoulder. "He spun around so fast. A dove had flown down by his face and it spooked him."

"Oh . . ." she groaned, lifting her hand, pressing it to

her hair. She felt dirt on the strands, the whole event downloading and coming back to her. "He used the bird as an excuse to attack me," she mumbled. The up and down motion of the litter aggravated her left knee. She was lying beneath several thick wool blankets, strapped in.

"Yeah," Noah growled, "the bastard was just waiting to charge you."

"What happened after I got hit, Noah?"

"He charged you once you were down, striking at your metal leg. And then as I ran toward him, he turned and his hind hoof caught you in the side of the head, knocking you out."

"Damn . . ."

Giving her a tender look, he lifted his hand and barely grazed her dirty cheek. "This wasn't your fault, so don't go there."

She saw Shay running from the house, out the gate and down to the gravel parking lot where the ambulance was parked. "Where's the stud?" Dair asked Noah.

"Harper got him and he's in his stall. The vet's coming. We think he broke his right front leg when he tried jumping over the arena fence." And then he added darkly, "Just deserts. That's an animal who isn't safe for anyone. He needs to be put down."

"He hates humans," Dair agreed weakly, feeling the pain radiating upward from her knee. "What did I do with my knee? Where's my prosthesis?"

"Well," Noah said, "it's pretty beat up. It took the bulk of Champ's attack. Harper is going to bring it along in a minute, but it's pretty well destroyed, Dair."

Groaning, she saw Shay arrive, breathless, her blue eyes dark with worry.

"Dair, are you okay?"

"I'm fine," she whispered. "I'm alive, that's all that counts."

The litter halted and one paramedic opened the rear doors. In moments, they had slid her in on the gurney and into the ambulance. Dair saw everyone looking at her was concerned.

"I'm going with her," Noah called to Shay.

Harper ran up, out of breath, carrying Dair's badly dented prosthesis. "I'll follow you in the truck. You'll need a way to get back to the ranch."

"Oh, dear," Shay said, studying her prosthesis as Noah slid in beside the gurney in the ambulance.

"Yeah," Noah said, "if that stud hadn't attacked her there, he'd probably have broken her leg, maybe her pelvis. I'll call you once we know something about Dair's knee, Shay." He hopped into the ambulance.

"Okay," Shay called. "Stay in touch! If you need anything, let us know."

Noah lifted his hand. "We will." He saw Harper running down the slope to get in his truck to follow them.

The doors shut with such finality that Dair closed her eyes for a moment. One paramedic drove the ambulance. The other firefighter, in his midthirties, remained with her. He hooked her up to a blood pressure monitor and made sure she was comfortable for the fifty-mile ride to Jackson Hole. Glad that Noah sat next to the firefighter, on a bench against the wall, she saw how upset he really was. Things settled down quickly after the paramedic, named Jason, called the ER at the hospital and gave all her medical stats to the person at the other end. He gently pulled the covers aside and placed a chemical ice pack on her left knee, as well as a pillow beneath it to support it and take the strain off it.

"How does that feel?" he asked her.

"Good," Dair said. "Thank you . . ."

Jason nodded and brought the covers back over her legs to keep her warm. "Just rest. We've got a damned good ortho doc up in Jackson Hole. He'll take good care of you."

Dair grimaced. "Do you know if he works with amputees? I'd bet everything that he's very unfamiliar with amputees."

"He just left the Marine Corps. He was one of the head ortho surgeons at Landstuhl Medical Center in Germany."

Relief shot through Dair. "That's really good news."

"Yeah," Jason agreed, sitting down, giving Noah a quick look. "His name is Dr. Elliot Radke. You'll like him. He's a cool dude. And he's on duty at the hospital right now, so I'm sure you'll be assigned to him."

Dair hoped so. She glanced up at Noah, whose gaze had never left hers. "I'm glad you're here," she said, reaching out her hand in his direction.

Noah nodded, his elbows resting on his knees, hands clasped between them. He lifted his hand, encasing hers. "Are you in any pain?"

"My head aches a little." She touched her dusty hair near her left temple. She felt a swollen lump. "But I'm far more worried about my left knee. It hurts a lot." Noah's face tightened and she saw turbulence in his dark gray gaze. His fingers grew firmer around hers, as if to comfort her.

"Well, let's get there. I'm sure they'll x-ray your knee first, and we'll see what happens next. I'll be with you every step of the way, Dair. I'm not leaving your side." Reluctantly, Noah released her hand.

The ice pack was helping with the swelling of her knee. Glad that Noah was so close, she felt more stable with his hand around hers. Inwardly, Dair worried about her knee. Torn ligaments? Torn tendon? ACL injury? She didn't know, and it scared her badly. She needed that knee to be strong because that joint was the only thing between her being mobile or being reduced to a wheelchair for the rest of her life. She wanted to cry, but fought back the urge. Just having Noah nearby helped her emotionally and she drowned in the melting look he gave her.

"Everything's going to be all right," he soothed.

She knew he didn't know the mechanics of her knee. She hadn't either, until the ortho people at Bethesda had taught and trained her knee to be as strong as it could be to support the loss of her lower leg and foot. If only this attack hadn't happened! Closing her eyes, she felt deep depression stalking her. She'd wrestled with it for over a year after losing her leg. The last few months, she'd felt so free and happy, so many things going so well in her life. And now this.

Noah kept his game face in place once they admitted Dair to ER at Jackson Hole. It was a middle-sized hospital and they weren't that busy, which was good. It meant that Dair would be quickly seen and taken care of. He remained at her side at all times and stood guard when they wheeled her into a cubicle where blue fabric curtains were drawn open. One of the nurses, a blonde in her twenties, pulled them closed to give them some privacy. Noah walked over to the gurney where Dair lay. Her hair was mussed and filled with the sand from the arena. Her clothes were dusty, as well. He could see the turmoil in her gold-brown eyes, her brow wrinkled with worry.

Halting near her right shoulder, moving a few tendrils away from her cheek, he said, "It's going to be okay, Dair," slanting a look in her direction as he moved his hand tenderly across her shoulder, where he could feel her tension.

"I've been so careful not to hurt that knee," she whispered brokenly. "If it's bad, I don't know what I'll do, Noah." She gave him an anxious look. "I have to be able to be mobile. I can't be stuck in a chair."

Moving his hand across her shoulder, Noah said, "We'll take this one moment at a time, Dair."

The curtains parted. A physician in a white coat, a stethoscope around his neck, short blond hair and blue eyes, entered. On his name tag it read: Radke, E., MD.

"Hey, I hear you tangled with a pissed-off stallion, Dair," he said, smiling, holding out his hand to her. "I'm Doctor Elliot Radke. I'm the ortho man around here. How are you doing?"

"Better now that I know you were at Landstuhl," she said.

He released her hand. "Yeah, I'm one of them." He laughed. Turning, he held out his hand to Noah. "And you are?"

"Noah Mabry. Dair and I live together."

"Good to know." Radke devoted his attention back to Dair.

"So? You've been through Bethesda or the Naval Medical Center in San Diego?"

"Bethesda, Doctor. I was a WMD dog handler in the Army over in Afghanistan."

"Tough job," he said, losing his smile. "Let me examine that leg of yours." He carefully removed the blanket from her lower body.

Noah remained close, wanting to keep contact with Dair. The doctor seemed warm, friendly, and it was just what she needed right now. Dr. Radke brought the gurney into a semi-upright position so she could lean comfortably against the support. Her pant leg had been cut off above her knee by the paramedics. The knee was the size of a cantaloupe, and even to Noah, it looked pretty awful. Plus, the skin was rubbed raw, bleeding a little here and there. "The stud hit her prosthesis at least four times, down on the metal part of the leg," Noah told Radke.

"Is the prosthesis here?" he asked, moving his hands gently around Dair's swollen knee as he carefully examined it.

"Yes." Noah left the room and went to retrieve it. Bringing it back into the cubicle, Noah held it up in both hands so the doctor could look at it.

"Wow," he murmured, giving it, and then Dair, a look, "that stud meant business, didn't he?"

Dair snorted. "I don't remember most of it. Noah, here, saw it all."

"Paramedic said you suffered a level-two concussion. We'll look at that in a minute," Radke said, moving his hand down her residual leg, pushing here and there, but gently. "I'm going to carefully move your joint around, Dair. You'll tell me when it hurts?"

Nodding, her whole focus was on her knee.

Noah watched as the doctor slowly moved her joint one way, and then the other. At some angles, Dair stiffened. The doctor would instantly stop, allowing the knee to go back to its normal position. And then he'd slowly stretch, pull, or twist her knee in another direction. It hurt Noah to see her stiffen, knowing she was feeling pain. Finally, Radke was done with his exam and he eased her leg down on the gurney, keeping his hand just above it.

"I suspect a torn ligament," he told her. "I'm going to have my nurses take you to get a CT scan to prove it."

With a moan, Dair said brokenly, "No . . ." That

meant six months for it to heal. "I won't be able to use my prosthesis . . ."

Noah held her hand, hearing the absolute despair in her voice. "What does that mean, Doctor? She can't wear her prosthesis?"

Radke shook his head. "No, unfortunately she can't. Maybe starting at the third or fourth month, but that means she's coming up here to my ortho center and getting therapy as well as exercises to strengthen it in the meantime."

Miserably, Dair whispered, "I'll be bound to a chair. I won't be able to do horse training, Noah."

He heard the tremble in her strained voice, saw tears edging her eyes. "Don't worry, we'll work around this, Dair."

"But," she said, "I'm useless without my leg!"

"Nah," Radke said, "don't go there." He gave her a kind look. "Let's get the CT scan. I'll know a lot more after looking at it, okay? Don't jump to conclusions just yet."

Dair gave a bare nod, staring in anguish at her injured knee.

Noah moved away as the doctor checked the side of her head where she'd taken a glancing blow from the stud's hoof. It was swollen, but the good news was the doctor said she was fine.

"You'll have a headache off and on for a day or two, I'll bet," he told her. "Maybe dizzy on and off, also. In about a week, you'll be back to normal, Dair." He examined her arm where the stallion had bit her. "Nasty," he muttered. "You're going to have this lump for a few weeks, but it's the least medically important and will heal up on its own."

"Tell me that same thing about my knee after I get through that CT scan," she told him.

Radke smiled and jotted down some info on his tablet. "I got all kinds of work-arounds up my sleeve for you, so don't go there. Okay?"

Noah could see the anxiety subside in Dair's eyes as the ortho doctor left the cubicle. She was gripping her dusty hands and he could feel her ballooning anguish over the accident. He slid his arm around her slumped shoulders. "It doesn't matter, Dair, if you have a torn ligament or not. Okay?" She lifted her head, utter misery in her expression. "No one is firing you from that job. It's yours. If you have to be wheelchair bound for a while, we'll figure out things you can do to help me at the arena until it heals up."

"But there's eight horses in training, Noah! And if I can't use both my legs, I can't train. Then, it all falls on your shoulders because there's no one else who can take that load off you."

"There's always work around, Dair. I don't want you going to the worst-case scenario just yet." He squeezed her shoulders a bit. "Your job is safe. You're living with me. Nothing changes. No one at the Bar C is going to abandon you because of this accident. We'll make this work. We're a team."

Dair listened to Elliot Radke's interpretation of the CT scan taken earlier on her injured knee. She was back in her cubicle in the ER, waiting for the results. She liked the man. He was upbeat, kind and sensitive toward her. Most of the surgeons at Landstuhl that she'd dealt with after her leg was amputated, were just like him. He was a bright spot in her life right now. Her last hope. And having Noah nearby, his hand rarely leaving her shoulder, helped her so much more.

"To put this in English," Radke told them, standing at the end of the gurney, "Dair, you have a partially torn ligament. Now, it's not a bad tear. It's only about thirty percent of the ligament, and that's good news for you."

"How is it good news? I still can't wear my prosthesis, Doctor."

"Not for the first six weeks," he agreed, "but depending upon how well you do your exercises, which I'll give you before you leave here, we might be able to put you back on your feet with a little tinkering on your socket. Now"—he went to the corner where her prosthesis was propped up against the wall—"this socket is pretty well destroyed," he said, holding it up for her to look at closely. "You're going to need a new limb. That stud tore the hell out of the center metal area and bent some other things on it that can't be repaired."

Dair's heart sank. "Even if I could come back and stand on my legs in six weeks, Dr. Radke, the VA will never have me fitted for another prosthesis that quickly."

"You're right," he said, setting the prosthesis in the corner and returning to her gurney. "But here's a game changer in your favor. I happen to be one of the ortho doctors working for a manufacturer that is looking for amputees to try out their new, super-duper prosthesis. I'm on the board and I make recommendations, and I'll get you into the program. It's free. All you have to do is get properly fitted for it, give the team feedback about it, and wear it. The company is BiOM. Have you heard of them?"

Her heart raced. "Well, yes, I have. BiOM produces the most advanced prostheses in the world. They're considered the best."

Radke smiled warmly. "It's true. Dr. Hugh Herr owns it. He's associated with Biomechatronics, a research group at the MIT Media lab. They're doing groundbreaking work for amputees."

"He's considered the most brilliant inventor in the field of limb replacement and rehab," she said, suddenly excited, feeling hope drizzle through the darkness inhabiting her. "You can really get me a replacement limb through BiOM?" She could barely believe how good this news really was.

Nodding, Radke said, "I'll have my staff put your name up for consideration and I'm sure BiOM will accept you, Dair." He pointed to her knee, which he'd fitted with a brace around it to give it stability. "All we need is for your knee to lose the swelling and then wait six weeks to see where that ligament of yours is at. With all the advancement in BiOM, they may well be able to produce a socket and suspension system that will allow you to begin to use the limb at that time." He added, "You're young, you're a military vet, and that means you'll work consistently at your exercises to help make that happen."

"For sure," Dair whispered, feeling mildly in shock over her turn of good fortune.

Radke shifted his gaze to Noah. "I'll give you the address of my clinic. I've already called over to my office supervisor, Eugenia Ross, and she's going to have a file of information and instructions on Dair's exercises that she's to do daily."

"We can drive over there as soon as you release her from this ER," Noah agreed.

"That's gonna happen right now. You can pick up her prescriptions here at the hospital pharmacy up on the second floor." He turned to Dair. "Now let this cowboy take care of you. Okay? I know you're a big girl, a vet who has seen her share of combat, but sometimes it's good to lean on your partner for a bit, eh?"

Dair felt heat moving to her cheeks. "Yes, Doctor. I'll do that."

Noah gave her a look that double-checked it. She managed a partial smile and saw his light gray eyes grow warm.

"Okay, so I'll be seeing you at my office in seven days, Dair. By that time, we should have everything in place and I'll be able to tell you that you're going to be looking forward to getting the most advanced prosthesis in the world and that you'll be able to wear it in about week six. Sound good?"

Did it ever! She reached out, shaking Radke's long, spare hand. "Yes, sir, it does. Thank you for *everything.*"

He leaned over, giving her a light embrace and patting her back. "We take care of our vets around here. Don't ever forget that. Okay?"

Tears jammed into her eyes as she watched the doctor leave the cubicle. "Okay," Dair choked out. The nurse came in and pushed the front curtains aside so that they could leave. She brought up a lightweight wheelchair.

"Now, Dr. Radke has these real sporty, bright red models he keeps here when he's on duty," she told Dair. "Have you ever been in a chair like this one?"

Dair knew it was an ergonomic sports-type model wheelchair, one that amputee sportsmen and -women used. "No, but it sure looks sleek."

She smiled and brought it over to her. "Well, he's loaning it to you. He thought you were a real outdoors type and would probably want to be active, plus your arm and hand strength will match this chair's capability," she said.

Grinning, Dair said, "He's right."

Noah came over, lending his hand to her as she slid off the gurney. She felt his strength, his quietness, and it helped stabilize her. Sliding gently into the well-padded seat, she liked that the wheels were canted toward her; it made it easy to place her hands on them to move in any direction she wanted. Noah then released her hand and covered her lap and legs with a wool blanket. Dair was grateful. She knew people would stare at her odd-shaped residual limb.

"Do you want help?" he asked her.

"Oh, give her some, Mr. Mabry," the nurse urged. "I know she's the kind of woman who is very independent and young, but the doctor wants her to truly rest for the next three or four days." The nurse bent over, catching Dair's gaze. "Let others help you for a bit?"

"I suppose I can," Dair grumped.

"It's temporary," the nurse reassured her, patting her shoulder. "Go home now. I'm sure you're dying to get a shower to wash that dust out of your hair."

Wrinkling her nose, Dair muttered, "Yes, it's the first thing I'm going to do." Noah came up behind her, hands closing around the handles of her chair.

The nurse walked out with them. "Now, Mr. Mabry. You're going to have to help her wash her hair and such. The doctor wants her to have someone close by to help her for the next week. With that level-two concussion, she might suddenly get dizzy in the shower and she could lose her balance, falling and reinjuring that knee of hers. She needs your close support for the next few days."

Dair gave Noah a look that spoke volumes. He grinned like a little boy, amusement and tenderness in his gaze.

"Oh, we'll make it work," he promised the nurse.

Dair gave him a grudging smile and shook her head.

It felt odd for someone to be pushing her along the tiled ER floor toward the exit door in her chair. Given how her knee was throbbing, she was grateful to Noah for squiring her around the hospital.

They went to pick up her prescriptions and then Noah guided them out to the parking lot. The day was brisk and cold. Noah had thoughtfully brought her jacket in after shaking the dust off it. Now she hugged it tight to her body as he wove between parked cars to get to Harper's truck. Inside, Harper was busy on his iPhone when Noah approached the window.

He quickly put the iPhone away, climbed out of the truck, and came around to the passenger-side door. "How are you doing, Dair?"

Harper was always the optimist, and that was one of the many things Dair liked about the vet. She filled him in as he opened the door for her. Noah was being attentive. She wasn't going to be able to climb into that truck by herself, not with a bum leg. Instead, he leaned over her.

"Hold on. I'm going to lift you up and out of the chair and I'll slide you into the seat. You okay with that?"

Dair inhaled his scent and she nodded. "Yes, I guess I am." His eyes gleamed with concern as he carefully and slowly scooped her up into his embrace. Automatically, her arms fell around his shoulders. The bruised, bitten arm throbbed a bit, but it was nothing in comparison to her knee issue. There was nothing soft about Noah's hard, lean body, and Dair absorbed the unexpected contact with him. He smelled so good to her.

"Relax," he rasped, waiting for Harper to pull the wheelchair out of the way, "I've got you . . ."

And she did just that, relishing their closeness despite the thick, heavy winter jackets they wore. She wasn't a lightweight, but Noah lifted her easily up onto the black vinyl seat of the cab, carefully placing her legs so that her foot didn't accidentally hit the door. Grateful, Dair released him, whispering, "Thank you, Noah . . ." He was so close that she wanted to lean forward and kiss his stubbled cheek, but resisted. Dair told herself it was the shock and trauma making her feel so emotional, so needy and wanting him to hold her right now.

Noah brought the seat belt across her body and snapped it into place. "There," he murmured, "are you comfy?" He placed the blanket over her lap and rearranged it once more.

"Yes, I am." She saw Harper open up the rear cab door, fold up her sleek wheelchair, and lift it easily into place behind where she sat.

"I'll drive," Noah told Harper. "You hop in the back."

"Yeah," he said, "I've got a bunch of emails that need answering."

In no time, they were leaving Jackson Hole and heading south on Route 191. It was midafternoon and Dair leaned her head back against the head rest, closing her eyes, suddenly feeling exhausted. She felt Noah's hand on hers for a moment.

"You doing okay?"

Nodding, she turned her hand over and he squeezed her fingers and then released them. "Yes, just suddenly very tired."

"Shock," he said. "Go to sleep. We've got fifty miles to go before we get home, Dair."

She didn't need any coaxing. Just the low growl of the truck, the humming of the tires against the asphalt road leading toward Wind River Valley, soothed her fractious state. She'd taken some pain pills Dr. Radke had ordered for her. Maybe that's why she tired so quickly? Unsure, Dair moved her hand toward where Noah sat driving. She needed his touch once more. He made her feel as if everything would be all right. His fingers met hers and he weaved them between hers, holding them gently on the seat. Dair didn't want to have to explain why she'd done it. He gave her such a sense of calm in this chaotic world of hers.

Her mind rolled around like an aimless bowling ball in her head for a moment. She worried about her job, despite what Noah had said. She wondered what would happen to Champ. Had he really broken his leg trying to leap over that metal rail fence? What would Reese and Shay think of her getting injured? They had such high hopes for her. Would they be horribly disappointed in her? Especially since she had a minimum of six weeks before she could put her prosthesis back into place and be mobile once more? Her heart lingered sweetly on Noah. She liked being picked up and held by him. She loved his smell, part man, part alfalfa, and part sweat. Dragging in a long, ragged sigh, Dair succumbed to the darkness swirling around her. She needed to sleep and heal.

Chapter Ten

Reese knocked and entered the back door to Noah's home. "Hey," he called, sticking his head in the door, "how's Dair doing?"

"Come on in," Noah invited. "Dair is doing okay. I just made a fresh pot of coffee."

The rancher nodded and stomped off the dirt on his boots in the mudroom. "Shay told me an hour ago she was meeting Kira over here and they were going to help Dair get a shower and help wash her hair," he said, entering.

Noah nodded, pouring him a mug. "Yeah, the girls are still in the bathroom," he noted wryly. "Lots of laughter and giggles are floating down the hall every once in a while," he said, smiling a little. "I think they're having a lot of fun." He gestured to the table. "Have a seat."

Reese nodded, taking off his Stetson and setting it on a chair before taking the cup. "How bad is her injury?" he asked, sitting down opposite Noah.

Noah filled him in. "Dair's worried you're going to be disappointed in her because she's laid up for six weeks."

Shaking his head, Reese rumbled, "No way. Things like this happen. Ranch work isn't for the weak. Someone's always getting hurt. It's just part of the job."

"I agree, but she's worried. Maybe later, you and Shay can convince her she's still got a job here?" And then Noah added, "Otherwise, she's gonna be restless and lose the sleep she needs in order to heal."

"I hear you," Reese murmured. "We'll take care of it. She's done fine training, and is making the ranch and herself money."

"No disagreement," Noah said. "She keeps asking about that damned horse, Champ."

Shrugging, Reese said, "The vet came, said he'd broken his cannon bone on the right leg when he tried to jump that arena pipe fence. They took him in their trailer and the vet was going to put him down at his clinic."

"I should have told Dair not to take him into training. I had a really bad feeling about that stud, Reese."

"No one's fault. From what Shay said, the little girl was out there crying and begging Dair to 'fix' her new horse so she could keep it." He gave Noah a wry look. "Which one of us can say no to a crying child?"

"Yeah," he muttered, sitting back, his hand around the mug, "I know. But next time? If I get that feeling, I'm going to refuse. I'll say no to anyone who wants a bad horse trained. I'm not making that mistake again."

"It's okay. Things like this happen when you're growing a training business," Reese said, giving Noah an understanding look.

"She's got a great ortho doc," Noah said, filling him in on Dair's healing schedule. He saw Reese's face relax.

"Ligaments take six months to heal," Reese said, "but if the tear is small, which it sounds like it is, she could start getting mobile sooner than that, with a new prosthesis and gym work."

"I'm going to call Mike Barton at his gym in Wind River tomorrow morning. I want to set up a schedule for taking Dair in every other day so she can do Dr. Radke's exercises to strengthen that left knee."

"Good. We'll pay for that gym time, Noah. Our health insurance probably won't cover it, but we will. Tell her that, okay? I don't want her thinking her whole life has been suddenly upended again and she's lost everything. In Shay and my eyes, she's here to stay. This is just a pothole we all have to deal with, but we will."

"Yeah," he sighed, "that's pretty much where she's at right now. But I think if you and Shay could sit down with her, and tell her she still has her assistant horse training job, that will go a long way toward her getting better faster."

"We will," Reese promised.

Women's laughter floated down the hall. Reese grinned. "Sounds like the three girls are having a good time in that bathroom together."

Chuckling, Noah said, "It's been a party since they all crowded in there."

"Still, it's nice to hear them laugh," he mused, smiling.

"Much preferred to tears, that's for sure," Noah agreed.

"How do you think Dair is going to take Champ having to be put down?"

"Personally," he said. "She'll feel partly responsible when none of it was her fault."

"Horses can spin on you so damned fast that you don't have a chance to move or dodge them," Reese growled, frowning. "I didn't see Champ, so I didn't get to size him up."

"You probably would have had the same reaction I did. Even Dair felt something was 'off' about Champ, but the girl's tears made her say she'd try to retrain the damned stud. I should have stepped in and just said no." Noah scowled.

"Don't go there, either," Reese warned. "You're still getting to know one another in this work arrangement. Things happen, that's all."

"Well, I'm going to take over the training of the horses for Dair, for now."

"And I'll go muck out stalls for you. Shay has another military vet, a Special Forces sergeant, coming in tomorrow for an interview. He might be a fit for the Bar C. We need to hire at least two more wranglers."

"That's good to hear. Hope he's a fit." Noah grinned a little, holding Reese's gaze. "You're gonna trade in your accounting job for a pitchfork and wheelbarrow for a while, huh? Helluva change for you."

Giving him a sour smile, Reese said, "Garret's out in Jackson Hole on a big construction job. If he was here, he'd pitch in and help, too."

"Ask Harper."

"Yeah, I'm going to. I figure if he and I do the mucking out of the stalls, it'll go twice as fast as one wrangler doing it. Don't worry about it. We'll get it fixed."

Noah heard the door to the bathroom open. He saw steam escaping from it, moving down the hall along the ceiling until it dissipated. "Uh-oh, here come the girls," he teased Reese.

Dair felt so much better as Shay and Kira supported her, her arms over their shoulders as she used her one leg to move slowly down the hall toward her bedroom. Their arms were around her waist. They had washed her hair, added a conditioner, and then dried it. Even better, they'd gathered up that thick, dark mass into two cute pigtails. Kira thought it made her look like a young college-age woman. It was wonderful to have all the dirt and sand of the arena scrubbed off her body. Kira had gone and gotten her a soft gym top and loose trousers. They'd put a thick, warm sock on her right foot and then placed her tennis shoe over it. The lower left leg of the trouser flopped around because she no longer had on her prosthesis.

They took her into her bedroom, where they halted in front of her sleek ergonomic wheelchair. Kira had the brake on it, but placed her hands on the handles of it to keep it steady while Dair turned and then carefully set herself down into it.

"Dair? You look tired. Do you want to lie down for a while?"

"No, I'm starving to death. I'll take a nap after I eat."

"Woman after my own heart," Kira said. "I'm going to put on that knee brace. Then, let me wheel you out to the kitchen?"

Dair wanted to do it, but she loved their maternal nurturing, too. She remembered Noah's conversation about letting others help her right now. "Sure, that would be nice. Thanks, Kira."

"How's the knee feeling?" Shay asked later as they walked down the hall toward the kitchen.

"Much better. That warm water really helped."

"We need to get some ice on it, too," Kira reminded her.

"Maybe when I lie down for a nap," Dair said. She saw Reese and Noah at the table, drinking coffee. Her heart took off because she missed him being close to her right now. Noah fed her something no man had ever given her before: genuine care. The other relationships she'd had were all based on wanting sex. How different Noah was from her other experiences. At odd moments when she'd glance at him, she'd see that look in his eyes: a man wanting his woman. That didn't frighten her though; Noah didn't flirt with her, nor did he do anything inappropriate to make her feel as if she were being stalked for the sake of wanting sex from her.

Noah stood, and he smiled at her as they came into the kitchen. Reese also stood, nodding toward her, concern in his expression.

"Hey," she said to them, "I'm starving to death."

"How about I make you a turkey sandwich?" Noah asked, pulling out two chairs and removing them so she could sit at the table in her wheelchair.

"Sounds good," she said, giving him a grateful look.

"Make four?" Shay asked. "It's past noon and we haven't eaten either."

Noah grinned. "I got enough to go around," he assured them.

Kira joined him. "Mustard, ketchup, and mayonnaise?" she asked, going to the fridge.

"All the above," Noah said. "People can tell you what they want on their sandwich."

"Grab sweet pickles?" Shay called, sitting down next to Dair.

"I'd like a slice of cheese on mine," Reese added. "How about you, Dair?"

"Noah knows what I like on mine, so I'm set, thanks."

Kira brought over mugs and the pot of coffee. "You're looking better, Dair. More color in your cheeks now," she said, sliding the filled mug into her hands.

"I'm feeling better," she said, relief in her tone.

"That's good news about the doc giving you a new prosthesis," Reese said.

"Don't I know it," Dair said, sipping the hot coffee. "When I saw how busted up my other one was while I was in the ER, my heart dropped. I knew the VA would take months and months to get a replacement for me."

"Well," Noah called over his shoulder as he quickly put the sandwiches together, "Dr. Radke is taking care of you now. He's a helluva lot better than the VA."

Shay gave her husband a loving look. "Despite everything, you have some good luck on your side, Dair. From what you were telling me and Kira about that prosthesis, it's going to be a top-of-the-line model. The latest generation. That's exciting!"

"It is," she said. "And I'll be able to flex the foot, which will help me to move around. It will give me a lot better balance and I won't have to compensate so much with the rest of my body, like I did before."

Noah brought over two plates, sliding one over in Dair's direction and the other one to Shay. Kira brought the other three plates. Soon, they were all sitting at the table enjoying a late lunch together.

Dair was glad Noah took the chair at the end of the table, their elbows near one another. He winked at her at one point and she smiled, warmth flowing strongly through her.

"How's the knee doing?" he asked her.

"Better."

"She needs an ice pack put on it later," Kira reminded Noah.

Nodding, he said, "Will do."

Dair missed Garret's company, but he'd be home on Sunday morning to cook their Sunday afternoon dinner, which everyone looked forward to. "Kira? Did you let Garret know what happened to me?"

"Yes, I called him earlier, a bit before you guys got home," she said.

"Where's Harper?" Noah said, lifting his head.

"Candy, one of our quarter horse broodmares, is just

about ready to foal," Reese told them. "He wanted to stay with her at the foaling stall for a bit, see how she's doing."

"Couldn't you make him a sandwich, Noah?" Dair asked. "Take it out to him when we're done?"

"I will," he said.

"He won't like that he missed having lunch with all of us," Shay said.

Dair knew Harper was just as family oriented as everyone else here at the table.

"He loves foaling," Shay said. "He's a midwife and the horses know it."

They had three quarter horse broodmares who were due to foal in March and April. Candy, who was a seven-year-old bay, was due at any moment. And Harper was a true nurturer, good at mothering the broodmares. Many times, a mare waited until the human had left her stall to drop her foal. But not with Harper around. They usually dropped their foal when he sat on a low stool in a corner of the stall, just keeping the mother quiet company.

"I wish I could go out there and be with him," Dair said to no one in particular, finishing off her sandwich.

"I've been thinking," Shay said to everyone. "We need to build a wooden sidewalk from the homes here, down to the arena. At least until we can put in a concrete one after the weather warms up in June. That way, Dair, while you're in the chair, you can go up and down to the barn and corral areas as you please. The inside of the arena is all concrete, so that would be easy for you to navigate. Then you could go visit the broodmare section any time you wanted."

"That's a great idea," Reese told his wife.

"We've got plenty of two-by-fours stacked in the

other barn," Noah added. "The weather is supposed to be good the next two days."

"Heck," Kira said, "we could all roll up our shirt-sleeves and have that sidewalk built in two days. I'm great at measuring and cutting wood."

"And I'm deadly with a nail gun," Shay volunteered, suddenly enthused.

Reese nodded. "Noah and I could lay the framework out for it today. We've got five hours of daylight left. How about it, Noah? You doing anything else?"

He grinned and gave Dair a warm look. "Yeah, I'll help out."

"Harper will want to stay with Candy, though," Kira said. "I'm sure the group of us can make quick work of getting a sidewalk built."

Dair wanted to cry, and she gulped several times, deeply touched by their idea, their enthusiasm, and their caring for her. Noah laid his hand on her lower arm and she looked up at him. There was something so beautiful and intense in his gaze at that moment, it stunned her. And then it was gone. She felt his fingers close gently around her lower arm in a caress.

"What do you think, Dair?" he asked, his voice thick with feelings. "Does that sound doable for you? Would you use it?"

Clearing her throat, she gave all of them a grateful look. "Yes . . . that would be wonderful. I could feed and water the horses in the barn, you know. I could cut open a bale of hay, use my chair to take the flakes to the horse stalls. Give them their ration of oats. That would take off some of the load all of you are carrying because I can't do my normal job for a while." She needed to feel as if she could do something, anything, to be of help to the team.

Reese nodded. "Sounds good to me, Dair. You let us

know what you can do once we get that sidewalk in place. We'll all pitch in to help, and that way, no one gets a sixteen-hour day out of this." He grinned over at her. "We'll use whatever help you can give us. Okay?"

It was more than okay with Dair. "I-I just feel so bad that I've put everyone into this position," she told them, her voice hoarse as she looked each of them in the eyes.

"Don't even go there," Shay warned, shaking her head. "Getting injured wasn't your fault. That was a mean stallion. No one is upset with you. We're just glad he didn't kill you. You could have been hurt a lot worse."

Dair frowned, feeling Noah's hand leave hers. She so badly wanted constant contact with him right now. She was still in shock; that's what made her feel like that. "What happened to Champ? How is he?" she asked everyone. Instantly, she saw their expressions close.

"When he tried to jump out of the arena, Dair, he didn't make it. He broke his right cannon bone," Reese offered, regret in his tone.

Staring at him, her mouth dropped open. "Y-you mean he's dead?"

"We had the vet come out with his trailer to examine him. The vet said he broke that leg. He took him back to his clinic," Reese said. "He had to put Champ down. There's nothing that can be done for a horse with a broken leg. I'm sorry."

Wincing, Dair closed her eyes, tucking her hands in her lap beneath the table. "Oh," was all she managed to choke out. Tears burned beneath her eyelids, but she refused to allow them to fall. Finally, getting a handle on her stunned feelings, she opened her eyes. "He was a badly abused horse," she whispered. "I thought I could slowly bring him out of it, turn him into a useful animal."

Noah shook his head, giving Reese a grim look. "Dair, in my experience, Champ was too far gone. He was at least ten years old. He had an ingrained pattern of distrust of humans in him for his entire life."

"I feel so sorry for Joy, the little girl," Dair whispered, distraught. "Does she know what happened?"

Reese said, "Yes. I called her parents earlier and spoke to them. Frankly? They sounded almost relieved, because both of them worried about Champ. They aren't even horse people, but they picked up on the stud's mean disposition. They worried for their daughter."

Grimacing, Dair said, "I sensed that."

"We all did," Noah added gently. He held Dair's watery stare. "I'm really at fault here. I knew the stud was big-time trouble. Like you, I allowed a little girl's tears to sway me from what I knew to be true." His voice turned heavy. "If I had to do it all over again, I'd tell the parents no, that we wouldn't try to train Champ, and explain why. By not doing that, I got you hurt." Reaching out, he squeezed her hand resting on the table. "And I'm damned sorry about that. It was my responsibility to make the final decision on this, and I screwed up."

Dair started to protest, but Kira said, "Look, we live on a working ranch. Stuff like this happens, Noah. You did the best you could. I'm sure Dair isn't blaming you for this."

"God, no," Dair said, giving him an anguished look. "I had a part in this, too, Noah. I begged you to let me try to work with Champ for a week to see if he'd come around."

Reese said drily, "Noah, when you've got two females,

one crying and the other pleading with you? You'll *always* defer to what they want, no matter what you think."

The table broke into knowing laughter, everyone's head bobbing in unison over that classic comment.

Noah removed his hand, giving Dair a sad look. "Never again will I do that. If I sense something about a horse, you and I will discuss it in private. We'll both make the determination together, and not be swayed by a little girl's begging and tears."

Nodding, Dair said, "Yes, I completely agree."

Noah tucked Dair into her bed with a pink afghan that had been knitted months earlier by Shay. She'd given it to him as an after-Christmas gift. "There, are you comfy?" he said as he straightened. Dair lay on her right side so that her left knee and residual leg were resting on a supportive pillow.

"I am, thank you," she said, holding his stare. "What a day, huh?"

"Yeah, one we'll be glad to see go." He smiled a little. "I'm meeting Reese down at the barn to look at those two-by-fours we've got stacked in that one barn. If they're good, we'll start laying them out, measuring, and get you a nice sidewalk you can spin your wheels up and down on."

She smiled tiredly. "You're all incredible. I wish I could help you make it."

"No," he said, leaning over, moving a few dark strands away from her cheek, "you need to rest. You've had a tough day, Dair."

The brush of his fingers, roughened but warm, grazed her skin. "I'm just glad Reese and Shay are going to give me a second chance."

"They always will," Noah assured her. "Listen, I have to run. I'll come in once an hour just to check on you. Okay? In case you need anything?"

"You don't have to do that, Noah—"

"But I want to," he told her, his hands on his hips, holding her stare.

"Okay," she whispered, closing her eyes. "But don't wake me if I'm asleep."

"Wouldn't think of it. Rest. Sleep as long as you need." He stood there, watching her thick black lashes rest against her pale skin. What Noah wanted to do was slide in behind her, curve himself around her body, and hold her, warm and safe. There was so much he wanted to tell her. His hands dropped from his hips and he felt a powerful urge to kiss that cheek of hers.

Unsure of where they stood with one another, Noah cautioned himself to remain patient. They were getting along well until this happened. And now her focus was torn back to her rehabilitation. Thanks to him for not following his own damn instincts, he'd put her life in jeopardy. Guilt-ridden, he couldn't resist and leaned over, using his index finger to lightly graze her high cheekbone. Dair was already deeply asleep because she didn't move. She was exhausted.

He stood there, torn, not wanting to leave her because he'd seen the effect he'd had on Dair since the injury occurred. With every contact, she relaxed a little more. He could see the look in her eyes, that fear of being once again rejected because she was an amputee. Noah couldn't imagine all the hellish emotions she'd gone through since the accident. Dair was more worried about losing her job than the damage done to her knee.

Everything within him wanted to protect her, give her happiness instead of the rough life she'd had. She was a vet, and deserved better. The fact that the VA would not be able to replace her badly damaged prosthesis in a short amount of time made him more than angry. If not for Dr. Radke, Noah was very sure he'd have done something—anything—to get her prosthesis back to her a helluva lot sooner. Noah had his own issues with the VA, among them, the long waits. When he'd gotten out of the military, it had been a six-month wait time for him to see a doctor about his PTSD. He'd learned very early on not to trust the VA or rely on it for anything because it didn't care. While he'd heard good things from other vets in other states, he'd experienced the other side of the VA. It was upper management and the federal government that was making life incredibly harder on vets who deserved far more than this. Only people like Shay and Reese, vets taking care of vets, who were essentially putting out a hand to help them.

Forcing himself to move, he took one last, long look at Dair. She had one hand beneath her cheek, the other peeking out from beneath the pink afghan. She lay curled up, almost in a fetal position. The pigtails made her look so young, and his heart mushroomed with so many emotions that he kept closeted away from her. Was there something between them? Sometimes, Noah thought so.

He quietly closed the door to her bedroom and made sure his boots didn't echo down the hallway toward the kitchen. The sun was out and he could see the blue of the sky through the kitchen windows. It was a good day to build that wooden sidewalk for Dair's wheelchair. Something good and clean flowed through him as he pulled on his thick sheepskin vest, settled the Stetson on his head, and picked up his leather gloves.

Outside, he could see Reese coming from the barn with a huge wheelbarrow load of those wooden two-by-fours. Kira and Shay were already down at the main barn, getting the sawhorses set up after they measured the length of each piece of wood planking. Harper was probably enjoying the sandwich Noah had made earlier for him, delivered to him by Shay. He was happy being allowed to babysit Candy. Smiling to himself, Noah opened the door and went outside.

The air was brisk and just above freezing. It felt sharp, clearing his mind. Hoping that Dair would sleep long and hard, allowing the shock to leave her body, Noah looked forward to dropping in once an hour just to look in on her. No longer did he want Dair to think that no one cared about her. Because it was clear to her this afternoon at the kitchen table, everyone did care for her. And he'd seen the softening in her gold-brown eyes, the acceptance that she was important and counted in all their lives. That she was valued. Noah was sure that realizing the Bar C wranglers were here to support her return to health had helped her drop off to sleep. It would begin a long healing process, but he'd be there with her, every step of the way.

Chapter Eleven

"Well?" Noah asked Dair as she sat in her chair at the top of the newly created wooden sidewalk in two days. "What do you think?"

Dair was surrounded by everyone as they waited for her to speak. The sun was setting behind the Wilson Range, and pink-edged clouds hung over the peaks, northwest of the ranch. "It looks wonderful," she told them, smiling. "Thank you so much."

Shay came and placed her hand on Dair's jacketed shoulder. "We should have thought about this the weekend we had the arena raising this past summer," she told Dair. "Because we need to make this place handicap available, too."

Reese came forward, standing next to Shay. "As soon as the weather turns warm and stays about fifty-five degrees, we're going to get a concrete truck in here and we're going to lay a real sidewalk that's wide enough for two people or anyone with a hardship. It needs to be done." He gave Dair a fond look. "You just reminded us to put this higher up on our to-do list, is all."

Dair felt some of the guilt slide off her. "So this was already in your plans?"

"Absolutely," Shay said, patting her shoulder. "We need a sidewalk so our boots aren't always either muddy or covered with snow. Plus, we wanted the arena accessible to all people."

Noah stood on the right side of Dair. "Would you like to give it a whirl?" he asked, gesturing to the gently sloping plank sidewalk.

"Sure," she murmured. Everyone stood back so that she could maneuver the lightweight chair.

"We also," Reese pointed out, gesturing down the expanse, "made it less steep for you. We didn't want you wheeling out of control." He grinned over at her.

Dair laughed. "Hey, it can happen! Thanks for that, too," she said as she pushed off, her hands running along the wheels. To her delight, it was wide enough so that the chair, if she made a judgment error, wouldn't tumble off the edge and tip into the gravel on either side of it, throwing her on the ground. Everyone had been thoughtful about making the sidewalk wide enough, but also used a switchback design to create a less severe incline so she could easily control her movements downhill, and also make it much easier for her to push herself up the path to their homes.

Noah followed her down, a shadowy figure beside her, his boots crunching in the gravel beside the walk. Dair knew he was worried she might need help, but she really didn't. He hadn't been around amputees enough yet to realize they are very, very adept at getting around without any help. She could feel his protectiveness toward her and it was like a wonderful, warm embrace. At the bottom, the wooden walkway was built out into a slight fan-like platform, evenly meeting the concrete sidewalk around the arena. It was an easy, seamless transition and she stopped, turning the chair around.

Noah stood there frowning, critical of everything, judging by his expression.

"This is great," she said. "Easy peasy."

"Well," he murmured, walking up to her, "what about going up that incline, now? Can you do it on your own?"

"Watch," she told him, giving him a wicked smile, pushing forward on those lightweight wheels. In five minutes, she was up on the wooden walk, wheeling quickly toward the rest of the people standing at the top, watching her progress with smiles of approval.

When she made it to where they were standing, they started clapping for her. Grinning, Dair could feel the sweat that had broken out beneath her jacket. The incline wasn't easy, but it was negotiable.

Noah had walked behind her, and she knew he was unsure if she could make the trip, but she had. Her biceps were aching, not used to such a workout, but every day she traveled up and down this walk, her muscles would respond, and pretty soon, she'd do it without even thinking about it. It would become muscle memory. Noah came around her chair, assessing her closely.

"I'm fine," she assured him.

"You've got sweat on your brow," Reese noted.

"Well," she said with a laugh, "it is a workout, but it's nothing I can't deal with. So, no worries, okay?" She gave everyone a smile. They all nodded, and any concern dissipated in their collective expressions.

"Well, it's time to feed the horses," Reese told them.

Noah asked Dair, "Do you want any help going into the house?"

Shaking her head, she said, "No, go ahead and feed." When the homes had been built this past summer, a wide wooden ramp had been installed to each door of the houses. Shay had wanted the homes to be available for military vets who might have handicap issues and they'd also built wider doors inside to ensure that they could get a chair through without getting stuck.

Shay and Kira ambled over to her.

"You look like you've been running a marathon," Kira noted.

"Are you okay, Dair?" Shay asked.

"I'm fine. In a week, I'll have that sidewalk down pat, so don't worry, okay?"

"I'm not used to being around an amputee," Kira admitted quietly, giving Dair a warm look. "If you ever need anything, you know you can call me or Shay on the phone."

Reaching out, Dair squeezed Kira's hand. "I know that. So, go home and do your translations. I've got to start supper for Noah and me."

"Okay," Shay said, reaching out, touching her shoulder, "see you later! Tomorrow's a new day for you, Dair!"

Kira reached over, giving Dair a quick hug. "Get inside. It's going to be cold tonight."

Dair loved those two women. They were, after all, military vets like herself. An incredible bond had formed among the three of them, because now, two days in a row, Shay and Kira had come over to help Dair get a shower and wash her hair. They didn't mind, and often told her they liked being of help to her. Everyone left, walking to their respective homes. As she made her way up the ramp to the house, she spotted Ray Crawford coming out of the last home at the end of the row. She rarely saw him, but noted his slight limp as he walked toward where he had his pickup parked. What was he doing out at this time of night? Dair opened the door to the house and saw him climb into his truck and leave, the headlights shooting glaringly into the dusk.

Wheeling inside, her focus lingered on Crawford. Shay was beside herself because she knew her father continued to drink. Didn't the old man know it was hurting his daughter? Shay cared deeply for what was left of her family, and there were days when Dair saw how much it tore her up. Shaking her head, she quickly removed her jacket, muffler, and knit cap, along with her gloves. Noah had thoughtfully set a small bed stand at the end of the mudroom, where she could lay her gear. Being bound to a chair, it would be a struggle to stand up on her one leg, balance herself, and place her jacket and other items on the wooden pegs high above her.

Dair couldn't cook or work well at the kitchen counter from her chair. Noah had assured her he would take care of all the cooking, cleaning, and anything else until she could get mobile with a new limb again. *Six weeks*. It seemed daunting to her, and again, that sense of helplessness engulfed her. It had been with her at Bethesda as she acclimated to her prosthesis and learning how to walk again.

Reminding herself that Dr. Radke was like a guardian angel, Dair tried to move from that dark place within herself. She wanted to do something to help, and hated when she couldn't. Everything was out of her reach when she was in a wheelchair, the counter too high and the cupboards completely inaccessible. And right now, the doctor had given her stern orders not to try and use her good leg and hop around on crutches, unless absolutely necessary. The knee brace was there in case of emergency when she had to stand. Her left knee needed quiet and stability, not getting yanked around. If she lost her balance? Well, that could double the injury to her knee. And Dair wasn't willing to risk that for anything. If Radke could get her mobile in six weeks with a new limb if she strictly followed his orders, that would be a godsend. She just had to still her impatience and let these weeks go by.

Wheeling into the living room, she picked up the remote for the TV to watch the regional news. There was little else she could do, because Noah had put on a big pot of chili in the Crock-Pot, the smell making her stomach growl with anticipation. She was hungry. That was a good sign she was coming out of the shock. The remote slipped and fell on the floor. Making an unhappy sound, Dair saw it roll to beneath the wooden table that held the flat-screen TV against the wall. Wheeling forward, she leaned out, taking her injured knee off the foot pad so she didn't put undue stress on it. It gave her leverage to lean down so that her head was now beneath the table as she stretched, her fingers pulling the remote toward her.

Her eye caught something. Twisting a look upward, she saw something attached to the bottom of the table. What was it? Unsure, thinking that it might have to do with the TV reception or the DirecTV they used out here in the valley, Dair didn't bother it. The remote rolled toward her and she was able to grab it and then back out from beneath the table.

Straightening, she dropped the remote in her lap and wheeled back so she could watch the news. Everyone signed up with DirecTV, which was satellite fed, instead. And sometimes she knew the signals could be affected by a heavy snowstorm. Maybe that smaller antenna beneath the table helped boost the original satellite signal? Dair thought it might have something to do with that.

Noah ambled in half an hour later. He climbed out

of his winter gear, took off his boots, and traded them in for a pair of sneakers. The kitchen was filled with the mouthwatering scent of chili. He spotted Dair wheeling toward him. "Hey, you ready to eat? I sure am."

If daydreams could come true, he would walk up to her, lean down, cup her face, and kiss her until they melted together.

"That chili smells so good, Noah." Dair halted as he walked into the kitchen and rolled up his sleeves to wash his hands at the sink. "I wish I could help."

"It's okay, Dair. You're only going to be in that chair for six weeks at the most." He gave her a sympathetic glance. She had taken her hair out of pigtails, and it lay like a shining black cloak around her shoulders, framing her incredibly beautiful face. Every cell in his body reacted to the warmth resting in her gold-brown eyes as she sat at the edge of the kitchen, out of his way.

"Hey, that box under the table in the living room? Do you know what it is?"

"Oh . . . that. Yeah, it's got something to do with the satellite stuff."

That was good to know. "How's Candy doing? Harper still with her?"

"She's starting to move around in circles, a sure sign she's going to drop a foal in a bit." Drying his hands on a nearby towel, he gestured toward the Crock-Pot. "I'm going to go take him a bowl of chili and some bread and butter."

"Good idea," she agreed. "This is so exciting! I love seeing foals born."

"Well, Candy seems very happy that Harper is with her. She'll make a circle and then goes to rest her head on his chest. Wish I had a camera." He grinned.

Dair stayed out of the way while Noah quickly spooned out the thick, fragrant chili, and sprinkled it with shredded sharp cheddar cheese, slapped some butter on four pieces of whole wheat bread, and hurried out the door to the barn to go feed Harper. She smiled, feeling her heart swell with so many good feelings toward Noah. He thought of others first. It was a good sign in her book, because she'd known enough selfish men in her life.

In ten minutes, Noah was back, rubbing his cold hands together to warm them up.

"I'll bet you that by the time we get done eating, Candy will have foaled."

"And I bet Harper was happy you brought him something to eat."

He chuckled as he filled two yellow ceramic bowls with the chili. "For sure. It was such a good idea that Reese had that broodmare suite heated. It's cold out there, probably dropped into the twenties already. In the suite, it's a nice fifty-five degrees, just right for a mom ready to give birth. It will also help the foal."

"The foal won't get cold or contract pneumonia," Dair agreed.

He set the bowls on the table. "Come on," he urged, pointing to one side of the table. "What I'd like to do is eat, and then I'll wheel you down there. Kira, Shay, and Reese are waiting for Harper to call when the foal's been born. They're eager to see the new baby, too."

"Sounds great," Dair said, always enthusiastic over a foal being birthed. "Good thing they know to stay away until the foal is born."

"For sure. There's broodmares who will stop the birthing process if there's a crowd of onlookers around. Seen it happen too many times." Noah placed the platter with buttered bread between them. Going back to the counter, he brought over two glasses of water and then sat down.

The cheese-covered chili melted in her mouth. Noah had also added a thick dollop of sour cream. Her stomach growled. She hadn't eaten much since the injury, but now she was starving. They ate in companionable silence, just the sounds of their spoons scraping their bowls.

Noah had just finished his first bowl of chili when his cell phone rang. He pulled it out of his shirt pocket.

"Harper?"

"Yes. Candy just dropped a beautiful jet-black filly. She's a beauty. Mom and baby are fine. Come on down. And bring me a second bowl of chili? And while you're at it, four more slices of bread?"

Laughing, Noah said, "You got it. We'll be down in about ten minutes. Did you call Shay and Kira?"

"They're next on my list."

Noah told Dair, "She's a black filly. That's a rare color."

Finishing off her chili, she said, "Truly, it is. I love black. It's my favorite color in horsedom."

"Well," Noah said, "you may be of some help."

"How?" She munched on the last piece of bread.

"I was talking to Harper when I was down there. He said that Candy is really a sweet mare and she doesn't mind if someone is in the stall with her and the foal. I was thinking that maybe tomorrow you might wheel on over there and make friends with them. See how Candy responds to you and how the foal reacts to you. Because Harper has to leave for a job south of here for the next week. He won't be around to handle the foal like it should be handled in order to introduce it to humans."

"But, I'm in a chair."

"So what? Let the foal come to you. You can pet her, rub her head, neck, or any part she turns toward you.

Didn't you do this to your foals your grandmother's broodmares birthed?"

"Well," Dair said, hesitating, "yes. We'd make sure those foals were completely bonded with us, and not afraid of humans."

"Think you could do that for Harper while he's away on that job?"

"I can try. I've never been around horses and been stuck in a chair."

"I'll be with you at first. We'll see if it works or not. Okay?"

She smiled. "You're good for me, Noah." She saw his cheeks turn ruddy, a sudden bashfulness come to his gray eyes.

"I don't know how you can say that, Dair. I put you back in your chair by not being responsible toward you."

She stared at him. "What? That you didn't speak up about Champ?"

"Yes," he said, giving her an apologetic look. "I'm the boss. It's my job to make the tough decisions. Tears always rip me up. I'm a sucker for any child or woman who cries." His mouth quirked. "If I had just followed my gut, you wouldn't be sitting in a chair." He abruptly got up, taking the dirty dishes with him.

Swallowing her shock over his sense of guilt, there was little she could say. Noah scrubbed the dishes in the sink, his broad back toward her. She could feel the churning of his emotions, some anger, some frustration, and his disappointment in himself. Mouth tightening, she wheeled over to within a few feet of where he stood at the sink, rinsing off the dishes.

"I don't blame you, Noah." Dair said it quietly. He snapped his head in her direction and she could see the full weight of how he felt. There was raw, gutting guilt there. Opening one hand, she pleaded, "Look, no one's to blame for this. We all made decisions. I'm as much to blame in this situation, if you want to look at it that way." Her heart was beating hard because she didn't like seeing Noah this upset. He wasn't angry with her. He was angry with himself. She could see it in the flash of his gray eyes, the way he tensed unconsciously.

"Right now," he said, his voice low and thick with feeling, "I know I put you there. I don't want to argue about this with you, Dair. You're in training under me. I let you down. That makes me feel pretty damned disappointed with myself. And you're paying the price."

Sighing, she whispered, "Don't do this to yourself, Noah. I spent a year and a half after I lost my leg, beating the hell out of myself. It does no good." She watched him scowl as he placed the dishes into the dishwasher. Closing it, he turned and placed his hands on the slender arms of the chair, his face six inches from her own. "You deserve nothing but sunshine, Dair, after all you've been through. I like you way more than I should. Because of that, I allowed you to sway me from what I knew. That wasn't your fault. That was all on me."

More shock rolled through her. Noah was so close, so vital and alive. He was masculine, the power of him as a man, radiating off him. She picked up that scent of his, and she found herself inhaling it deeply. The stubble on his face, deepening the natural hollows of his cheeks, accentuated that sense of coiled power within him. Her gaze dropped to his mouth and she felt an incredible longing course through her, throwing her into a maelstrom of emotions.

Her hands tightened in her lap as she felt the full force of him connecting with her. Worse, she was yearning for him. His admission that he liked her way too much threw her off balance. What did that mean?

She wasn't angry or upset with him. Dair whispered, "You can't bluster at me, Noah. I'm not going to blame you for what happened to me. I'm a big girl. I wear big girl panties, in case that is lost on you." For a moment, she saw his chagrin change to amusement. And then he broke her gaze, bowing his head for a moment.

Noah straightened, holding her defiant gaze. "Big girl panties, huh?"

"Yeah," she growled.

He scratched his head, giving her an amused look. "Never heard that saying before."

"Well, you aren't a girl, either," she said, losing some of the defiance in her tone. Lifting her finger, Dair shook it up at him. "I won't let you take all the blame for this, Noah. I had a part in it, too. So I'm paying the price. I disregarded my gut hunch on Champ, too. I knew he was dangerous. I sensed that he wouldn't change. I was just as swayed by the little girl's tears and pleading as much as you were. So? Blame us for having soft hearts and not listening to our heads."

He sighed, giving her a wry look. "I'll always be sorry I helped put you in this present situation, Dair."

His apology made her wince because she could see the regret in his expression. "We'll get over this together, okay?" She wanted desperately to ask him what he meant by liking her too much. Noah had never made a move to show her he had any interest in her other than being a kind, compassionate person. What did he mean by that statement? It was on the tip of her tongue to ask when his phone rang.

Noah answered. It was Harper.

"Hey, I can sure use another bowl of that chili, Noah. Are you going to come down here soon?"

"You have a hollow leg, Harper," he growled. "Yeah,

we'll be down shortly." He slipped the phone into his shirt pocket.

"Harper's still hungry?" Dair asked, grinning.

"Yeah. The guy is lean as hell and he eats for three people. Want to go down and see the little filly with me?"

"In a heartbeat," Dair murmured, glad that they were off the other topic. She was discovering that Noah had a very sensitive conscience. With a shake of her head, she turned and wheeled into the mudroom to don her winter gear while he fixed another huge bowl of chili for Harper.

There was a tenderness in Noah's eyes as he handed her the wrapped bowl of chili that he'd put on a tray across her lap for her to hold on the trip down to the barn. He'd also wrapped up four more pieces of bread that had been slathered with butter. And added a thermos of black coffee.

"You're a good friend to Harper," she said, tucking all of it onto the tray as he pulled on his winter gear.

"Like to treat people as I want to be treated."

"Is that your mom or dad's teaching?" she wondered when he went and opened the door.

Walking behind her chair, he gripped the handles with his leather gloves. "Both of them. I like their stand-up morals and values."

She twisted a look up at him, her head tipped back. "I like who you are, Noah. You're a good man." And he was. For an instant, she saw her softly spoken compliment reach out and move him. And then, just as quickly, he hid his reaction.

"On some days," he muttered. "Let's go, pardner . . ."

The lights from their house as well as the ones at each barn entrance provided plenty of light to see where Noah was pushing her chair, and Dair could barely contain her excitement. She spotted Shay, Reese, and Kira gathered down at the door to the main horse barn. They were waiting for them, and that touched her heart. Only in the military was there such unspoken camaraderie among a unit of people. And there was no mistake about it: Even though they were civilians now, scrambling to survive in their new world, they were doing it together. In some ways, as Noah wheeled her up to the huddled group in the freezing night air, Dair looked at the military like a beehive of sorts.

Everyone was a worker bee doing something for the good of the whole hive's survival. The military was exactly like that. Everyone had a career designation, was trained up for it and contributed through constant teamwork within their squad, platoon, or company. It grew to be a battalion or division, but it was the same hive. Every one of them was a worker bee in the military. It was no different here on the Bar C, either.

She saw Shay give her a huge, happy smile as they rolled up to the group.

"A black filly, Dair! She's so cute!"

"You guys already saw her?" Dair asked.

"Yes," Reese said. "We didn't want to all go in at once and make the mother tense. Harper took us in, one at a time." He smiled. "She's a cutie. Strong, curious, and has no fear of two-leggeds."

"That's great," Dair said, eager to see the newborn. "How's the mom doing?"

"Oh, she's fine. This is her fourth foal, from what Harper said," Shay told her. "She's an old pro at this."

"Then you're heading home?" Noah asked them.

"Yep," Kira said. She patted the arm of his jacket.

"Go in and see her. Harper's moaning that he's hungry enough to start eating two-by-fours." She laughed.

"The guy has a perpetual hole in his stomach," Noah groused, smiling sourly as Reese opened the door and he pushed Dair into the warmer interior of the barn.

Dair inhaled the wonderful scent of sweet timothy hay along with the alfalfa hay stacked in another area of the huge three-story barn. The broodmare suite was away from the rows of rented box stalls. She'd been there a couple of times, marveling at how well it was conceived and designed.

Noah turned her chair and pulled her through another door that led to the suite area. It had low lighting, but not so dark that they couldn't see. She'd been there with Harper, whose expertise was in breeding and foaling, a number of times earlier. He'd shown her the suite that looked more like a penthouse than a box stall.

"There he is," she said excitedly, pointing down toward the other end of the concrete aisleway.

"Yeah, waiting for his food," Noah said, chuckling.

Dair held on to the tray but lifted her other hand, waving at the cowboy dressed in a thick sheepskin jacket, tan Stetson, and his nearly threadbare Levi's. As Noah had told her before, Harper never threw anything away, not even his jeans when they should have been tossed years ago.

"I can hardly wait to see the little filly," she whispered, suddenly emotional.

"It's going to be special," Noah agreed thickly. "First, we'll feed this bear of a man and then he'll take us into the suite." Slowing the chair, he lifted one hand to smooth Dair's long black hair away from her shoulder.

Drawing in a swift, soft breath, Dair turned, twisting to look up at him, surprised by his intimate touch as he moved the strands aside. Her scalp prickled pleasantly and her heart opened over the unexpected gesture. There was something in his eyes, but she was too afraid to interpret it. At least, not yet. That look sent a river of fire flowing strongly throughout her body, pooling hotly below, and there was no way not to feel herself coming alive in a way she never had before.

Chapter Twelve

Dair couldn't keep from making a happy sound as Noah wheeled her into the large, airy broodmare suite. It was fifty feet long and twenty feet deep, giving the pregnant mare an opportunity to pace around in the glass-enclosed area. Reese had ordered bulletproof glass for the front of the stall. Only the sliding door was of heavy oak and had a set of Dutch doors, allowing the mare to poke her head out of the stall if she wanted.

Harper grinned widely and walked out to meet them in the aisleway. "Hey, you got some food for me, Dair?"

Laughing, she held up the tray. Noah had thoughtfully placed a large spoon, a napkin, a bottle of water, a thermos of coffee, plus the food. "Here you go," she said.

"Thanks," he said. "Hey, go take a look at mama and baby. They're doing fine. I'm gonna go over to that bale of hay, sit down and eat. I'm starving to death."

"You already had one bowl of chili," Noah reminded him with a grin. "It's that perennial hollow leg, pardner. Either that or you won't sleep tonight because of indigestion."

Harper tittered and walked with the tray to the bale of timothy hay sitting along the opposite oak wall. "I know. My mother always said I was born with a tapeworm in my gut."

Noah laughed and so did Dair. "We'll just stand quietly outside the stall."

"Yeah. When I get done, and when that pretty little filly gets done drinking her fill, I'll take you inside one at a time."

Straining her neck as Noah wheeled her down the aisle, Dair caught sight of the tiny black foal who was less than an hour old. She had her thin, long legs spread out like a tent to stay upright as she assertively bumped her mama's milk sac and suckled noisily, gulping and drinking as fast as she could.

"Ohhhhh, she's so pretty!" Dair whispered, turning, catching Noah's smile.

"Yeah, pretty, well built, and she's a winner," he agreed, critically looking at the foal.

Candy, the mother, a red sorrel, lifted her head as they quietly spoke to one another. She nickered softly, remaining in the center of the straw-covered stall, her ears up, alert as they slowly approached.

Noah placed the chair in the vicinity of the shatterproof glass wall. He set the brake and said, "Let's just stand and watch. I don't want the filly to be disturbed from getting her fill of milk."

"For sure," Dair agreed, absorbing Noah's presence, his hands resting on the handles of the chair. Dair could feel the heat of his body and it just made this experience so much more special for her. She grinned and said, "Wow, look at her little brush tail waving back and forth like a clock ticking." Dair knew the importance of assessing the strength of a foal less than an hour old. And this filly was strong! She was constantly head-butting her mother's milk sac, suckling noisily so that even Dair could hear it from behind the glass wall. The mother would turn and lick the baby's black, fluffy fur, smoothing it down here and there across the back. Candy was a wonderful mother, as Harper had told her before.

"This is one of the best things about being around horses," Dair whispered, tipping her head upward, meeting Noah's gaze. "I love working with broodmares, helping with the foaling process. The are so cute!"

Noah laid his hand on Dair's jacket, giving her shoulder a gentle squeeze. "You're just a natural mother, is all," he said.

The heat of Noah's hand transferred through her heavy coat, and Dair had never felt so happy as right now. The black filly moved around, those tiny, slender legs of hers still unsteady, but she was bound and determined to stay upright to get that milk. Candy hung her head, her eyes half-closed.

It was always amazing to Dair how strong the broodmares were after the foaling process. It took them an hour or less, once in labor, to deliver their foal. They remained standing, taking care of their baby and then semi-dozing as the foal suckled, just as Candy was doing right now. She had lots of straw stuck in her red mane, and Dair itched to get in there and pull it out, to give the mare a nice curry and soft brushing down to make her feel better.

They stood there quietly, watching the filly eagerly drink her fill. And when she was done, her spindly legs collapsed beneath her and she plopped down on the thick, cushiony wheat straw spread throughout the suite.

The foal then stretched out, nestling her face into the straw, and promptly fell asleep.

Dair laughed softly. "What a little sweetie that filly is."

"Yeah," Noah said, smiling, keeping his hand on Dair's shoulder. "She's a real tiger. But that's a good sign. She came out strong and ready to take on the world."

"That's right," Harper said, coming up and standing next to them. He rubbed his belly beneath his sheepskin vest. "That was really good chili, Noah. You outdid yourself. Must be Dair's influence on you."

"Yeah," Noah deadpanned, "you're asking for digestive nightmares if you go to sleep with that second bowl of hot, spicy chili in your gut, Harper."

Harper pulled off his Stetson and pushed his fingers through his short brown hair. His gray eyes were the color of old silver that hadn't been polished, and he was lean and lanky. "I have a stomach made of cast iron, Mabry, so no worries. The hotter it is, the more chili peppers in it, is fine by me." He flashed them a smile.

"Well," Dair said, "you're a glutton for punishment, Harper."

"Maybe," he murmured, giving them a wicked look. "I'm going into the stall. I don't want to wake the baby, but I want to give Candy a little TLC. She's half asleep herself."

Dair watched the wrangler quietly enter the suite. The straw was so thick it was up to his knees as he carefully walked through it. What she really liked about the suite was that the floor beneath it was hard-packed clay soil, covered with thick rubber mats, not concrete. Reese had been very thoughtful about every aspect of creating a large, safe foaling stall. Even though the straw was thick and deep, a small foal had tiny little hooves, and if they ran, bucked, or suddenly whipped around the stall within a few hours of being born, they could slip on slick concrete. But if their little hooves struck the hard, safe rubber with treads on it, they wouldn't slip or slide, putting them in danger of snapping one of their fragile legs.

Dair was glad it was those three-inch-thick mats and the clay beneath it, for so many reasons. They acted like the earth itself, shock absorbers. She didn't like concrete anyway, because shoed horses easily slipped on it. But most horse facilities had concrete aisleways, and there was no getting around the possibility of injury.

She watched Harper work quietly with Candy, who looked exhausted. Who wouldn't be after foaling a baby? Candy weighed around a thousand pounds, and generally speaking, foals were ten percent of the mother's weight. She guesstimated that the filly was around a hundred pounds at birth. Big, black, and incredibly feminine looking, this foal was going to be a looker, no question. Harper had a soft dandy brush and he was gently smoothing it out across Candy's thick winter coat. Dair knew the power of touch with animals, and she could see the tired mare truly appreciated it, blowing softly through her nostrils, along with an appreciative, soft snort. Harper then picked out all the straw in her mane and tail that she'd accumulated while on the floor of the stall birthing her daughter.

"I think it's his Navy medic side expressing itself," Noah said. He knelt down on one knee next to her chair so he could meet her eyes. "He's always been a big softy. When he was over in Afghanistan, he helped birth about forty babies off and on through different deployments. He could never be with the mother because of Muslim law over there, but the midwife would come out of the hut and ask him for help or directions."

"That's wonderful. Harper told me he is working at becoming a paramedic right now. Once he finishes his college courses, I'm sure he'll get hired either by the fire department here in Wind River, or he'll have to move away and work at the hospital in Jackson Hole. I hope he gets an invite by the fire department to join and stay here with us, Noah."

"Oh, I think it's already a done deal," he said. "The fire department captain has talked at length with him and he knows he's got another six months of college. The chief has already offered him a job when he graduates."

"Really? I didn't know that."

"Yeah." Noah gestured toward the wrangler in the stall. "He doesn't want to leave the Bar C. He's already talked to Reese and Shay about staying here, paying full monthly rental on the house he's living in, and still working for them during his off days from his fire department schedule."

"Plus, I think he loves broodmares and foaling too much to walk away from that end of it, too."

"For sure," Noah agreed. "He's got a real special touch with animals and they love him. Since I've been here, he's sorta taken over all the broodmares and foaling duties."

"He's good at it. Just because he was a Navy medic doesn't mean he can't transfer that wonderful healing ability to animals."

"Right on." Noah met her gaze. "So, we aren't going to lose Harper to Jackson Hole. He's already got a job waiting for him at the fire department."

"That's such great news," Dair agreed, watching as Candy nuzzled into Harper's vest, nibbling on it and then licking the roughened sheepskin. She laughed. "Candy loves him!"

"Yeah, the three broodmares all have a crush on Harper, and that's good. You want someone with that kind of gentle quietness around a mare who's in pain, pacing and trying to foal. She's exhausted and wants to get rid of that foal in order to stop the contraction pain. Harper just lends a calm and quiet environment around them. I've seen all our broodmares drop healthy babies into his waiting hands. The mare will sometimes stand to deliver, and that's quite a fall for the foal coming out of her. Harper has been there every time to catch the tyke as it was birthed, and gently lower it to the stall floor so it isn't injured or shocked by the drop."

"The mares must truly trust him, Noah, because I don't know many who would allow a human behind her like that while birthing."

Nodding, he said, "Yeah, I've seen men kicked and sent flying by a broodmare when they try that."

"Me, too," Dair agreed. "Harper is so special. I wonder why he doesn't have a woman in his life?" She looked up at Noah. "Really. He's so darned handsome and he's a nice guy. What's wrong with this picture?"

Noah sighed, resting his arm on his knee. "It's a long story, Dair. He was married once to a woman named Camille. He was in the Navy, attached to a Marine Corps company in Afghanistan at the time. He was married to her at twenty-one. Like all of us, Harper got PTSD. His marriage to her broke up three years later and it devastated him. He's still friends with Camille, but she's engaged to be married to a doctor who has three girls and is divorced. Harper knows he has bad PTSD issues and I think, even though he hasn't said anything to us about it, he doesn't want to get involved with another woman until he can get through the worst of his PTSD. He doesn't want to make another woman miserable like he did Camille."

"That's so sad," Dair murmured, watching Harper gently rubbing Candy's withers. He was giving the mare what she called a horsey massage, and all horses loved to be massaged just as he was doing with his long, spare hands. "He's such a decent dude."

"Yeah, but like all of us," Noah said, catching her gaze, "his night hours are when the PTSD nightmares and flashbacks stalk him. And he loses half a night's sleep three or four times a week."

"Just like us," Dair muttered unhappily. "I hate it, Noah. I really do."

"It's no way to live," he quietly agreed. "But at least in Reese and Shay's case, they fell in love even though both of them had severe PTSD."

"Yes, but they both know the issues and know what to do to protect the other partner from a bad flashback or nightmare," Dair pointed out.

"Yes, in their case, it worked. Kira and Garret were in Special Forces. They were together in the same A-team for three years. And they both have PTSD. There's another happy ending. They live together and are in love with one another."

"Well, it appears to be working well here at the Bar C," she noted.

"Yes, it is," Noah said, "but you're new here, Dair. So much of the environment here is due to Shay and Reese Lockwood. They're fully invested in military vets who are injured by combat, physically, mentally, or emotionally. Shay originally set this ranch up when she came home to take over the reins of the operation because her father had that stroke at forty-nine. It was her vision, her heart, to help all of us."

"She's an incredible role model," Dair agreed, her voice thick with emotion. "She deserves a Medal of Honor."

"Really," Noah agreed. "Oh, Harper's gesturing for us to come on in the stall." He slowly rose, smiling down at her. "Ready?"

Was she ever! "You bet. But I worry that Candy might spook when she sees me in a chair."

"Let Harper handle this, okay? He's not going to put you or Candy at risk, but he's got the mare's trust."

Dair wasn't sure, but trusted Noah. Harper had already slid open the huge oak stall door and was standing in the entrance. He had a big smile on his face.

"Dair? I'm going to ask Noah to step aside, and I want to wheel you in here just beyond the sliding door. Candy will want to come over and sniff you out. You know how that goes."

"Yes, I do. Are you sure about this, Harper? I don't want to scare the mare or the foal. I know I look odd in their eyes. I'm human, but I don't have two legs like you do."

"No worries," he murmured, taking the handles of her chair and easing her into the stall. He'd tamped down some of the straw so the wheels would sit firmly. Noah slid the door shut, remaining outside. He ambled over to the glass end of the stall, watching, his hands draped over his hips.

Candy lifted her head, her dark brown eyes assessing Dair as Harper called her over. The mare shook her head and then stepped over to Dair.

"Now, she'll just smell you all over," Harper said, leaning down near her ear.

"I know the drill," Dair assured him. "I'll just sit real quiet."

"That's it," he assured her, patting her shoulder.

Candy, like any other horse, smelled and sniffed Dair's hair, face, her clothes, the chair itself, curious about the wheels, and, finally, her one foot encased in a sneaker. Dair loved the warmth of the mare's moist, timothy-hay breath on her face. Horses were very thorough in smelling something they didn't know. The mare wasn't afraid of her, and that was good. She was all curiosity, and Dair knew that Candy was going to make sure that Dair and the contraption she was sitting in, were not a threat to her newborn.

"She's relaxed about you," Harper murmured, pleased, as he remained beside her. "Candy likes you. If she licks you, that's a sign of great affection from her to you."

Candy was licking Dair's clasped hands in her lap.

Dair laughed softly. "Are you sure it isn't the salt on my hands she wants, Harper?"

He chuckled and leaned his hand slowly forward so as not to startle the mare. "Nah. There's a nice mineral salt block for her in the corner of the stall over there. It's low enough so that she and her foal can lick from it all they want. She's licking your hands because it's her way of letting you know that she trusts you. A good sign, but I'm not surprised. Are you?"

Shaking her head, Dair smiled into Candy's huge face. She had a wide white blaze down the middle of it, just like her foal. "No, not surprised, Harper. But I'm glad you're here to make introductions. I think if you weren't, Candy would be jumpy about my chair and the fact I'm not walking like the other humans she's used to seeing and dealing with."

"Probably right," he agreed amiably. "You okay with me leaving you? I want to check out the little tyke while she's sleeping. Get a closer inspection of her when she's not a tornado tearing around this stall."

Grinning, Dair said, "Yeah, go ahead." She saw Candy follow Harper, who slowly and quietly walked over to where the foal lay sleeping heavily. Candy then devoted her attention back to Dair, satisfied that her foal was not in any danger. The mare gently nuzzled Dair's chest.

Dair smiled, slowly lifting her hands and rubbing each side of the mare's long head. Reaching her ears, she moved her fingers into each of them, a favorite for a horse because they couldn't scratch their own ears inside if they itched. Candy groaned, her head resting more fully against her, trusting her and enjoying her ears being gently scratched and then massaged.

"I think you've made a good friend," Harper said softly, grinning as he continued to inspect the filly without touching her. She was sleeping like a proverbial log, dead to the world around her.

"I think I have, too, Harper. Candy is such a loving horse." She began to smooth her hands along the horse's jawline. There were lots of itches that never got scratched beneath the horse's jaw, and that's where Dair went next.

Candy gave a pleased snuffle, eyes closing as she rested her head against Dair.

Smiling, Dair leaned forward a little and placed her cheek against the white blaze down the front of Candy's face. She smelled so good, the sweetness of being horse combined with the mare having nibbled on a flake of timothy hay strung from the ceiling in a nylon netting bag that she could easily reach. All of Dair's tension bled out of her body as the horse entrusted herself to her. It was a thrilling warmth that skittered through her wide-open heart. She could feel how exhausted the mare really was from that labor and birthing process. Continuing to ease her fingers around that region beneath the horse's jaw, scratching it and giving Candy pleasure, Dair closed her eyes, happiness tunneling through her.

There was nothing like an animal loving her in return, in its own unique way. The past few days of her own trauma melted away as this thousand-pound horse, her hooves on either side of the chair as she continued to rest her head against Dair, righted her world once more. Animals had always done that for her, and now was no different. Dair had always loved horses. Her grandmother said it was her Comanche blood. Dair had been so fortunate to have spent nearly every weekend at her grandmother's home just outside Laramie, where Rainbow had given Dair the lifetime gift of learning how to work with, and love, horses.

Candy made another long, soft snuffle, content just to lean into Dair and be patted, scratched, and massaged. She was so tired, and Dair knew if the mare could, she'd lie down to sleep, too. But with a newborn, the mother usually remained on her feet the first twenty-four hours, to be available for her hungry little charge when the foal would suddenly wake up and head to the udder. It struck her that, like Candy, she too was exhausted emotionally by what had happened to her. It formed another emotional bond between her and the weary mare.

"Uh-oh," Harper chuckled in warning, "the baby is awake! Get ready!"

Candy lifted her head, looking toward Harper, who had stood up, giving the foal room to sit up and then stand up, on stronger legs this time.

Dair smiled as Candy left her and walked over to where Harper stood so that her foal could nurse once more. The little filly was all flailing legs for a moment as she rolled over on her back and then grunted, struggling to get herself upright once more. She wasn't used to pushing her weight around, and her front legs splayed out in front of her. She grunted again, pushing off with her hind legs.

"We need to name this little black filly," Harper called to her.

"I thought Shay gave them names."

Shrugging, he said, "If there's a new foal, then at our weekly Friday night meeting, we all put names in a hat and choose the one we like best."

"That's a great, democratic idea," Dair said. She always looked forward to the weekly meeting that was mandatory for all the vets. Often, Shay would ask psychologist Libby Hilbert, who lived in Jackson Hole, to drive down and act as therapist-moderator for their meeting. It was always a lot of fun and laughter, and sometimes, tears. Libby was a nurturing mama bear, taking care of all of her cubs. She was at the forefront of PTSD research, and was an international expert on the condition. Everyone loved the widow who had two grown children. Maybe it was her red hair, green eyes, and freckles that endeared her to Dair. Libby didn't act like a therapist among them. Even the guys opened up to her. And that allowed all of them to heal just a little bit more at each session. Besides, Garret always baked a pan of cinnamon rolls, Shay made the coffee, and they sat in that large living room like a family. And they were family, there was no question in her heart and mind.

"I think I'm going to choose the name Ebony for her," Dair told Harper, who was watching the foal's awkward antics to get to her feet once more.

"I like that name," he said. "She's a very prettily marked girl with four white stockings, that big, wide blaze on her face, just like her mama."

That was true, Dair agreed. Ebony made a quick leap into the air and landed right at her mother's side. She knew where the milk was located and proceeded to snake her thin neck and tiny head beneath her mama's belly and butt that sac swollen with the good stuff.

Grinning, Dair turned to see Noah standing slouched and watching the horses through half-closed eyes. Her heart swelled even more with need of this man. She knew Harper didn't want more than one stranger at a time in the birthing suite.

"Maybe Noah would like to come in now?" she asked Harper.

"In a moment. I want Ebony to drink her fill, and then she's going to want to check you out. I want the little girl to get used to seeing people in chairs, too. Okay?"

"Sure." Dair lifted her hand toward Noah, who smiled and gave her a wink in return. She knew he loved babies of all kinds here on the ranch. The small herd of Herefords that Reese and Shay kept were for breeding purposes only. They'd calved last year, and soon would be dropping five more starting in April.

As soon as Ebony was done getting her fill of milk, she whirled around, scampered like mad around her mother's hindquarters, and raced around in a semicircle. Ebony came to a sliding halt when she saw Dair sitting there. Instantly, she picked up her legs, prancing toward her, big dark brown eyes sparkling, tiny ears pricked forward, and her tail straight up like she was carrying a flag. Dair had to smile as the filly came to a halt directly in front of her, fearless. Of course, her mama wasn't giving a sharp, snorting sound which meant "danger," and so the little tyke stretched out her neck, woofed loudly, and smelled Dair. Her tiny teacup muzzle stopped at her hair, and Ebony enthusiastically began to chew on the strands.

Laughing, Dair slowly raised her hands so as not to startle Ebony, and eased her tiny mouth off her now very wet strands. Right now, she had no teeth, just those wet gums that were chewing eagerly on the strands. "No, you don't eat hair, little one," she said in a soft tone. She rubbed her hands over Ebony's tiny ears, and the filly leaned into Dair's palm as she began to lightly scratch inside of them. Ebony closed her eyes, laying her head into one of Dair's hands while being scratched by the other.

"She likes that," Harper praised.

"Bold little thing, isn't she?" Dair murmured to him, smiling.

"Yes, she's like her father, the stud. He's big, bold, and fearless in that same kind of way, but not mean like Champ was."

Nodding, Dair left Ebony's ear and smoothed her fingers across her velvety muzzle. The filly drowsily opened her eyes, lifted her head, opened her mouth, and sucked on several of Dair's fingers.

"No," she said to Ebony, "I'm not your mama." She pulled her fingers out of the foal's mouth. Foals were born without teeth, but soon they would come in. Her shiny pink gums caught Dair's fingers again as she withdrew them with a laugh.

Harper chuckled. "She likes the way your fingers taste, Dair."

Wiping them on her jeans, Dair nodded and watched as the foal then took off, scampering around her chair and around Harper, who stood still. She then leaped playfully around her mother. Ebony made two leaping, jumping circuits around Candy before she dived beneath her mom's belly to get another shot of warm, nutritious milk.

Harper walked up to Dair. "Ready to leave? At least for now?" he teased.

"Yes. Noah will love coming in here."

"From the look on his face, for sure," Harper said. As he turned Dair around in her chair, Noah came over and slid the door open so she could leave.

"Well," Noah asked as she came out of the stall, "did you enjoy yourself?"

Dair melted beneath his gray gaze, feeling that tightening of need that always seemed to be strung between them. "I loved every second of it. Your turn."

Harper placed her chair so that Dair could easily watch everyone within the huge stall. He took Noah in and then slid the door shut. She couldn't help but smile. Noah and Harper were like brothers. Although they didn't look alike, they had that same whipcord body type. Lean but strong. And Noah had been strong for her in so many ways. She felt so much happier now, watching Ebony leave her mother's milk to go sniff curiously around Noah, the strange newcomer. Harper had been dead-on about the filly's boldness. Nothing fazed the little tyke. Dair's lips lifted into a fond smile, and she wanted to spend hours just sitting there watching the filly's antics, absorbing Noah's laughter, and watching the delight and amusement come to his expression as Ebony doted on and adored him, as well.

Just one visit had lifted Dair from the darkness that occurred after her injury. If she'd been back at Bethesda, she'd have had to fight, claw, and scratch her way out of her depression over a week's time. But one tiny black foal, Harper's kindness, and Noah's care for her, made all the difference. Dair didn't feel as if her world had been shattered, any longer. It had been rebuilt, and she sat there, stunned by how quick a turnaround she'd made emotionally from the accident. It had been Harper's nurturing, Candy and Ebony's trust in her, and something even more important: Noah's protectiveness and thoughtfulness toward her. He didn't try to smother her, knowing that she was independent and not going to be a victim of what had happened to her.

When Noah knelt down on one knee, little Ebony came racing around her mother and slammed into him, nearly knocking him over. Luckily, Harper was nearby and kept the foal from stumbling over him, righting her so that she could give a shrill little whinny, and off she went again! Dair couldn't stop laughing as Noah looked bemused and got up out of the straw, dusting himself off.

"I guess," Harper said loud enough for her to hear, "Ebony thought you were her new play toy, Noah. An odd looking foal just like herself."

That brought laughter inside and out of the broodmare suite from everyone.

Chapter Thirteen

Noah tried to tame his physical reaction to Dair as he helped her out of the chair once they were back in their home after seeing Candy and her foal. Her hair smelled of sweet timothy hay, a perfume to him. He'd brought her into her bedroom, locked the brake on the chair, and grabbed her pair of lightweight aluminum crutches for her to use. Dair had asked him for a hand to leave her chair and balance herself on her one foot.

This was their nightly routine, and it was something he always looked forward to because it meant being close to her for just a little bit. If she knew how torrid his dreams were about making love with her, holding and kissing her, Noah was sure she wouldn't want him anywhere near her. But tonight was different. He'd seen how soft and vulnerable she'd become after being with the foal, Ebony. He was sure the rest of the wranglers would approve of the name tomorrow evening when they had their weekly Friday night meeting with Libby.

"Okay," he murmured, "you ready?"

Dair nodded. "Ready."

Noah liked that she was independent, but he worried about her head injury and the possibility that she could get dizzy when she was taking a shower by herself. Kira and Shay had helped her for a bit, but now she wanted to do it on her own. What if she slipped? The bathroom door was closed, and unless Noah stood right outside of it, he wouldn't hear Dair fall. Knowing her perseverance and pit-bull stubbornness had gotten her this far, he wasn't going to share his concerns with her. He'd mentioned it to her in passing the other day, and he saw the set of her jaw and the flash of determination come to her eyes. At that time, Dair had told him she didn't want to have to ask people all the time to help her. That she had to learn to be mobile on her own. Understanding where she was coming from, he said nothing more. But the damned urge to help her was always there within him. He found himself biting back a lot of thoughts he knew Dair wouldn't agree with. She'd never been fully protected by her parents. This streak of independence was fostered by her parents' decisions—mostly her mother. He had so many personal questions for her.

"Okay," he murmured, standing in front of her, the footrests out of the way so she could place her foot on the floor, "let's do it." He held out one hand to her while holding her crutches in the other. There was pleasure thrumming through his hand as her fingers curled trustingly around his and she pulled herself upright. Dair was strong. She was constantly working out in the small gym that was over at the main house where Reese and Shay lived.

Dair moved close to him and he inhaled her sweet scent as he released her hand, sliding his arm around her waist so she could stabilize herself against him. He handed her the crutches and she took one of them in her free hand, slipping it beneath her arm. For a moment, Dair hesitated. She looked up at him, her face inches from his, staring deep into his eyes. This was different. And new. Noah wanted to kiss her, pure and simple. He saw her gold-brown eyes widen marginally, and her lips part. There was a sense of openness that he felt with Dair as she leaned a little more against his body. The contact was electric. Heat plunged deeply through him and he felt his erection respond instantly. Searching her eyes, he saw yearning in them, and so much more that he was afraid to interpret.

His mind spun in those split seconds. Dair felt so good against him. She was entrusting herself fully to him for the first time. An errant thought occurred to him—that being with Candy and her foal had allowed Dair to drop the walls she hid behind, that the animals had opened her up in a new way. She had remained open with him. It was startling. But wonderful. Noah wanted a more personal relationship with Dair, but it had never happened. Until now. He swore she looked like she wanted to kiss him. The terror of making an incorrect assumption was just as real. His arm was curved around her shoulders, and made his desire for her soar as never before.

To hell with it. He was going to kiss her and take the fallout from her later. He leaned down, his eyes tracking hers, watching for any sign of fear or rejection. There was none. Their breath mingled, his nose an inch from hers. Unable to believe that she wanted his kiss, Noah saw nothing to indicate otherwise. His hands were occupied. He wanted to frame her face with them, but couldn't. The warm, soft strength of Dair's body resting against his made all other thoughts dissolve in the boiling heat erupting within him.

Noah grazed her parted lips gently, with invitation. He wasn't about to plow into her like the typical alpha male would. No, he didn't want her shocked by his aggressiveness. Dair had had enough of that with her father. He didn't want to be like that with her, anyway. Her mouth moved against his, tentative, but so mind-bending to Noah, that he mimicked the same tender movement. Tasting her for the first time sent another wave of burning need through him, and he fought to control himself for both their sakes. He felt her arm tighten just a fraction around his waist, felt her lean shyly upward to meet and connect fully with him. Elation soared through him. He felt giddy, like a little boy who had just discovered the treasure of a lifetime. He absorbed the movement of her lips against his, her honesty, her trust in him as he curved his mouth fully against hers for the first time. Dair closed her eyes and so did he, lost in the building heat and promise simmering between them, finally fulfilled.

There was a poignancy flowing through Noah as Dair's mouth met and matched his. The kiss deepened and he felt her body melting against his as she entrusted herself to him. Not wanting her to fall, he remained anchored so she had something steady to lean against. His mind began to dissolve as her lips parted more and he felt her tentativeness disappear. In place of it was her breath arcing, a little ragged, as she fully invested herself in him. Sheer joy raced through him along with surprise that Dair was actually kissing him in return. This wasn't one-sided, as he'd thought. Her lips were wet, gliding against his, her breath matching his shortened breath, her arm tightening even more around his waist as she pressed her breasts fully against his chest.

His whole world melted, his mind erased, his body flaming and throbbing as Dair's lips blossomed beneath his. There was such beauty in the moment for Noah. He swore he could feel the quiet joy flowing through Dair, felt her fingers now moving against his rib cage and back, stroking him, letting him know she was enjoying this communion that had sprung up between them suddenly and without warning. Never had a woman tasted so good. There was no coyness or games in the way she explored him. It was her honesty that totaled Noah, as their mouths reluctantly separated from one another.

Slowly, he opened his eyes and drowned in her gold ones. Noah saw such hunger in them, flecks mixed with the light sienna color. Dair hadn't pulled away from him. It was more than just about balance, his faltering mind told him. Dair *wanted* to be against him, wanted to feel her body connecting with his. Luckily, she couldn't feel his erection swelling beneath the zipper of his jeans. His hands weren't free, and it frustrated him. Noah gave her a lopsided grin.

"I wish I had my hands free," he said roughly, watching amusement come to her eyes.

"I wish you did, too."

His erection hardened over her husky words. Swallowing hard, he savored the feeling of Dair resting against him, never wanting her to leave. "I wasn't expecting this," he admitted.

Dair shook her head. "Me neither . . ."

"Maybe it's been coming over time?" He searched her eyes, seeing lust in them, but also something else, more beautiful, that he couldn't interpret.

"I think so, Noah." She cleared her throat and stopped stroking his back. "Maybe seeing the foal did it."

Noah could feel how shy and tentative Dair had become. He didn't see regret in her eyes for kissing him. There was still yearning there. "A foal always makes me vulnerable, too," he admitted.

"Are you sorry you kissed me?"

He smiled a little, liking her boldness. "Not one bit. You?" He saw her lips twitch.

"No. But I don't know where this will lead, Noah."

Feeling her fear about the future, he shrugged. "Let's walk that path a day at a time and see where it brings us. You're in charge here, Dair. We just need to talk about it so we don't make stupid assumptions about one another. That's what will get us into trouble."

Nodding, she whispered, "I agree." And then she stared up at him. "This changes everything, Noah."

"Yes, it does. Are you okay with it? Or do you want to move out and live with Harper in his house?" Noah wasn't going to assume anything. He saw an instant regret come to her expression.

"Why . . . no. Do you want me to move out?"

"No. But I had to ask. I don't know what you're thinking."

Her mouth quirked and she looked away for a moment. "That's fair. I guess . . . I guess I'm not used to talking so honestly with a man I just kissed. That's on me."

"Well," he soothed, "the only reason I know it's good to talk is because I lost my marriage to Chandra because I was locked up and never communicated. I swore that if a woman ever interested me again, I was going to make sure we talked a lot and often. I don't want a possible relationship dying because I didn't open my mouth or ask important questions." He saw a flare of understanding in her eyes.

"I'm not really good at that, either, Noah."

"Let's work toward it, huh?" He leaned down, kissing her wrinkled brow. "Let's take this one day at a time. Talk a lot. Ask questions? Make comments." He straightened. "I'm not going to push myself upon you, Dair. I'm not going to attack you out of nowhere. You need to come to me and tell me what you want. That way, I'm giving you the room you need."

She compressed her lips. "Fair enough. I appreciate that, Noah. Thank you."

"Are you ready for the other crutch?" He saw some pinkness come to her high cheekbones and realized how fragile she really was. Dair projected this individual toughness and bravery, but now he was seeing the tender side that she hid from the world. Noah felt privileged to see it, to feel it, and that she trusted him enough to reveal herself. More elation swept through him as she released her arm from around his waist, took all her weight on her right foot, and he placed the other crutch into her hand.

Dair was an old pro at being on crutches, and Noah stepped aside so that she could make her way into the bathroom to take her shower. Earlier, he'd made sure that a fresh towel, washcloth, and another towel for her hair were within her reach. Every day since being injured, she'd wanted to handle her bathing alone, without help. Noah made sure shampoo and conditioner were on the shower-stall shelf. They were little things, but he knew how much they meant to someone in Dair's situation. She was teaching him what she needed without asking, because he was a keen observer. And Dair had already thanked him for his insights into some of her needs as an amputee.

As he watched her leave the bedroom and swing easily and confidently down the hall on her crutches, Noah stood there, feeling euphoric. Rubbing his chest, he had never felt happier than when he'd kissed Dair. It had happened so unexpectedly. But it had been such a beautiful coming together. Most of all, it was mutual. That is what stunned him as nothing else had tonight. Dair had wanted to kiss him as much as he'd wanted to kiss her. Still in pleasant shock, he moved her chair toward her bed after pulling back the sheet and covers for her. Everything was within her reach.

Still stunned by their kiss, Noah moved to the kitchen, tidying up for the night. Until Dair got her replacement prosthesis, he was taking care of the cooking and cleaning for them. He didn't mind. He'd lived here alone before she came into his life. As he wiped down the granite surface of the counter with a cloth, he felt that bubbling, joyous feeling percolating through him. His erection was killing him. There was so much he wanted to do for Dair, to love her, to let her know, in his eyes and heart, she was whole to him regardless of the loss of one of her limbs. Sometimes, though, he would see something in her eyes, maybe shame, maybe a sense of hesitancy, when she allowed herself to get close to him. Was it because of the amputation? Noah wasn't sure. It was so damned hard for him to talk, to open up. But if he wanted to explore what they might have, he had to communicate. He had to do it no matter how uncomfortable, how awkward he felt. As he finished wiping the counter down, he rinsed the cloth beneath the faucet.

Noah felt even more tentative, the more he thought about their kiss. It was near nine p.m., and he knew both of them would be in bed by ten. Ranch work was brutally physical. But his heart simmered with so many dreams, so many desires, that Noah knew he'd probably not sleep well tonight. He wouldn't ever regret their kiss. It opened up a whole new window of possibilities. He had no idea where it would lead them or where their potential relationship might go.

A blizzard hit Wind River Valley the next morning. Harper and Noah cleared off the wooden sidewalk for Dair. And then he came back to the house and wheeled her down to the barn first, so she could start feeding all the horses. Harper was waiting for Dair and he would help her while Noah went about his duties training the horses in the nearby arena.

Harper would cut open a bale of timothy hay, hand Dair two flakes of it. She would place them in her lap and then wheel over to a horse's stall, unlock the door and slide it open, tossing the flakes to the awaiting horse, who nickered his or her thanks. Dair felt good this morning, even though she hadn't slept much the night before. Ruthlessly asking herself why she had initiated that kiss with Noah, she wasn't sure of her answer, and that drove her crazy. Dair wheeled to the next stall and slid the door open. Harper set two more flakes into her lap.

"You sure you want to continue to do this?" Harper asked.

"Absolutely," she said. Harper had a tendency to want to coddle her, and Dair would have none of it. "I need to pay my way around here," she called over her shoulder, giving the flakes to the horses.

Harper grinned, walked down the aisle, picked up two more flakes, and placed them into her lap. "No one around here is going to bother you on not hauling your fair share of the load around here, Dair. Is that what's worrying you?"

"No," she said, moving to the next stall to deliver the flake of timothy. "Doing this type of work is a good upper-body workout for me. I have to keep my arms and shoulders strong, for obvious reasons."

"Gotcha. So? Are you gonna keep working out over at Reese and Shay's gym?"

"Not so much, because this is a helluva workout, Harper," she said with a grin. She smiled more as Harper wriggled his dark brows. He was an easy person to be around, but then, he had been a medic in the military and he was a healer at heart.

"Well, don't forget. We have our Friday evening chat with Libby tonight."

"Wouldn't miss it for the world," she said.

"That's because Garret's making us his world-famous cinnamon rolls."

"When's he going to be back? It's a blizzard out there," Dair said. "He's got fifty miles to drive in this stuff to make it home by this evening from Jackson Hole."

Harper looked out the huge, open doors to the barn. "Well, as far as blizzards go, this one isn't that bad, and it's moving fast. It's supposed to have dumped its load of snow by noon today. The plow trucks are out in force, so I think the highway through Wind River Valley will remain open." Flashing her a grin, he said, "Don't worry. You'll get his nice, hot cinnamon rolls tonight."

Laughing, Dair took the proffered flakes from him. "Hey, I swear Garret could quit his construction jobs and make a business out of baking cinnamon rolls. Really."

"Oh, Shay's told him that, too, but I don't think Garret wants to be tied down to being in a kitchen twenty-four seven. The guy was Special Forces, you know? They're strong outdoor types. And he's no exception."

"So am I," Dair said, tossing the flake into Jeb's stall. He was a nice black quarter horse gelding. She moved onto Ghost's stall. "I couldn't stay in an office or house too long. I need fresh air and sunshine."

Laughing, Harper gestured to the thick veil of snow falling outside. "Well, living here, you get nine months of snow and three months of sun. Just remember that."

"HEY!" Ray Crawford yelled, launching himself through the open door of the barn. "What the hell is a gimp doin' in here?"

Dair's head snapped up. She saw the short, wiry rancher charging toward them. His face was twisted with rage, his fists at his sides. As he got closer, she could see he was aimed right at her. Dair turned her chair around after sliding the door closed to Ghost's box stall. Harper was down on the other side of the aisle, cutting open another bale of timothy hay.

Tensing, Dair held the rancher's small, angry brown eyes. His face was triangular and covered with at least three days' worth of gray and brown beard. He was dressed in a denim jacket and jeans, a black baseball cap over his longish hair that hid his ears.

Crawford halted in front of her. "Who the hell are you?" he ground out, glaring at her.

"I'm Dair Wilson, Mr. Crawford."

He breathed hard, looking with disdain at her chair. "I suppose my stupid daughter hired you?"

Feeling attacked, her heart rate roared upward, her fingers tightening around the wheels of her chair. Dair rolled back a few feet, trying to get away from him. His breath wreaked so much of alcohol, she wanted to gag. Dair heard Harper hurrying up toward them, his boots slapping hard against the concrete of the aisleway.

"Yes, sir, she did," Dair replied quietly, watching him warily.

"You're USELESS!" he roared, shaking his finger in her face. "What the hell has gotten into her? You've got no legs! And she's payin' you to do *this*? Throw hay into box stalls? What the hell! This is *my* ranch!"

Harper moved between them. "Ray, you need to leave," he snarled. "You have no right to come in here and start yelling at anyone who works at the Bar C."

Dair moved her chair around Harper. Anger was amping up in her, and she snapped, "Mr. Crawford, you'd best leave. You're drunk."

Crawford swore, pushing Harper aside with a sharp jab of his elbow, making him fall backward. He charged Dair.

Dair grabbed her wheels and kicked out with her right leg. Crawford slammed into it, letting out an "oomph!" He took a swipe at her with his fist. She ducked and jerked one wheel of her chair around, jamming her foot in his gut, pushing him away. But the force with which he charged her knocked her chair up on one wheel. In seconds, Dair was slamming down onto the concrete. She heard other commotion. And then, she heard Noah's voice ringing through the barn.

Dair slammed down to the right, pinning her good limb for a moment. She felt pain in her right cheek as she fell full force onto the cold concrete. Crawford had staggered backward, rolling to the floor, swearing. Struggling, Dair was trying to get free of the chair when she looked down the aisleway. Noah was running toward them, his face set, his eyes blazing with rage. All his focus was on Crawford, who was shaking his head and clawing clumsily to get to his hands and knees.

Harper quickly came to her rescue. Placing himself between her and Crawford, he let Noah take care of the angry, drunken rancher.

Noah hissed Crawford's name, leaning down, reaching out with his gloved hand and yanking the older man upright to his knees. He smelled the heavy alcoholic cloud around the bastard.

"You sonofabitch!" he growled, hauling him to his feet, slamming him into the oak wall.

Crawford snarled and cursed Noah, raising his fist.

Noah blocked his attempt, realizing the man was drunker than hell. But Ray was in a rage and tried to flail at him with his fists, missing him. "Stop!" Noah yelled at him, pinning him to the wall so he couldn't charge Dair again. He'd seen it all, and he wouldn't allow Crawford to strike her again. He couldn't take his eyes off the older man, who was still wriggling and kicking out, trying to force him to let go. Every cell in his body wanted to land a solid punch into this sick bastard's face. Noah heard Shay's scream echoing down the passageway from the barn opening.

"Stop it! Stop it!" she shrieked, flying down the concrete aisle toward them.

Noah didn't hit Crawford, as badly as he wanted to.

Ray spit and snarled, trying to get loose. Noah held him right where he was. He then saw Reese running up the slope toward the barn, too. Breathing hard, Noah glared at Crawford.

"Stop fighting. You're going nowhere."

Shay came running over to Dair to help Harper get Dair out of the tangle with the chair.

Reese came to a halt next to Noah, glaring at Crawford.

"What happened here, Noah?"

"Talk to Dair and Harper."

Reese turned, walking over to them.

In moments, Dair was back in her chair, Shay and Harper surrounding her, protecting her in case Crawford, who was still jerking around, got free of Noah.

Swearing under his breath, Noah, in one swift move, turned Crawford's face toward the wall, captured his hands and yanked them behind him. Grabbing some rope from his back pocket, he tightly tied Crawford's wrists. He let go and the rancher stumbled around.

"You bastard!" Crawford spat. "I'm going to haul your ass up on assault charges! I'll put you where you really belong!"

Noah gave him a lethal smile. "Try it," he rasped, and jerked the shoulder of Crawford's jacket, pinning him back against the wall. "You're going nowhere. You're the one who assaulted Dair. And we have witnesses."

"Are you all right, Dair?" Reese asked, leaning down, his hand on her shoulder.

Dair gave a jerky nod, her gaze never leaving Crawford, who was still cursing and kicking out at Noah. "I-I'm fine."

Reese gave her a strained look. "What happened? Can you tell me?"

In as few words as possible, Dair told him everything.

"I'll second what she said," Harper growled. "Crawford attacked her. If Dair hadn't used her good leg to stop his forward motion, he had his fist cocked and was going to hit her in the face."

Grimly, Reese glanced over at his wife. Shay looked absolutely shocked, white faced, her blue eyes filled with anguish. "I'm calling the sheriff," he told her.

"Y-yes. This isn't right. My father shouldn't be attacking anyone. Especially Dair." Shay patted Dair's dusty jacket, trying to give her reassurance.

Reese crouched down in front of Dair, his hands on the arms of her chair, looking her over intently. "Do you need an ambulance, Dair? What about your leg?"

"No, I'm fine. A few bruises is all. Ask Harper. He's a medic."

Harper grimaced. "You should be seen by Dr. Radke, Dair. You took a helluva spill in that chair. And your right knee took the brunt of that fall."

Dair shook her head. "My right knee has some scratches, but that's all. It feels fine." She looked at Reese. "Just get that drunken asshole out of here."

A grin partially leaked out of one side of Reese's thinned mouth. He slowly rose, patting her left arm. "We're going to." He looked over at Shay and Harper. "Will you take Dair back to her house? And Harper? Can you check her over medically once they are home? Just in case?"

"I'll stay with her, too," Shay volunteered, her voice wobbling with emotion, her gaze on her combative father, who had unceremoniously sat down on the floor with a disgusted grunt.

Reese leaned forward, kissing Shay's cheek. "Everything's going to be okay," he said thickly. "Let me handle this? You stay with Dair."

Tears tracked down Shay's taut cheeks. "Y-yes, go ahead." She sobbed, pressing her hand against her mouth as she stared at belligerent, cursing Ray, who was now glaring up at her.

"This is all your fault, Shay!" Crawford roared. "This is on you!"

The concrete walk between the barns was slippery, so Dair was glad Harper was willing to push the chair for her, Shay with her hand on her shoulder, walking quickly beside her. The wind blew fiercely, and by the time they arrived at Noah's home, they had a lot of snow to shake off their clothing. She felt numbed out, and realized she was in shock.

Chapter Fourteen

Kira joined Shay over in the kitchen at Noah's house. Dair felt completely cosseted by the two women. It was Harper's calm under fire that helped the situation as well. He carefully checked Dair out medically, from the swelling and bruising on her right cheekbone, to gently palpating and moving her right knee around. He went to the bathroom and found some sterile pads and a tube of antibiotic gel, and cleaned up her scratched cheekbone.

"I'm not putting a bandage on it," he told her as he crouched next to her chair, taking care of the area. He looked up at Shay, who was distraught. "Can you get me a cloth and fold some ice cubes into it for Dair?"

"Of course," Shay whispered, turning and hurrying into the kitchen.

Kira came around and knelt down on one knee, her hand on Dair's dusty thigh. "What can I do for you, Dair?"

"I need some clean jeans," she muttered, frowning.

Kira rose and said, "I'll get them from your bedroom and help you change when you're ready."

"Thanks," Dair said.

"How about a stiff drink?" Harper teased.

"No thanks. Crawford is drunk enough for all of us."

"I didn't hear anything," Kira said, coming back with a clean set of jeans in her hands as she halted and looked toward them. "I was in my office translating a letter into Arabic."

"Just as well," Dair muttered.

"Crawford's crazy," Harper growled. "He's a loose cannon around here." And then he glanced up as Shay returned with the cloth and ice cubes. Giving her a look of apology, he added, "I'm sorry, but your father has crossed a line."

"Yes," she whispered, apologetic as she handed Dair the cloth to press against her swollen cheekbone, "he has. We need to try and get the court restraining order to stop him from ever returning back here."

"What got into him?" Harper demanded, finishing his care for Dair. He stood up, scowling over at Shay.

"This has been coming on for a while," she said. "We were going to talk about it tonight at our weekly Friday meeting."

Snorting, Harper went to the sink and scrubbed his hands with soap and water. "We still will."

Dair saw how devastated Shay was. "I'm really sorry this happened. Your father just came out of nowhere. I didn't even see or hear him coming."

Reaching out, Shay touched her shoulder. "I am, too, and this was *not* your fault, Dair."

Lowering her voice, Dair asked, "Was your father like this with you and your mother?" She saw pain flit across Shay's darkened blue eyes.

"Yes, all the time."

"That's horrible," Dair growled, reaching out and touching Shay's arm. She wore a lavender knit sweater with a pair of jeans. "I'm so sorry. This whole situation has to be hell on you, Shay."

Kira said, "Clean clothes are ready. Can I help you change?"

Dair nodded her head. "Yes, I can use a little help."

Harper came over and said, "I'm going to go to your father's house, Shay. That's where Reese and Noah are staying with him until the sheriff, Sarah Carson, arrives. If you need me, just give me a call."

Shay nodded. "I'll go with you."

Dair felt sad for Shay, seeing the desolation in her expression as she turned and walked to the mudroom, gathering up her jacket and winter gear. Harper followed. Soon enough, they were gone and the house became quiet.

"I'll stay with you after we get you changed into clean jeans," Kira said, "if that's all right?"

"Yes, I'd like that. We still have to finish feeding all the horses, Kira."

"Well, why don't we do that once we get you into a set of clean clothes? I'll leave a note on the door so Noah knows where we're at. Fair enough?"

Dair liked the woman vet's attitude. Kira never tried to coddle her as Harper did. Giving her a faint smile, she handed her the cold cloth. "My cheek feels better. Can you put that in the sink? I'll take care of it later after we get done feeding the horses."

"Sure."

It didn't take Dair long to get rid of her dusty jeans and trade them in for a clean pair. She washed her hands in the sink and then wheeled out into the living room, where Kira was standing by the picture window, the drapes pulled aside.

"I just saw two sheriff's cars pull up at Ray's home,"

she said over her shoulder. "Sarah Carson is with them. That's good."

"Who's Sarah?" Dair asked, wheeling over and seeing the two vehicles parked outside Crawford's home.

"She is the sheriff of Lincoln County, where we live," Kira said. "A really cool woman. She's the only female sheriff in Wyoming."

Eyes narrowing, Dair saw two deputies emerge from each car, four in total. She saw Reese meet them at the door, gesturing for them to come into Crawford's house.

"Hey!" Kira said, suddenly excited. "Look! Garret's here! He just drove in!"

Dair grinned. "Did you know when he was coming home?"

Kira laughed. "Not really, just sometime today. Will you be okay for a bit? I want to go meet him. He doesn't know what's going on and when he sees the sheriff's cars in the driveway, that's going to send him into a big worry."

"Go ahead," Dair urged her. "I'll be fine here."

Kira leaned over, gently hugging Dair. "I'll be back in a bit. I'm sure Sarah or one of her deputies will be over here to take your statement. Noah will be with them."

"Sounds good," she said. "Go see your guy."

Kira gave her a silly grin. "He's been gone all week, Dair. I swear, I'm gonna hogtie that Spec Forces guy to the bedroom bedposts and not let him out of the room for at least two days! You may not see us for a while!"

Laughing, she watched Kira hurry to the mudroom, grab her winter gear, and take off out the door. She watched through the picture window, warmth in her chest as Kira ran full tilt up the slight slope, past all the houses, to the main parking lot where Garret had just parked his big three-quarter-ton truck. It was nice to see something beautiful and loving in lieu of what she'd just experienced with Crawford. Moving her hand over her swollen cheek, which was starting to throb, Dair missed Noah's calming presence.

As she sat there, she saw Garret Fleming get out of the truck, a hard look on his face. His expression changed to one of vulnerability when Kira flew up into the parking lot, arms wide open. Dair smiled softly. Garret was a big man and Kira was so tiny in comparison. He lifted her off her feet, twirling her around, kissing the daylights out of her. Dair wanted to do the same to Noah. That kiss . . . that kiss meant everything to Dair. It was soft, tender, and exploratory. She loved Noah's softer side. After her father was so abusive to her and her mother, she didn't want a man who was all brawn and force. She watched Garret gently set Kira down on her feet, his arm around her shoulders to steady her. They kissed again. For a long, delicious time.

Dair couldn't imagine her life without Noah in it. She'd become so accustomed to him being in the house. He made her feel at peace, and that wasn't something she felt often, except at her grandmother's home. There, she always felt safe and calm. Noah gave her so much, much more. For a moment, Dair felt shaky inside. She recognized the reaction too well. When she was a WMD dog handler and they were out with Special Forces black ops teams, the danger was always high. After completing the mission, she'd let Zeus sit between her legs while they were being helicoptered on a MH-47 back to base. And then, her insides would turn into trembling jelly in response to not dying, but living. It was a delayed reaction to the danger they faced daily.

Pushing strands of hair off her uninjured cheek, Dair watched as Garret and Kira walked to Crawford's house and disappeared inside. She didn't want to be over there. Crawford was an angry drunkard. A mean one. Feeling so very sorry for Shay, she now understood clearly what the other woman had grown up with. And Shay was so damned kind and caring with everyone else. She could have turned into an abuser like her father, and carried that sickness through the family line, but she hadn't. Shay had taken that experience and done just the opposite. Even more respect for her flowed through Dair. Getting a taste of Crawford's explosive, unexpected rage, had her insides quaking. She felt like she'd been in a life-and-death situation with the rancher. The look in Crawford's bloodshot, red-rimmed eyes scared the hell out of her. For a split second, as he came at her, Dair thought she was going to die. It brought back times when her father Butch would attack her. She was fairly sure Crawford wasn't trying to kill her. Rather, roaring that the ranch was his, he was trying to scare her off by assaulting her. The unspoken message he was sending was that if she stayed, he'd attack her again. Dair knew the type. Her father, Butch, was a mirror image of him.

She left the picture window. Dair didn't want to imagine what was going on inside Crawford's house, and wheeled out into the kitchen to make herself a pot of coffee. She wished someone would come back to the house so they could wheel her down to the barn to finish up the feeding. Fretting about it, she pulled a leftover omelet she found in the fridge, which she could reach. Early on, he'd placed the microwave on the counter, near the edge, so that she could roll over and use it. She did. All together, it made a tasty breakfast for herself.

Dair had just finished with her breakfast and was wheeling the dirty dishes over to the sink when there was a knock at the mudroom door. She heard it open and close.

"Hi," the woman in the sheriff's uniform said, sticking her head around the corner. "I'm Sheriff Sarah Carson. Are you Dair Wilson?" She stomped the snow off her black, shiny boots and entered, a notebook in one hand.

Dair dried her hands on a towel sitting on the counter and extended her hand to the tall, attractive sheriff. "Yes, I am. Nice to meet you, Sheriff Carson."

"Call me Sarah." She looked longingly at the pot of coffee. "Any chance I can pour myself a cup and we can go sit at the table and talk? I need to take your statement."

"Of course. Cream's in the fridge," Dair said, gesturing toward it.

"Nah, I like it black and strong." She walked to the counter, opening the cabinet door and finding where the mugs were located. "Would you like some, Dair?"

Smiling a little, Dair realized she liked the woman. "No, thank you." She appeared to be in her late twenties or maybe her early thirties. Sarah was her height, she would guesstimate, around five-foot-ten inches or so. It was her heart-shaped face, her sharp green eyes that missed nothing, that made Dair relax. This woman had confidence to burn. But she wasn't arrogant about it, and Dair knew the difference. She wore her dark brown nylon jacket over her tan uniform. Maybe it was Sarah's soft mouth that somewhat eased the mantle of power this woman carried. Dair wondered how she'd become the sheriff of the county. She wheeled to the kitchen table and locked the brake, waiting for Sarah.

In no time, Sarah had taken off her jacket and hung it over the back of the chair. She sat down, took a quick sip of her coffee and then opened her notebook.

"Everyone's got electronic tablets to write their reports on," she said with a grin, pointing to her paper and pen, "but I'm such a non-geek that I like handwriting my reports. I'm sure someone will force me to do it the new, computer-age way sooner or later." She chuckled. "That's good coffee, by the way. Thanks."

Dair nodded, watching the sheriff quickly shift into law enforcement mode. "How's Crawford doing?" she asked.

"Drunker than hell. We gave him a Breathalyzer and he's probably drank half a bottle of whiskey, according to the numbers." She wrinkled her nose. "You're new to Wind River, aren't you?"

"Yes." Dair filled her in with a few short sentences about how she came to the Bar C.

"Noah Mabry is pressing assault charges against Mr. Crawford," Sarah told her. "My deputies are reading him his rights, and then they're taking him to the Lincoln County jail. He'll be arraigned by a judge tomorrow sometime." She pointed to her book. "Now, give me your side of what happened. And leave nothing out if you can help it, Dair."

In ten minutes' time, Dair had explained what had occurred in the barn. She'd seen Sarah's eyes turn dark, felt her anger as she finished the story.

"I'm really sorry this happened to you, Dair. Noah had told me when I was taking his statement, that you'd just been injured by a stallion who turned on you, destroying the prosthetic you used. This really sucks."

"I'll get a replacement," Dair said. "For now, I'm

hobbling around on crutches or forced into using this chair." She placed her hands on the wheels.

"Had you ever had a run-in with Mr. Crawford before this?"

Shaking her head, Dair said, "I would catch brief glimpses of him from time to time when he left his house to drive to his condo in town, or when he came home here to the ranch."

"Did you ever trade words with him?"

"Never. I was always far away when I caught sight of him."

"So, what do you think triggered his rage this morning?"

"He's drunk," Dair muttered, her brows dipping.

"I see," Sarah murmured, giving her a look of care. "Harper used to be a medic and I know he's working toward his paramedic license right now. He said he checked you over. Do you want to go to the hospital just to make sure? The right side of your face is going black and blue on you."

"No, I hate hospitals," Dair said darkly. "Spent too much time at Bethesda after I lost part of my left leg. Can't stand being in them." She touched her hot, throbbing cheek. "Harper said I banged it good. He pushed and pressed around, trying to see if I'd fractured it, and he said I hadn't. I'll be okay. Thanks for asking, though . . ."

"Okay," Sarah murmured. "I think that bruise is going to catch the lower part of your right eye, too, from the looks of it. You hit that concrete pretty hard?"

"Yeah, I guess I did." Her lips quirked. "I'd rather mess up my face than my left knee, which has already been injured by that stallion. I was worried about injuring it more when Crawford attacked me."

"But Harper said it was fine, too?"

"Yes. He's really good at what he does, Sarah. I trust him. I have an appointment with Dr. Radke, my ortho surgeon, in a week. I'll tell him what happened and he'll very thoroughly check that left knee of mine to make sure it's okay."

"Good," Sarah said. Folding her notebook closed, she held Dair's gaze. "Now, you have a choice to make here, Dair. Are you going to press charges against Mr. Crawford? Because clearly, he assaulted you, and that's a felony, not a misdemeanor. That means if you do press charges, he's going to jail, bail will be set, and then he's going to go through the court system for injuring you."

"I know."

"Noah's pressing charges because he says Crawford tried to hit, kick, and bite him."

Uncomfortable, Dair said, "I'm not sure if I want to or not, Sarah."

"Why?"

Looking away for a moment, she said, "Because Ray Crawford is trying to get healthy enough to sue Shay and Reese to take back the Bar C."

"I'm aware of the situation," Sarah told her quietly. "But you shouldn't make a decision based upon your loyalty to Shay and Reese. Mr. Crawford assaulted you."

"But what will Crawford do if we send him to jail for a year or two? Will he come back here afterward? More angry? Sue Shay and Reese to get the ranch back, no matter how long it takes him? If I press charges, it just makes Crawford that much more angry and determined to take the Bar C back." Dair heard the frustration in her voice. "For all I know, he'll come back with a pistol or rifle and kill all of us, to get even."

Sarah gave her a nod, her face mostly unreadable. Dair understood why. Law enforcement, in her world, was akin to the military. She was sure that Sarah knew a whole lot more than she could ever tell about everyone, good and bad, in Lincoln County. But it wasn't something she could talk about, precisely because she held so many secrets. She saw the concern in the sheriff's green eyes, that sense of strength around her. Dair was glad she was the sheriff. She liked Sarah's demeanor and that she did not use her authority heavy-handedly.

"Between us?" Sarah said gently. "Mr. Crawford has made it known far and wide to anyone who would listen that he's intent on suing his daughter to take back the Bar C. It's coming, no matter what you decide to do, Dair."

Heaviness cloaked Dair's shoulders and she hung her head, staring at her hands tightly gripped in her lap. "I know Ray told Shay he'd do that."

"Were you hoping that by not pressing charges it would make Mr. Crawford back off? That won't happen." She opened her hands. "I was born here in Wind River Valley, Dair. I know everyone. And Mr. Crawford comes from a long line of male ranchers who were abusive toward their wives and children. He carried on that tradition with Shay and her mother. I'm sure that's not news to you, because Shay told me earlier that you knew about their family history."

"Yeah, she did tell me," Dair muttered, shaking her head. She frowned. "Can I have until tomorrow morning to make up my mind?"

"Sure," Sarah said, pushing the chair back and grabbing her dark brown baseball cap. She pulled a card from her pocket, sliding it toward Dair. "Just give me a call with your decision as soon as you can."

"I will . . . thanks . . . for everything, Sarah."

"I'm sorry we had to meet under these circumstances,

Dair. Word was getting around the valley that you're a wonderful horse trainer." She smiled. "You have a good name here, and that's something to be proud of. I'm also asking my photographer to come over here and photograph your injuries by Mr. Crawford for evidence." She lifted her hand. "I'll talk to you later."

Dair sat there feeling miserable. Just as Sarah opened the door to leave, she saw Noah coming in. They exchanged a few words out in the mudroom, and then Sarah left. Her heart leaped. She needed him right now as never before. When had Noah become so indispensable to her? It didn't matter, Dair told herself. He stomped the snow off his boots and then entered the kitchen, giving her an intense, cursory inspection.

"I'm okay," Dair said. "Is Crawford gone?"

"Yes," Noah said, coming over to her. He crouched down in front of her and reached out, grazing her uninjured cheek. "The deputies took him away. You're pale."

"Am I?"

He smiled faintly and slid his hands in a comforting gesture down her arms. "Anyone would be. How's your right knee doing? Harper said he examined you and said it was fine."

"It's okay." She felt her flesh tingling wildly in the wake of his hands gently moving down her arms. He rose and she missed his nearness, wanting badly to be embraced by him.

"Your one cheek looks pretty rough," Noah said. "Can I get you an ice pack for it?"

His thoughtfulness touched her, as always. "Yes. Kira made me one earlier. The cloth is in the sink. Just grab some ice cubes and put them inside it."

Noah moved to the kitchen and quickly created her ice pack, bringing it over to her. "Have you eaten, Dair?"

"I took that omelet you'd made earlier from the fridge and I saved half of it for you. It's in there, if you want it. I'm worried about getting the rest of the horses fed."

"Garret and Harper are doing that right now," he said. "Coffee smells good. I'm going to grab the last of that omelet. Want some toast?"

"No . . . thanks." Hungrily, she watched Noah putter around in the kitchen. He wore a bright red flannel cowboy shirt, the sleeves rolled up to his elbows as he washed his hands in the sink. "How is everyone doing?" she asked.

Noah snorted, turning and looking at her over his shoulder. "Let's put it this way: Tonight when we have our Friday meeting? It ought to be a humdinger."

"Garret looked pretty upset after Kira ran up and met him in the parking lot and told him why the sheriff's cars were here."

"Garret is not someone you mess with," Noah said, putting the omelet on a plate and then sliding it into the microwave oven. "When he found out what happened, he wanted to take Crawford apart, piece by piece, right there on the spot, in front of the deputies. And he could have done it."

"Wow . . ."

"Reese is the deadly one, though," Noah added, popping two slices of whole wheat bread into the toaster. "They untied Crawford once they got him into the living room. Reese and Harper just stood at the door and would not let him leave. He paced, screamed, cursed, and yelled at them, not necessarily in that order."

"How were you handling it?"

Noah scowled and turned, hips resting against the counter. "Not well, because I saw him try to hit you,

Dair. I wanted to kill the sonofabitch. I heard him screaming as he went into the barn. I was training a horse when I heard the commotion." His voice lowered, eyes flashing. "Crawford's lucky that I don't want to spend my life in prison for killing him. He's not worth it, when I have someone like you to come home to."

Dair felt his care, saw it burning in his narrowed gaze. "Well, I'm glad you didn't kill him. I want you around here, too, Noah." She saw the line of his mouth soften a little. There was a charged air of threat and danger swirling around him. He had been in the military, he'd seen combat, and she was sure he'd killed enemy. "I'm glad you didn't let your emotions run away with you," she whispered.

"Well, you were doing a pretty damn good job of defending yourself against him," he grunted. The toast popped up and he removed it and buttered it, placing it on the plate that had just come out of the microwave. He sauntered over to the table and sat down at the corner, their elbows nearly brushing one another. Holding out a piece of toast, he said, "Come on, eat a little. You're still in shock and your adrenaline hasn't crashed yet." And then he grinned. "I'll even put strawberry jam on it for you, if you want?"

She smiled and took the toast. "It's fine as is, thanks. Go ahead, eat. You have to be starved."

Noah ate hungrily, but he spoke between bites. "Sarah had one of her deputies take Crawford's statement. He lied his ass off. He said that you called him names and charged at him."

Mouth dropping open, Dair said, "That's a lie!"

"Sure it is. Harper gave his statement. And then, I gave mine. Our three statements are going to read the same. So it will make Crawford out to be the liar he is.

Besides, he failed the Breathalyzer test, and that's going to do him in with a judge or jury." And then he gave her a pleased look. "What Crawford doesn't know is that Garret had put video cameras in all the barns and arena. Garret is going to retrieve the video from that area where the attack occurred and hand it over to Sarah as evidence against Crawford."

Tearing the toast in two, laying it on the mat in front of her, Dair said, "I didn't know we had cameras out there."

"Yeah, it was Garret's idea as a safety feature. But now that video will show Crawford lied on his statement."

"Crawford doesn't respect any of us, Noah. He called Shay stupid. He's an abuser, pure and simple, with or without alcohol fueling him."

"No argument there," he said, finishing off the omelet. "He blamed Shay for bringing him the liquor he consumed this morning. Said she'd bought him a bottle of whiskey. Shay about dropped over dead on that one. It was a complete lie."

"Did the deputy taking his statement know that he was lying?"

"I'm sure he did, but he had his game face on and he acted nonjudgmental toward Crawford."

"I sat here with Sarah, and it's obvious she knows all about Shay and Reese's problems with Crawford," she muttered.

He chuckled, finishing off his piece of toast. "I don't know Sarah that well, but everyone thinks highly of her. She's the kind of person who tries to defuse situations and get people to talk and cool things down. Crawford was out of control and he was angry at everyone. He's threatened repeatedly to sue the sheriff's department for detaining him in his own home."

"Someone needs to permanently put that guy away."

"He's one of those dark humans who does nothing but spread toxic shit, unhappiness, and pain on anyone he touches or is around," Noah said, his voice grim.

"When he was coming at me . . ." Dair said, meeting his hardened expression.

"Yes?"

"I had the craziest thing happen for a split second. I saw my father's face over Crawford's face. And then it changed back. It really shook me. I wasn't thinking when he charged me. I just threw out my foot, hoping to stop him from reaching me with his fist." She saw Noah's gray eyes grow turbulent. He reached out, his hand enclosing hers.

"I'm so damned sorry I wasn't there to protect you, Dair."

She felt the warm roughness of his fingers around her cool, damp ones. "I guess," she choked out, "I'm more upset about this than I realized. I mean . . . I haven't seen my father since I was ten years old, when he broke my arm. It's crazy that I'd see his face over Crawford's." She searched Noah's narrowing gaze.

"I think some of us carry our past with us, whether we know it or not," Noah said gently.

Chapter Fifteen

Dair didn't have the courage to ask Noah to come and lie down with her. That's what she really wanted, but she knew it was the wrong time with everything in such an uproar. "I think I'll nap for a little while. You have horses to train."

He grimaced. "I do." He rose. "Do you need anything else, Dair, before I head to the barn?"

Giving him a kind look, she shook her head. "I think I just need to be quiet for a while and rest."

"You know where I am. You can call me on the cell phone."

She felt his concern for her. "I'll probably go to sleep, but yes, if I need something, I'll get ahold of you." Noah hesitated, as if not convinced, but he didn't say anything.

"I'll come in between training sessions, and just check on you. I'll be quiet about it."

Dair nodded and wheeled out of the kitchen. Exhaustion was creeping up on her and she could feel it. In some ways, she felt like a punching bag, getting hit with a one-two strike. First, her left knee was torn up. Then, Crawford attacked her out of the blue.

Going to her room, she left the door ajar, situated herself on top of the unmade bed, and promptly closed her eyes. Her mind was active and refused to shut off. Lying on her back, hands clasped across her stomach, she was torn between filing assault charges against Crawford or not. Noah had the balls to do it. Why was she hesitating? Dair knew it wasn't like her. She'd always had the confidence to make split-second decisions, especially as a WMD dog handler in a dangerous situation.

How much she'd changed! As she lay there, she thought about those changes and what had brought them about. She thought she knew herself pretty well, but life was brutal sometimes. Losing a leg had crippled her confidence in herself, she realized. It wasn't the first time she'd met this feeling of low self-esteem. She didn't like to admit it, but with Crawford trying to strike her with his fist, it made her aware as never before that she was no longer capable of fully defending herself as she used to be when she was in the military. The loss of her lower leg had thrown her into a completely new world, and she still felt vulnerable in it.

Dair gave herself credit. When Harper was knocked off his feet and Crawford came at her, she did defend herself the best way she knew how. And if Noah hadn't come in, along with Harper scrambling back to his feet, Dair knew she would have been wide-open to a second attack by the drunken abuser. Both men had come to her aid in different ways. Her mouth twitched. She hated feeling helpless like this. It bothered the hell out of her. Running over other possible scenarios of how to defend herself, Dair came to the glum conclusion that without wearing a weapon on her person, she would have been victim to Crawford's next attack. That hurt. A lot.

Hot tears formed behind her closed lids. She hated feeling stripped of her own power to protect herself. Dair remembered how defenseless she'd felt when her father would skulk around the house, like an IED ready to explode momentarily. It never ended in the ten years he lived there. He was always like that. A threat. And more than once, he'd struck her and he'd hit her mother.

Sometime after that, Dair's last thought was that their meeting at Shay and Reese's home tonight was going to be filled with tension. She sank into a dreamless, healing sleep, with no sure answers to anything in her life. Being an amputee brought a sense of being open to attack. She wasn't whole. Not any longer.

Libby Hilbert sat in an upholstered, flowery-fabric chair in the expansive living room of the Lockharts' home. Dair sat opposite her in the makeshift circle where all the wranglers sat in wooden chairs brought from the kitchen table.

The forty-year-old widow had her long red hair pulled back from her oval face with purple barrettes that complemented the silk blouse of emerald green that she wore beneath her black wool pantsuit. Dair had enjoyed seeing Libby once a week, because the psychologist wasn't like most therapists she'd met at Bethesda. There was no arrogance. Instead, she was maternal, gentle, and had a soft voice. Her green eyes were large and it was easy to read how she felt.

It was seven p.m., and Garret had faithfully made hot cinnamon rolls, much to everyone's delight. Her stomach was tight with fear. Dair felt as if she were back in her home as a child, waiting for her father to explode and then come after either her or her mother.

Noah sat on her left, next to her wheelchair. On her right was Shay, and next to her, Reese. Harper sat to the left of Libby while Garret and Kira were to Libby's right. They all looked somber. She noticed that hardly anyone had eaten much of the delicious, warm cinnamon rolls. There was an edgy, unsettled energy swirling among all of them, and Dair knew it was because of this morning's melee with Crawford.

"Tonight," Libby began, "we need to talk about what happened this morning out in the barn." She gave Dair a sympathetic look. Shifting her gaze, she glanced over at Shay and Reese. "Perhaps we should have an update on your father, Shay?"

Shay grimaced and clenched her hands in the lap of her dark brown corduroy slacks. "He's in the Lincoln County jail on charges of assault. He's going before a judge tomorrow morning."

"And how are you feeling about this?" Libby asked.

"Horrible," Shay admitted, giving all of them a look of apology. "I-I never expected something like this would happen."

"But Ray abused you and your mother, right?"

"Yes . . . yes, he did."

Libby gave all of them a moment to allow the information to sink in. "What we really have is an abuser loose among all of you," she said, her gaze meeting each person in the living room. "Is there anyone else here who has come out of an abusive childhood?"

Dair's stomach clenched. There was so much her wrangler friends didn't know about her yet. "Me," she whispered. "My father beat up me and my mother." She felt shame in admitting it, but at the same time, it felt freeing to release that dark, deep secret she hid from everyone. Noah's hand moved to her hands in her lap, squeezing them, comforting her. Giving him a quick glance, she saw turmoil in his eyes, but felt his protectiveness, too. And it felt good. That gave Dair the courage to add, "My father was not an alcoholic. He was bipolar. And he took recreational drugs. My mother pleaded with him to get help, but he said he was fine."

"Do you want to share what happened to you at ten, Dair?"

Knowing that Libby was going to bring this up, because Dair had discussed it with her the second week she'd arrived at the Bar C, she gulped and gave a jerky nod. In as few words as possible, she shared it with the group. Dair could see the horror in Harper's widening eyes. As a medic, he understood a bone being broken in a child's lower arm, the force that it took. Garret's face grew dark and stormy. Kira already knew, and so did Shay and Reese.

Libby allowed it all to sink in.

Garret spoke up. "My old man's the same way. A mean, abusive bastard."

Dair held his gaze. Some of the tension in her dissolved.

"I was lucky," Harper said. "I've got a great set of parents."

"So do I," Reese admitted.

"Mine are decent, too," Noah added.

"Dair? You're the one who took the brunt of Ray's attack. How are you feeling right now?" Libby asked.

Noah's hand tightened for a moment over hers. Giving him a look of gratitude, Dair felt her mouth going dry. "I guess I realized that I can't protect and defend myself like I could when I had two good legs under me."

"Feeling vulnerable?"

"Horribly," she admitted, her voice barely above a

whisper. "I was in the military, I worked in black ops. I felt totally confident in Zeus, my WMD dog, myself, and the men I was with." She rolled her shoulders, looking at each person in the room. "Now? I feel like half a person. I wouldn't have come out of that scrape this morning if Harper and Noah hadn't been around to help me. I had no way to protect myself, and it's a horrible feeling to admit that."

Silence fell over the group.

"Are you angry with Ray?" Libby asked.

"Yes," Dair admitted.

"When your father would abuse you, did you feel anger then?"

"Of course."

"What did you do with it?"

Dair snorted. "I was a kid, Libby. What could I do? I'd run and hide. Sometimes in the closet, sometimes under my bed. I wanted to disappear. I wanted to become invisible."

"Understandable," she said, giving Dair a gentle look. "When your father hit you, what did you do?"

"Tried to get away."

"Didn't you want to hit him back?"

"Sure," she said, "but I was afraid if I hit him back, he'd kill me, or worse, go after my mother."

"How does this morning's assault upon you bring back similar feelings from your childhood?"

Dair felt devastated by that question and rubbed her brow. Roughly, she said, "I wanted to hit Ray hard, with my fist. But I couldn't because I was lying on my side in a face-plant in the middle of that aisle, and the wheelchair pinned me so I couldn't move."

"But this time," Libby pointed out, "you did fight

back. You kicked out at Ray and it knocked him off his feet."

"There wasn't much choice, looking back on it, Libby. I was scared." And then she gave Noah a glance before continuing. "When Ray came at me, for a split second I saw my father's face overlaid on his. It shocked me. And that's when I got really scared."

Giving a thoughtful nod, Libby said, "That's not unusual. I'm sure you have lots of stored feelings and hurt from your father abusing you."

"Probably," Dair admitted bitterly.

"When you were a child, if you could have called someone for help, who would it have been?"

"The police."

"Did your mother call them?"

"No, never. She was afraid he'd kill her. I was afraid he'd kill both of us if we tried to get help."

"Is that why you haven't pressed charges against Ray Crawford?"

It felt as if she'd been hit in the solar plexus, and Dair closed her eyes for a moment, trying to contain all her emotions. Noah's hand on hers steadied her. She opened her eyes, staring across the room at Libby, whose expression was nothing but compassionate. Her voice hoarse, Dair said, "To tell you the truth? I *wanted* to press charges. Sarah asked me after the interview what I wanted to do. I wasn't sure. I was waffling." Cutting an apologetic look at Shay, she said to her, "I didn't want to cause you any more pain than you were already in. I was afraid if I pressed charges that Ray, once he got out of jail, would be ten times more angry and do everything in his power to take the Bar C away from you."

Shay nodded, wiping tears from her eyes.

"Was your decision based upon your past, Dair?"

Sighing raggedly, Dair held Libby's thoughtful expression. "When you put it that way? Yeah, it probably was. I was afraid Ray would come back here when he got out and shoot all of us."

"Often," Libby said quietly to the group, "when we've been abused and powerless to stop it, we behave just as Dair did. She was young, and couldn't run from it. The one parent was incapable of protecting Dair, her child. And so, when a similar threat comes along, no matter our age, we tend to react the same way, even though the events are different, we're older and we're more mature."

Dair stared at her, compressing her lips. "I think Ray is fully capable of coming back here once he gets out of jail and killing all of us if he could."

"Because that's what your father told you, right? He'd come after you and kill you and your mom?"

Anger surged in Dair, and she realized it had no place in this session. Libby was helping her to see a pattern in her life. She got that. She'd had way too much therapy at Bethesda in group sessions with other vet amputees, not to realize what she was doing. The anger dissipated. Giving Libby a sour smile, Dair said, "I see it now. Thanks." She saw Libby's green eyes glisten, but there was no triumph in her expression, just sadness for her.

"I knee-jerked," she told Shay. "I was afraid if I pressed assault charges against your father, it would cause you and Reese even more trouble after he got out."

"Oh, Dair," Shay said, getting up. She went over to her, sliding her arms around her shoulders and squeezing her tightly. "It's all right. My father hurt you. He deserves whatever he gets," she mumbled tearfully against her neck and shoulder. Releasing her, Shay crouched down, gripping Dair's hands. Tears were running freely down her face. "You have every right to press charges. We are no longer victims. Part of ending that mindset is to realize that we have choices now, Dair. You don't have to run to a closet or slide under your bed anymore. My father deserves to be charged."

Reese came over, his hand on Shay's small shoulder as he looked down at Dair. "We'll deal with Crawford after he gets out. I feel he'll take a legal route to try and get the ranch back. I don't think he's that stupid as to come onto Bar C property with a weapon. Besides, as a felon, if he's convicted, he won't be allowed to carry a firearm ever again. And you can bet that when they call us to tell us he's being released, we will be alert. Neither Shay nor I want you to worry about possibilities like that, Dair. You do what is right for you. Okay?"

"Yes," Shay whispered, her voice trembling, holding Dair's gaze, "you do what is right for you. My father hurt you. You're not a victim anymore. You don't have to be." She squeezed Dair's hands and rose, sliding her arm around her husband's waist.

Her gut was tight and aching. So many old feelings from the past, ugly, frightening ones, moved through Dair. She sat there hearing everyone agree with Reese and Shay. Noah moved his hand gently across her tense shoulders, trying to give her some solace. As Reese took Shay back to her chair, Dair lifted her chin, staring at Libby.

"Okay, I'm going to press charges."

"What a night," Dair muttered as she stood carefully on her one foot, holding on to Noah's upper arms as she balanced herself. The session had lasted until ten p.m., and a lot of dirty laundry got aired collectively by the group.

"It was a good night," Noah said, cupping her elbows. "You were very brave." He stared into her darkened eyes. "That couldn't have been easy to talk about in front of everyone."

There were only six inches between them, and Dair relaxed, allowing her weight to shift to her one leg. "You helped me, you know?"

"How?"

"It was as if you knew when I needed your touch," she whispered. As exhausted as she was emotionally, her heart opened to Noah. He looked tired and stressed, too. Everyone was. Lifting her hand, she caressed his jaw, feeling the stubble beneath her fingertips. "You were there for me, Noah. I'm not used to that, but it was so good, so steadying to me when I felt like emotionally I was flying apart inside."

He smiled down into her eyes. "I wanted to be there for you, Dair. You haven't been protected very much in your life, and I want to be the man who is there for you—if you want me." He took her hand, opened it, placed a soft kiss in the center of her palm, and then released it.

Her palm tingled. As tired as she was, she needed Noah. "You're like a shadow warrior," she accused, smiling a little. "Never seen, but always there, just around the corner when I need you."

"Well, I wasn't exactly doing my job this morning," he protested.

"You have the ears of a wolf, I swear."

"It was an intuitive feeling, Dair." He slid his fingers through her loose black hair, watching the bluish highlights dance through the strands. "You are beautiful, courageous, and I've been waiting since this morning to hold you . . ."

"Hold me, then," she whispered, sliding her arms across his shoulders. Never had Dair wanted anything more as Noah gave her a burning look, stepping forward, always sensitive to the fact that she was carefully balanced on one foot. She relished his arms sliding around her hips, caressing her lower back and gently asking her to lean against him. He would hold her safe. It was in his eyes, the yearning, the need for her in them, that allowed her to trust him. She uttered his name, surrendering over to him, feeling how strong Noah was, his muscles hard, hers softer and rounded against him. She nestled her face against his neck, relaxing, feeling his hand move slowly up and down the center of her back, comforting her. It wasn't sexual. It was human tenderness of the best kind, and Dair absorbed it, starved for just this kind of care right now.

"You smell so good," he muttered, his face pressed against her head, her hair tickling him here and there.

"I can't smell that good," she managed wryly. "I need a shower." She sighed. Sliding her fingers along his nape, the corded column of his neck, his short hair silky between her fingertips, Dair pressed her left cheek against him, her lips caressing his throat. She felt Noah tense and then relax. There was no way for her not to feel the thickness of his erection growing rapidly beneath his jeans, pressing into her belly, awakening her, warming her until a new ache formed and wanted to be tended to. His fingers moved across her shoulders, massaging them lightly, and she groaned with appreciation.

"Feel good?" he rasped, kissing her hair.

"Does it ever . . . I didn't realize how tense I'd become."

"Hey," he said, mirth in his voice, "that was one helluva therapy session for all of us tonight. But it was the roughest on you, Dair."

Nodding, eyes closed, she absorbed his caresses, that simmering fire glowing hotly in her lower body, needing him in every possible way. "I'll survive," she said. "Don't stop doing what you're doing, Noah," she urged, sliding her fingers downward, feeling his muscles react as her fingertips skimmed his back. Never had anything felt so right to Dair as this. Each time he caressed her spine, tiny tingles widened in the wake of his fingers.

"I wish . . ."

"What?" he rasped, moving her hair to one side, kissing the nape of her slender neck.

"I wish I had two legs."

"To do what with?" he teased, feeling her beginning to melt against him as he kissed and then licked that erotic area of her neck.

"To move closer to you," she said, her voice turning amused. "To push my hips against yours. It's a little tough to do it on one leg."

He laughed quietly with her. Noah eased her away from him just enough to hold her drowsy, lustrous gaze. "Tell me what you want, Dair. If I can, I'll give it to you." He threaded his fingers through her cloud of hair, watching how it affected her.

Gazing into his stormy gray eyes, she whispered, "Will you hold me tonight? I want to be with you, Noah. I don't know where this is going, but I'm willing to follow my heart, my need for you, what you give me . . . what I want to give to you . . ." She saw his expression flare with surprise and then turn turbulent with so many emotions. "Talk to me? Tell me what you're thinking? What you're feeling?"

He searched her eyes, his hands stilling over her hips, holding her gently against him. "If what you want is to be held, I'll do that for you, Dair. You're exhausted. You need rest. You're still in shock over what happened this morning." He leaned over, brushing her lips. "I'll just hold you. If you want anything more, you have to tell me and how much further you want to go. Okay?"

Relief flooded through her, tears burning in her eyes as she drowned in his warm gaze. "Yes . . . that's what I need right now, Noah. I need to be held."

"Then," he rasped, "you've got it."

Dair didn't have the courage to tell him how inept she felt, that she wasn't whole. She'd not been touched by a man since she'd lost her leg. There was such hesitation and fear within her. Fear of rejection. Fear she was disgustingly ugly. But Noah had already seen her leg without the sock on it. She'd looked for revulsion in his expression and there was nothing except sympathy. He didn't avoid looking at her residual limb. He wasn't fazed by it in the least, and that surprised her. It had given her the courage to ask him to sleep with her tonight. To hold her. She slid her hand across his shoulder, caressing the fabric near his collarbone. "Th-thank you. I feel pretty shaky inside and outside of myself right now."

He nodded. "Dair, you got assaulted this morning. Anyone would be shaken. Do you need some help in the bathroom? Getting your shower?"

"No . . . I'll manage, thanks. But if you could bring me my nightgown, that would be good."

"Sure," he murmured. "Ready to sit in the chair again?"

"Yes," she said, and for the first time allowed him to help her, instead of insisting she do everything herself. Noah was teaching her that it was all right not to be so independent all the time. He was so different from the relationships she'd had before, and it made her feel even more unsure of herself with him. He was so new to the world of men she'd known. Never had a man ever said he'd just hold her in bed, without sex. Not that she'd ever asked a man to hold her. How many men would do what Noah was offering to do for her? Probably none, her mushy brain reminded her as Noah pushed her to the bathroom and opened the door for her.

As good as his word, he brought in her nightgown, her brush and comb.

"Your bed or mine?" he asked as he paused at the open door.

"Yours," she said. "It's king-sized and has plenty of room." Because she was worried about her left knee and her limb. Maybe Noah would be sickened by that limb possibly touching him? She didn't know, and was too exhausted to think anymore about it. A larger bed would give him room to avoid her limb if he was repelled by it. Everything was so tentative within her. Giving him a searching glance, she asked, "Are you sure you want to do this, Noah?"

If she had any doubts, they melted beneath the tender look he gave her.

"I'm positive. I'll hold you as close or as far away as you want, Dair. You just need to speak up and let me know. Okay?"

It was such a huge leap forward in their growing relationship. The assurance in his expression told her he was being honest. The care in his deep voice flowed over her, removing some of the anxiety she was feeling so sharply within her. "Okay . . . good . . ."

"Once you get cleaned up and out of here, I'll help you get situated on my bed. It's taller than yours and you might need some help getting up on it."

Dair hadn't even thought that far ahead. "Oh . . . yes, you're right. Okay . . ."

He smiled a little. "Get your shower." He quietly closed the door, leaving her feeling alone, and yet like a needy beggar who wanted him more than anything else in her life right now.

Chapter Sixteen

Dair knew she'd have a lot of trouble on one leg, trying to lift herself up onto the high king-sized mattress. With Noah's quiet, patient help, sliding his hands around her waist, he lifted her up onto the bed. Earlier, he'd pulled down the sheet and covers for her. As he released her, she gave him a grateful look. "I would have struggled."

"Yes," he said, gesturing to her right knee hidden beneath her lavender flannel gown, "but your right knee is swollen and you don't want to abuse it, either. At least, not right now."

"I agree," Dair said, tugging down the gown that hung to just below her knees. Inwardly, she flinched over her left limb sticking out, looking alien, she was sure, to him. But if Noah felt that way, she didn't see it in his eyes.

He leaned over, picking up the sheet and covers, pulling them up to her waist. "Stay warm, okay? I'll be back in about twenty minutes. I'll take a fast shower." He grinned.

Nervously, she smoothed the bright quilt top made

up of colorful patches of old, worn velvet fabric. "I'll see you then."

Watching Noah grab his pj's from the drawer and leave, a ragged sigh broke from her lips. Was she doing the right thing? Was it fair to ask Noah to hold her tonight? She could see the bulge in his jeans and knew he had a partial erection. Dair was no neophyte to sex and knew that a man was swift to arousal. And she knew he could be uncomfortable or even in pain from such an erection. She didn't mean to do that to Noah. Was she being selfish? *Probably.*

Studying her swollen right knee made her feel queasy. Crawford attacking her was a direct reminder of her father grabbing and shaking or hitting her. And how she felt right now was how she'd felt as a child. At those times, it was her mother who came and held her afterward, fussed over her, and tried to comfort her when her father finally stormed out of the house. He would disappear for hours on end. When he returned, he was quiet and sullen, glaring at both of them. But at least, he wasn't going after them again.

Smoothing the nubby velvet patches on the quilt with her hand, Dair felt torn. She had to talk to Noah. She wouldn't be able to go to sleep if she didn't ask him more questions. Noah's openness, and coaxing her to speak up, were new for Dair. And she wasn't good at speaking out. But at least Noah was patient, and he listened, and that was so much more than any other man had ever given her. It gave Dair the courage to speak up when he returned to the bedroom.

Noah saw that Dair was leaning up against the quilted dark purple velvet headboard. Her hair was down around her shoulders and covered her breasts.

She had pulled the covers up to her waist, her fingers restless and fretting. He wore his pj's for her. Normally he only wore the bottoms, but tonight he wore the top, too, not wanting her to feel uncomfortable with his upper body naked. He closed the door and shut off the overhead light. The look in her gold-brown eyes was one of turbulence, and he could feel her anxiety. A nightlight near the door gave just enough light so that a person could find the door if they needed to.

Moving to his side of the wide bed, he pulled the covers down but left hers in place. Noah emulated her by sitting up against the headboard with plenty of space between them. "You look like you want to talk," he said, cocking his head in her direction, catching her worried gaze.

Dair licked her lips and whispered, "Yes. I-I'm feeling really awkward about this, Noah."

"Tell me why." He kept his hands to himself. His erection was still present, but less so as he exerted control over himself for her sake. He couldn't completely make it disappear, but he hoped it showed Dair this wasn't about a sexual arrangement between them. Did he want that? Yes. But he wanted Dair to come to him, tell him what she wanted from him, what she wanted to share with him.

"Well," she uttered, looking off into the darkness and then turning to his gaze, "I'm feeling odd, Noah. As tired as I am, my mind is screaming along at a thousand miles an hour. I wonder if my asking you to hold me in bed was wrong. I wonder if it's fair to you."

He raised a brow. "You've had a rough day, Dair. Anyone, including me, would want to be held. That's natural, don't you think? When you're hurting, it's not odd to want to be held." He saw her brows dip, her gaze settle on her tightly clasped hands in her lap.

"Well . . . when you put it like that . . ."

"Didn't you feel that way after your father would hurt you?" he asked her gently.

"Yes . . . always. My mom would come into my room, hold me while I cried, and try to comfort me . . ."

"I'm glad she did that for you." Sitting up, he turned and crossed his legs, resting his elbows on his knees as he studied her. "I want to be there for you, Dair. This isn't about sex. It's about one human helping another. That's where I'm at with this arrangement. I'm not going to try and bother you in any way that makes you uncomfortable. I want to help you, not make you feel anxious and worried and on guard against me."

"I-I've never done this before with a man, Noah."

He gave her a wry look. "I haven't either, but that's okay. My heart knows you need some care right now, Dair. I'm willing to do it for you. I try to put myself in other people's shoes and do the right thing for the right reasons."

"This isn't fair to you, though."

"In what way?"

Dair rubbed her wrinkled brow and muttered, "You have an erection."

He looked down at himself. "That's true, but just because I have one doesn't mean I'm going to act on it, Dair. I'm drawn to you. I have been from the first day I saw you. You're beautiful, intelligent, and we share a lot of laughs, a lot of searching talks with one another. I'd be lying if I said I didn't enjoy being around you, working with you, because I do." He saw her eyes grow teary, saw her fighting them back. Dair had never cried around him. She was a passionate, emotional person, but Noah knew that she probably learned as a very young child not to cry in front of her father. She'd learned how to stuff her feelings and hide them. That was the last thing he wanted her to do around him, but she had ten years of terror from her father branded upon her. She didn't realize she could handle her feelings differently as an adult.

Opening his hands, he paused. "Do I want to love you? Yes, I do, Dair. But that's something I'm not going to act on unless you want the same thing. Are we clear about that? I'm not going to touch you in a way that you don't want or approve."

Giving a jerky nod, she said, "I'm glad you said that, Noah. I wasn't sure . . ."

He laughed sourly. "Men get erections in a heartbeat. But that doesn't mean they're going to be a Neanderthal and act upon it and attack the woman that arouses them like that." He saw a grudging smile pull at one corner of her mouth, saw her shoulders begin to relax. "I'm just as nervous as you," he admitted, seeing surprise flare in her eyes. "I want to be your safe harbor tonight. I'm afraid I'll touch you in the wrong way by accident. I want you to feel relaxed and safe if I hold you, Dair. I'm the last person who wants to see you tensed up and waiting to be jumped on by me."

Shaking her head, she whispered, "You've never been that way with me, Noah. That's why I asked you, because you already make me feel safe enough to ask you these things. You always have."

"That's good to know," he said, holding her widening eyes that made his heart beat faster. In so many ways, Dair was still trapped in that pattern as a young child, always expecting the worst from a male. Expecting to be controlled by him. He understood the pattern and his heart ached for her. "What is bothering you, because I can see something else. Want to share it with me?"

Swallowing hard, she made a loose gesture toward

her left limb. "My leg. I know it's ugly looking. You may not want to be touched by it. It might turn your stomach or something."

He smiled faintly. "You lost your leg in combat, Dair. You gave a part of yourself for your country. Why would I ever be turned off by it? By you?"

She touched her residual limb, moving her fingers across the bed covers where it lay. "I-I've not been with a man since this injury happened. I was afraid . . . afraid that any man would see my left limb and be disgusted by how ugly it looks . . . turned off . . ."

Feeling her struggling against the terror of being rejected, he rasped, "All of you is beautiful to me, Dair. Your residual leg doesn't define you any more than my leg does me. I'm drawn to you. I like you. I admire and respect you. I admit I've never been around an amputee on a personal level like this before, but nothing about you is a turn-off to me. I see all of you. Your loss of limb is a story of your bravery, where I come from. How could I think it, or you, are ugly? That's not a word that exists in my vocabulary." He dug into her anxious expression. "Are we clear on that?"

"Yes," she managed in a choked whisper, her hand protective over her left knee. "Thank you for telling me that. I've lived in terror and fear that if a man ever saw me naked that he'd be disgusted by my less-than-perfect body . . ."

Giving her a heated look she could not misinterpret, he rumbled, "Just the opposite, Dair. Is anything else bothering you that we should talk about?"

"No . . . I guess not. Thanks for putting up with me."

Noah knew that response came from an angry father. "Are you used to the men in your life being impatient with you?"

"Yeah . . . I guess so. I think it's time I made some

adjustments and quit tarring you with the same brush?" She managed an apologetic sliver of a smile.

Just seeing the hope, the trust burning in her gold-brown eyes made Noah want to weep for her. "I think so." He slid down into the bed. "Now, how do you want to lie with me?"

"Could I maybe just kind of lie close to your back? Would you mind?"

There was such tentativeness in Dair. He throttled his reaction. "Sounds good," Noah murmured, lying down on his right side. "Come on, ease up as close or far away as you want and get comfy. Whatever you want is fine with me, Dair." Noah hoped his words, his teasing, would put her further at ease. The only way she was going to discover he wasn't a sexual predator lying in wait for her was to get close to him and find out.

Noah felt her move, felt the mattress dip a bit, felt her tugging at the covers. It had to be awkward, without a complete second leg, to scoot over to him. Closing his eyes, he felt her heat, felt her body so close to his. His erection swelled in response, but he placed full control over his desire. It was so important to give Dair this sense of safety with him. He wasn't anything like her father, and she was truly beginning to realize that. And he was sure from what she'd offered to share with him that no man had ever extended this to her in this kind of situation.

She got close, maybe a few inches away from him, her arm tentative as she curved it around his waist. He allowed her whatever she needed. Finally, he heard her sigh and felt her arm relax fully around his torso.

"Okay?" he asked.

"Okay . . ."

"Shut your eyes, Dair. Go to sleep. Only good dreams tonight. All right?"

"I hope so," she whispered brokenly. "I'm so tired . . ."

Noah closed his eyes, but his mind and his body were wide-awake. Almost instantly, Noah felt Dair fully relax, her breath moist and warm against the nape of his neck, her head inches away from his on the same pillow. His heart opened and he felt such a powerful need to protect her from the world at large. With the exception of her mother's arms holding her after abuse by her father, he wondered if she'd ever found safe harbor. Noah doubted it, but he was going to be patient and wait Dair out. Sooner or later, if he could forge this new connection with her, she'd tell him. Again, her bravery made him want to weep for her. Dair had no idea what a fighter she really was, a true survivor. If she would let him, he'd show her just how powerful and beautiful she really was in his eyes and heart.

Noah awoke near dawn. The grayness around the window told him it was almost six a.m. He'd quickly dropped off to sleep shortly after Dair had. And he'd slept deep and hard. As he grew more awake, he became aware of several things at once. Dair, sometime during the night, had curved her long, slender body around his in a spoon-like position. She had snuggled tightly up against him, her breath on his shoulder, her brow, it felt like, resting against his nape. One of her arms was tucked around his middle. It was her small, soft breasts pressing against his back that made his whole body leap fully online. Rounded hips against his butt, her legs following the line of his, she continued to sleep. He didn't want to move. Savoring Dair, having her softer curves against his angular body, a powerful feeling flowed through him. How badly Noah wanted to slowly turn over, slide his arm beneath her neck, lay her gently on her back, and watch her awaken.

Even though his mind was swimming in nothing but heat and possibilities, Noah lay very still. Dair was plastered to him like glue. If he moved, he knew it might awaken her. Yet, as the light was slowly dawning, he knew that it was time for him to get up, get dressed, and get breakfast for them. In another hour, the horses had to be fed, watered, and then his training day started. *Damn.*

Every cell in his body pined for Dair in every possible way. His mind churned and his lower body fired up, leaving him unhappy, unable to fully control his growing erection. It wasn't her fault. And he didn't blame either of them. Closing his eyes, he gave himself another five minutes of absorbing Dair in every possible way before he had to ease away from her and get started with his day.

When those five minutes were up, Noah did his level best to slowly leave her tucked position against him. She moaned once, and he froze, hoping she'd go back to sleep. And she did. Hating to leave, knowing he must, he forced himself out of the bed, grabbing the clean clothes he'd laid out last night, and tiptoed out of the bedroom. Closing the door quietly, Noah scowled. For once, he didn't look forward to starting his day at the ranch. As he padded quietly down the hall, he went into her bathroom to shave, dress, and pull on his boots.

In no time, he was making them a breakfast of pancakes that he'd sprinkled with cranberries and pecans. Keying his hearing, he wanted to hear the bedroom door open, alerting him that Dair had awakened and was up and moving around. He'd left a chair near her side of the bed, to make it easier for her to slide off the mattress.

He'd made extra pancakes, wrapping them in foil and placing them on the counter for Dair whenever she did wake. Adding a Post-it note to it, he wrote that he didn't want her doing anything today but resting and giving both her knees a day off.

By the time the grayness lurked along the horizon, Noah was bundled up in his winter gear, cleaning off the snow that had accumulated along the wooden walkway the night before. He quickly spread salt on it to keep it from icing over again, in case Dair wanted to come down to the barns and arena in her chair. The sky above was dark, with lowering clouds, but he saw patches where he could see the sky above them. The blizzard had passed. Now, they might get two or three days of clear, cold weather, but at least the sun would shine.

Harper was already in the main horse barn, throwing in flakes of hay to hungry horses. Garret was giving them each a ration of oats or sweet feed, depending upon the horse. They greeted him, and Noah saw neither wrangler looked like he'd gotten much sleep last night. Noah admitted that the Friday night get-together had been hard on everyone.

"Have you seen Candy and Ebony?" Noah called to Harper.

"Yeah, Garret and I already took care of the brood-mare suite. They're doing fine. Ebony is eating Candy out of house and home." He grinned as he tossed Ghost, the gray quarter horse, a fat flake of timothy hay.

"What do you want me to do?"

"Nothing. Garret and I got this. How's Dair doing?"

"Dunno. She's still sleeping."

Garret came up to him. "That's a good thing," he said.

Noah nodded to the wrangler, who looked more like a tall mountain in his sheepskin coat and baseball cap with a black knit cap pulled down over his ears. "Yeah, it is." He wasn't about to tell them that they'd slept together. That was no one's business, unless Dair wanted others to know. If she did, she'd be the one letting that info out, not him.

"I don't see any lights on in Reese and Shay's house," Harper said. "Usually, they're up by now."

Snorting, Garret rumbled, "Last night emotionally totaled both of them. Especially Shay. Let them sleep. We'll take over anything that needs to be done around the ranch this morning. They deserve some downtime."

Wasn't that the truth, Noah thought. "Okay, you two have this. I'm going to start my training roster. I'll be in the arena if you need me."

"Go ahead," Harper said. "You have eight horses wanting to be out of their stalls," he said, and grinned.

Noah laughed, lifted his gloved hand, and left. Soon he walked past the second barn where the broodmares were kept and entered the arena, getting his gear ready for training. The place was quiet and chilly, but not freezing like it was outside. A lot of insulation had been placed into the walls, keeping the area a fairly constant fifty-five degrees. At night, the temperature lowered, but not to freezing.

Noah kept remembering Dair's conversation with him last night. When the chips were down, she came clean, was dirt honest and looked him in the eye. Despite her nervousness, her angst or anxiety, Dair held herself together to communicate with him. That said so much good about her inner strength and resolve. It did nothing but make him want her in a forever relationship.

Even as he brought out a young three-year-old quarter chestnut named Horace, a gelding with a flaxen mane and tail and reddish-colored body, Noah's heart lingered on Dair and their talk. Despite her anxiety and worry about getting close to him, in the end, she'd trusted him, or she wouldn't have been so close against him this morning. Whatever worries she had, based upon her previous experiences with men, he'd proven to her that he was trustworthy. He felt relieved. Noah wouldn't lie to himself any longer. He was falling in love with Dair, and he knew it. He'd been in love before and recognized the signs. The real question was what Dair wanted. Right now, she couldn't get around on two legs. Noah doubted she had time for any kind of personal relationship. There was no question she trusted him. But was it just a friendship thing with her? Or something deeper and more intimate? He didn't know.

The hours sped by. It was near noontime when Noah was finishing up with a pretty bay Arabian mare who needed to be gently broke, when he spotted Dair wheeling into the arena. His heart leaped with joy as he walked the sweaty mare over to the gate where she sat watching them. Hungrily, he searched her face, finding gold warmth in her eyes, her lips slightly parted. Today, she'd braided her hair into two plaits and tied them off with some red yarn. The red sweater she wore beneath her denim jacket brought out her Native American features. He smiled.

"Hey, how are you feeling?" He halted the mare and opened the gate.

"Much better," Dair said, smiling over at him. "You won't believe this, but I only got up an hour ago."

Noah laughed, in part out of relief. "Yeah, well, when you get hit by a Mack truck, it takes a bit for your body to get proper rest afterward." He led the mare out and shut the gate behind him. Turning, Noah saw that she was dressed in her regular wrangler clothes.

"Nothing for you to do down here today, Dair. Garret's here and he's more or less taking over for you for a while. He's in between construction jobs and wanted to pitch in and help Harper."

"I know. I saw him on the walk when I was wheeling down here. That's really nice of him."

"He's a stand-up guy," Noah agreed. "Follow me, I'm putting her away and I was heading up to the house to get lunch and see if you were still sleeping or not." He kept his tone light and teasing, watching Dair respond positively to it. She looked better than he'd ever seen her, and wondered if sleeping with one another last night had done it.

"Sure," Dair called. She waited for Noah to lead the mare into the main aisle of the box stall area before slowly wheeling after them. Dair moved slowly. She kept a good distance between them. She didn't want to scare the mare, who was cocking one ear in her direction.

Once Noah had put the horse away, he came up to her and crouched down in front of her, his gloved hands resting on the arms of her chair. "Well? Have you looked at your face in the mirror yet?"

She laughed and shook her head. "No, I avoid that if possible."

He smiled. "You shouldn't. You're a beautiful woman, Dair." Noah saw her smile slip a little. Coming out of an abusive home, from what Libby had told them last night, made a child feel ugly, unwanted and abandoned. He silently promised Dair he'd change her mind about herself if she'd let him. "Well? How late did you sleep?"

Groaning, she said, "Until ten thirty. Can you believe it, Noah? I've never slept that late in my whole life."

He sobered. "That's good. You needed it. Did you feel me leave your side this morning?"

"No. What time did you get up?"

"About six. I left you some pancakes in foil on the counter. Did you see them?"

Patting her tummy, she grinned. "Yeah, I ate all four of them. If I keep eating like this, I'll weigh two hundred pounds in no time."

He snorted and slowly rose. "You're underweight, Dair. You need the extra pounds. Want me to wheel you up to our home?" He liked calling it that. It warmed him with a dream he wanted to come true for both of them.

"Sure. Did you see? The sun's out."

"Yeah," he said, turning her around and pushing the chair along the aisle. "I've lived in this area long enough to become a sun hound. Between trainings this morning, I went out just to let that sun land on my hide. Warm me up." He absorbed her laughter.

"It feels so good to feel the sun on me, too. We have so little of it for nine months out of the year, from what Shay said."

"Shay's right. Makes June through September really special for all of us. We want to stay outside in that sun as much as we can every day." He wheeled her quickly up the wooden walkway. The sky was shredded with the last of the front's gray clouds, but the blue sky had deepened in color and the air was warmer. Noah saw Reese coming out of the house. "Have you talked to Reese or Shay yet?"

"No, I got up, heated up those wonderful pancakes, had coffee, and then took a long, hot shower."

"I wonder if they've heard from Sarah yet about Ray?"

"I don't know. Do you ask them or do you wait for them to tell you something?"

"Oh, I'll call over," Noah assured her. "They probably got up late this morning, too. Yesterday was rough on everyone." He saw Dair bob her head. "You look really good this morning."

"I feel a hundred percent better, Noah."

He wheeled her up the walk and into the mudroom. Helping her off with her winter gear, he hung everything on the wall pegs and wheeled her into the kitchen. "Hungry?"

"No," she said, tipping her head back, catching his gaze. "I ate those pancakes. You go ahead and make yourself lunch." She pointed to the counter as he drove her toward the table. "I made fresh coffee for us."

"Woman after my own heart," he murmured, turning her into the table and setting the brake on the chair. "How's your knees this morning?"

"The swelling in my right one is reduced by half and feels a lot better."

"Good. We need to get you in to see Dr. Radke sometime this week."

"Yes." Dair pointed to her left knee. "And it actually feels a little better today, too."

Giving her a teasing, burning look, Noah said, "When you sleep with someone your heart likes? It always makes you feel better."

Chapter Seventeen

Dair sat at the table watching Noah slap two turkey-and-ham sandwiches together for his lunch. As he brought over the plate and sat down opposite her, she said, "I called Sarah at the sheriff's department this morning and told her I'd charge Ray Crawford with assault."

Noah became somber. "How are you feeling about it?"

Shrugging, Dair said, "Okay. Libby made some good points last night at our meeting. I was acting out of my wound pattern, as she refers to it. With my father, the less he saw or heard me, the less likely he was to come after me."

"We all have those avoidance patterns," Noah said between bites. He pushed an open jar of sweet pickles toward her. "Want some?"

She smiled, pulling one out and chewing on it. "I have to go in this afternoon and fill out my statement."

"Can I drive you?"

"I was hoping someone could. I know you're super busy with those horses to train."

"Don't worry about it. I want to be there with you, Dair," he said, holding her gaze.

She nodded, giving him an appreciative look. "Sarah said that it will probably be a year before Ray's case comes before the court."

"Yeah, courts are clogged and backed up. I wish it could be a lot sooner."

"She said that he'll make bail, most likely."

Frowning, Noah said, "I wonder if the judge will prohibit him from coming back here to live?"

"I talked to Shay about that this morning before I called Sarah. I told her I was going to the sheriff's department to fill out a statement against her father. Reese got a lawyer many months ago, and he'd been on the phone with him before I had called over there. Their lawyer is going to go to that bail hearing and Reese will be there, too. He doesn't want Shay to attend. She's too upset about it all."

"Understandable," Noah growled, shaking his head. "She's given her father a lot, and all he does is bite the hand that feeds him."

"He's single-minded, that's for sure."

"I wonder if Reese wants company."

"I don't know. You might ask him."

"Yeah, I think I will. Do you want to be at that bail hearing?"

"No, not unless I have to be, Noah. I'm still really upset about it."

"I'm sure you are. Okay, after I eat, I'll mosey over to their home and talk to Reese in private about it. I know Shay is going through a lot right now."

"It's awful for her. I might feel bad about Ray attacking me, but she's lived with this abusive alcoholic her entire life. I don't think I could take it much longer, either." Her lips thinned. "I hope the judge stops him from ever coming back to the Bar C."

"Well, we'll see shortly if the lawyer can get a restraining order against him that will stick because the first one didn't," Noah promised her.

Darkness fell quickly in the winter at the Bar C. Dair had made supper earlier and they sat at the table. She wasn't real hungry because of the stress of the day. Unexpectedly, the judge had ordered Ray Crawford to come before him in the late afternoon. Her statement had already been sent over to the court, and she wondered if it was responsible for the rancher's swift appearance before the judge. She was sure they would never know.

"How are you doing?" Noah asked. He cut into the chicken breast that had been served with a tasty white sauce.

"Just . . . hanging in there, I guess."

"You need to eat."

"I know." She gave him a wry look. Noah had piled on the fluffy brown rice, and given her the biggest chicken breast in the baking dish. He wasn't subtle.

"I'm relieved the judge agreed to the restraining order, and Ray's not allowed to step back onto Bar C property. I know he has that condo in Wind River. Will he stay there?"

"He has money," Noah told her.

"Does he have a car to get around in?"

"Reese is willing to loan him one of the ranch trucks, which I think is pretty nice of him to do. I don't think I'd do it."

She studied Noah's darkening features. "Why wouldn't you?"

"Because the bastard hurt you."

Nodding, Dair felt her heart opening to him. "Last night?" Dair saw his eyes soften.

"Yes?"

"It's the best I've slept since getting wounded, Noah." She hesitated, and then forced herself to say, "And I know it was because you were beside me."

"I've never slept better than last night, either," he admitted quietly, holding her turbulent gaze. "I think there's something good and strong between us, Dair. What do you think?"

She cut into the chicken, frowning. "I know you're right." She set the flatware down, holding his intense gaze. "I keep going back to what Libby said about family patterns of abuse. I see myself in all of them. I never trusted men, because of my father. In my child's eyes, I guess, I overlaid my fear of him onto all other men that walked through my life, no matter how young or old I was."

"That wouldn't be unusual," Noah said. "My father is the opposite of that. I would imagine if he'd been your dad, you'd have trusted other males. You don't trust men, but you have good reason not to, Dair."

"I'm not sure I want to live in that pattern anymore, Noah. You've shown me time and again that you're trustworthy. Last night I was so scared you'd try and take advantage of me. But you didn't."

"I would never do that to you, Dair."

"My heart"—she pressed her fingers to her chest—"knows that. My head was screaming at me that it was a stupid idea to even ask you to hold me or be near me in the same bed."

"It's a torturous mental pattern for anyone," he agreed. "And it's a negative place to live. Look at Harper, Garret, and Reese. You trust them, don't you?"

"Yes, I do. But all of you are military vets, and I'm one of you. I didn't fear the military guys, although I was watchful of them. When I got into my team of guys, we were like brothers and a sister. And it's the same here with all of you guys."

"I think you're maturing and slowly breaking the pattern that imprisoned you, Dair. Last night I knew it was a huge step for you."

"Wasn't it for you?" She tilted her head, holding his amused stare.

"No, not really." Noah finished eating and pushed his plate aside. "I've always liked you, Dair, from the moment I met you. That hasn't changed. It's just gotten deeper, wider, and better. When you asked to sleep with me, I was fine with it. Happy, as a matter of fact. But I could see by the look in your eyes that you had a lot of fear to work through."

"You're really good at reading me."

"Because I like you a lot, Dair, I am sensitive to what you're thinking and how you're feeling."

She lost her appetite and put her half-eaten plate of food aside. "I'm not used to such honest talks with a guy, but you deserve my honesty, Noah."

"Okay," he said, "what would you like to talk about?"

She sighed and sat back in the chair, giving him a tender look. "You've always been there for me. You never raise your voice, you don't yell at me, and you don't make me feel bad. When I'm with you, I feel uplifted, happy and free. I like being around you. I love being in this house and living with you." Dair looked around the warm, quiet kitchen. "For me? Everything is perfect. I've never felt this relaxed or unworried. I know part of it is Reese and Shay's commitment to all of us wranglers, giving us a second chance, but it's more than that." She choked up, her voice suddenly emotional. "You are giving me a chance to reclaim my soul, Noah. I honestly don't think you care if I have two good legs or not." She saw his eyes grow lighter with amusement, felt that sense of protection invisibly wrapping around her, and she knew it was coming from him. "You make me feel safe for the first time in my life . . ."

Noah sat there, thinking about her emotional statement, watching her tear up and then push them back down deep inside herself. "What else?" he asked softly.

Pushing hair away from her temple, she gave him a fearful look. "I'm afraid to say it. Afraid it won't work."

"What wouldn't work, Dair?"

"You and me. I-I know you want me in your life on a more personal basis. I've been fighting it because of my past." She looked up and sighed raggedly, lowering her chin, holding his calm gray gaze. "It's easy for you, but it's not for me. I keep fighting the past that keeps trying to destroy my present. My heart wants you. My head screams the opposite." She swallowed hard, whispering brokenly, "I'm so tired of this war inside me, Noah . . ."

He nodded and slowly rose from the table and walked around to where she sat. "Come sit with me in the living room?"

Looking up at him, Dair felt hot tears pushing into her eyes. "Yes . . . okay . . ." She wheeled herself into the living room. He walked at her side and motioned to the couch.

"If it's okay with you, I'd like to have you sit beside me on the couch."

Dair needed those words so badly. Emotions sheered through her, a blaze of need and joy for Noah. She parked her chair and, with his help, climbed out of it. Noah eased her down on the couch and then he sat in the corner of it, offering to place his arm around her shoulders. He didn't force her into anything, allowing her to sit and make her own decision. Driven by her need of Noah, she scooted next to him, feeling his arm curve around her shoulders, bringing her gently against him.

"Just rest," he murmured, kissing her hair as she nestled her brow against his jaw.

Those two words winnowed through her like a healing breeze, quieting her wary mind and allowing her to hone in on her thudding heart and the feelings she had for Noah. She closed her eyes, surrendering to him. Her mind stopped yammering at her. She eased her arm across his middle, needing what he was silently feeding her. Dair didn't know how long she remained in that position against Noah, but nothing had ever felt so right to her.

Stirring awhile later, she lifted her head, resting her cheek on his shoulder, gazing up at him. "When I'm with you like this, my head stops yapping at me. And I feel nothing but happiness, Noah." She saw his mouth curve faintly, his gray eyes dark and intense upon her.

"It's because we share something good between us, Dair. Don't you think? You affect me the same way. I'm so damned happy when you're in my arms like this, I can't even put it into words. But I can show you." He leaned down, brushing her lips.

A low sound of pleasure came from Dair as she eagerly met his mouth, wanting another kiss with him. This time, Noah wasn't hesitant or careful about kissing her. As his mouth slid surely across hers, she felt his maleness, felt him controlling himself for her sake, but luxuriating in their joyful union with one another. His other arm came around her waist, his hand resting on her hip, keeping her close but not putting pressure on either of her knees. Never had a man been so sensitive to her and her condition. It brought up a deluge of old, buried feelings, of times when she hid in her closet from her father as he stalked in a rage around their home. She would cry, her fists stuffed into her mouth so she wouldn't make a sound. If she was heard, he'd come after her.

Hot tears squeezed out of her closed eyes, making trails down her face. Noah lifted his mouth from her lips, kissing each of her eyelids, kissing away the trail of tears that fell despite her trying to stop them. He just naturally opened up her vulnerability, made her want to weep for days and allow all that toxic fear of dying she'd had as a child to finally be released. He grazed her damp cheek with his thumb, lips resting against her brow.

"Go ahead and cry, Dair," he said gruffly against her temple and ear. "It's okay. I'll just hold you . . ."

Dair's whole body shook inwardly, as if his low, coaxing words were a key to unlock that door where so many old tears had been imprisoned. Her arm tightened around his waist and she pressed her face against the column of his neck, a sob tearing out of her. Dair lost track of time, pulled into the pain as her tears rushed down her face. There was no way to stop them and she gave up trying. Noah simply held her, moved his hand slowly up and down her upper arm, whispering soothing words to her.

Finally, the sobs lessened. Dair's heart ached. Her throat hurt from all those awful, animal-like sounds that had been torn out of her. Noah held her. Continued to whisper words of comfort to her as she lifted her hand, fingers trembling as she tried to dry the last of the tears on her face. Her eyes felt swollen and hot as she eased from his arms and sat up.

Noah leaned to the right, pulling some tissues from a box on the lamp stand next to the couch. He pressed them into her hand.

It meant so much to Dair when he slid his arm around her waist, lightly holding her, letting her know she wasn't alone with all that pain that had just exploded out of her so unexpectedly. He gave her more tissues so she could blow her nose several times. Placing them on the coffee table, she whispered, "I-I'll be okay . . . Thanks. . . ." When she forced herself to look up into Noah's face, her heart tumbled open. Tenderness burned in his eyes, and the tension that was normally in his face, was gone.

"Feel better?" he asked, giving her a faint smile, lifting his hand, removing several dark strands of hair from her cheek where they stuck to the shed tears.

"I-I don't know. Not yet . . . yes . . . maybe . . . lighter feeling . . ."

"You can always come into my arms and cry, anytime you want, Dair. I like holding you. I want to be there for you."

His words were a balm to the torn-up feelings still roiling through her. "So much is happening, Noah." She pressed her hands to her face.

"I understand. You lost your leg, then you were thrown out in the world to make it on your own." He moved his hand down her long back. "Then? You came here and a mean stud about took you apart."

"And then Ray Crawford had the same thing in mind," she rattled, pulling her hands away from her face, meeting and holding Noah's gaze. He gave her such stability.

"It isn't like you haven't gone through a hellish

blender of late," Noah teased quietly, splaying his hand in the center of her back.

Giving a jerky nod, Dair whispered, "And through it all? You were here for me, Noah. You never withdrew, you never broke my trust. You were always the quiet shadow in the background until I needed you." She sniffed, searching his tender expression.

"I always want to be there for you, Dair, if you'll let me."

His hand felt soothing to her fractious state, sliding lightly up and down her back. "Y-yes, I'd like that." It took all of her courage to add, "And I want to keep sleeping with you at night in your bed. I want to kiss you . . . love you . . ."

Noah's hand stilled on her shoulder, searching her watery eyes. "Are you sure, Dair? Because that would be a dream come true for me, but I want it to be your dream, too."

Sniffing more, she sat up, moving so she faced him, her right knee resting along his hard, long thigh. "You give me courage, Noah. Whether you know it or not, you do. Libby's right: I have to consciously break the patterns from my past. Once I recognize them, I can then replace them with more positive, healthy ones." She reached out, her fingertips gliding down his stubbled jaw. "More than anything, I've wanted you with me. I've had so many dreams about us sleeping together, loving one another, but I was afraid to admit it to you."

"Because so much else was happening in your life," he said, nodding.

"Yes. On top of everything else, my heart wanted you and only you. I'm afraid to call it anything yet, Noah. I sometimes don't think I know what love is. And I don't know . . ."

"Don't go there yet," he said quietly, taking her hand, squeezing it. "We have all kinds of time to figure this out, Dair. And with everything going on around us with Crawford? There's going to be a lot of upset to come."

"Poor Shay," Dair said, "I feel so sorry for her. She's hurting so much from all of this."

"Yes, but you know what? She has Reese, and he loves her. When you have the love of another person and you're going through crap like this? It helps so damn much."

Giving him a warm look, she offered, "That's what you've been doing for me ever since I got here."

"Then, let's let what we have, grow and blossom over time. I'm in no hurry, Dair. Are you?"

Her mouth quirked. "No, not in any hurry. I've never asked to live with a man, share his bed before. It's all so new to me. Scary, sometimes, but my heart feels driven to be near you, be with you whenever I can. You have no idea how often you said just the right words to me, or touched me, and it made whatever I was going through, bearable. You fed me hope, Noah. You always have." She saw his face crumple with so many emotions, saw the yearning in his eyes for her alone. It made her feel a rush of happiness she'd never experienced before.

"Then," he said, clearing his throat, holding her hand, "let's just keep doing what we're doing. I'll always be there for you, Dair. That's a given. I feel what you need to do is be assured in your own heart and mind that I'll be supportive."

"Yes . . . that's pretty much it, Noah."

"I want to take a chance on you, Dair. I've been in love before and years ago I lost my wife because of my PTSD. I learned a lot from that painful time. I do know what love is. I've matured since then, know a lot more about myself, my symptoms, and I've grown because of it. Libby, since I came to the Bar C, has helped me make some incredible breakthroughs about myself and my life. She's helped me be a better man . . . a better person."

"I think we all need someone in our lives to help us along," Dair agreed, absorbing the dry, rough warmth of his fingers around her hand. "You're that for me."

"Well," he said wryly, "it's always more than one person who digs us out of the ditch we've fallen into. But part of love is caring for the other person and being sensitive toward them and their needs."

"I think love means a lot more than just sex."

He nodded. "It's a part of it. A great part, but window dressing compared to the deeper human emotions, and how love in different ways can help us through those dark times."

In his eyes, she saw his grief over the loss of his wife. And she ached for Noah. "Maybe you were just too young when you fell in love with her?"

"Absolutely, although at the time, I didn't give it a second thought," Noah admitted. "I fell in love with her, married her, and then my long deployments, plus my PTSD, tore us apart."

"I'm really sorry, Noah. She must be a wonderful woman."

"She is. Chandra is happily remarried, has a little daughter, and her life is good. And I'm glad for her. We remained friends throughout the divorce. We just couldn't make it work at that age or stage in our lives."

Dair could see the regret, but also the maturity in his eyes and voice. Noah had learned from his divorce. And he knew what love was, and she did not. "Are you okay with us sleeping together?" she ventured unsurely.

"Yes, but you know what, Dair? If there's a time or place when you need to sleep alone, then do it. We're still finding our way forward with one another, and it's early in our relationship. We have a lot of trials and struggles before us, especially with Crawford. No one is sure what he'll do next. His court case is a year away. Will he respect the restraining order? He's impulsive and he never does what anyone expects."

"Would you not want to sleep with me at times?" She saw instant amusement jump to Noah's gaze.

"Never. But that's me. You have to listen to what your needs are, Dair. And if there are times when you want to be alone, we'll talk about it and let it be what it is."

Shaking her head, she muttered, "I don't think I'll ever want to sleep apart from you, Noah." She saw hope burn in his eyes, and his hand became more firm around hers.

"Well," he murmured, smiling a little, "a relationship is built on trusting one another, one step at a time. Talking. Gutting through the good and bad times together. Having you beside me, Dair? That's a dream come true to me. It always will be . . ."

When Noah padded into his bedroom later that night, he saw Dair in her flannel lavender granny gown, sitting against the headboard, a serious look on her face. Turning off the overhead ceiling lamp, the nightlight gave him just enough to see where he was going. He'd deliberately worn only his pajama bottoms because he wanted to see how Dair reacted to him. It was one thing to talk about sleeping together, but now it was real. He didn't want her to feel pressured or backed into a corner, thinking she had to have sex with him. His erection was there, but his own emotional quandary and worry over coming together, was keeping things tamped down for now.

"You still feeling okay about this?" he asked, moving to the bed, sitting opposite her, legs crossed, hands on his knees.

"Yes," she said. "Worried. Anxious. But I want to not only sleep with you, Noah, I want to be able to reach out and kiss or touch you if I feel like it, too."

Nodding, he saw her smooth the soft flannel so it lay below her knees. "Both your knees are injured," he said.

She gave him a wry look. "I know. I was thinking about that. Thinking how best to do this."

"It hurts more if you bend them?" He reached out, smoothing his hand across the arch of her bare foot. Massaging it gently, he saw her eyes grow dark with yearning.

"Yes. I can flex them about halfway, but I couldn't kneel at all."

"Well, that takes out a few positions," he said, giving her a grin. Above all, Noah wanted Dair to be looking forward to him loving her, not dreading it. And if her sparkling eyes were any indicator, she wanted this as much as he did.

"Sure does. Unless you want to hang me from the ceiling in some kind of harness," she managed, chuckling.

"No, I'm afraid I'm not into that kind of lovemaking. Are you?" He saw her cheeks grow a dull pink.

"No. I guess I'm terribly traditional, Noah."

He was also guessing she hadn't had that many sexual partners, either, from the way she reacted to his question. "That's okay. I'm thinking the good ole missionary position would be best for you and your knees right now. Maybe after you get healed up, we can explore." There was relief in her expression. More and more, Noah realized that because of her childhood, Dair hid most of her real reactions and feelings. Wanting to draw her out, he asked, "What do you think? What would be most comfortable for you?"

"I was thinking the same position."

"Okay, glad we got that out of the way." He smiled into her eyes. Her lips lifted and he felt heat flow through him. He was going to worship her, from her head to her toes. Noah didn't reveal that to Dair, but he knew she was nervous and so was he. "If I do anything you don't want, tell me."

"Sure."

"And if you're in pain because of your knees, you'll tell me. Right?"

"Oh, I don't think I'll have to say much. I'll probably freeze up like I always do when I'm in pain. You'll know right away."

"I have condoms," he said, motioning to the bed stand.

"I don't like them," she said, wrinkling her nose. "I'm on the pill, Noah. And I'm clean."

"I'm clean, too," he said. He smiled to himself as Dair scooted down next to him.

"Unbraid my hair for me? I love to have my scalp massaged."

"Sounds like a good plan," he murmured. Getting up on the bed, Noah settled behind her. Leaning near her ear, he rasped, "Relax. I'm going to pull you up between my legs and then I'll lean against the headboard." He was humbled when she completely relaxed against the front of him after he leaned back on the headboard. She settled against him and between his opened legs. Noah untied the red yarn around her braids, slowly easing the three strands apart as they fell between his fingers. "You have such strong, silky hair," he told her, kissing some of the strands.

"And what you're doing feels so good . . ." She sighed, closing her eyes.

Noah smiled as he released all her hair and then combed his fingers slowly through the shining, black cloud. Her hair smelled of timothy hay because she had not washed it yet tonight. Taming the silky hair around her neck and shoulders, he continued to place small, light kisses across the strands. "You are so beautiful," he rasped, leaning down, catching the hem of her gown and slowly easing it up across her knees.

Dair sat up, lifting her arms so that Noah could ease the gown over her head. He allowed the material to drop beside the bed. The grayish light outlined her small, proud breasts, the nipples hard, asking to be touched. Controlling his hunger for her, he invited Dair to come lie against him. He wanted to be slow, thorough, and build their passion based upon her needs. This was an exquisite exploration he'd been dreaming about since meeting her. Her body was slender but strong, and he silently lamented the loss of her lower limb because she had such long, shapely legs. Noah slid his hands slowly from her upper arms, feeling the velvet warmth of her flesh, to her lower arms.

"I want," he told her as he brought her palm to his lips, "to love you, Dair. You deserve to be worshipped . . ." He moved his tongue across her palm, hearing her breath hitch, her fingers curving in reaction to his gesture and then his kiss. He could feel her melting little by little as he touched her here and there. Nothing intimate, just allowing her time to get used to him, to his fingers trailing across her responsive body.

He watched as her chest rose and fell a little more

quickly, her breath shallowing out as he allowed her to reclaim her hand. Moving his fingers through her hair, Noah exposed her slender neck. There was such a sense of utter deliciousness to loving this woman he wanted desperately for his own. As he nibbled on the lobe of her ear, hearing Dair's swift intake of breath, her nipples hardening to points, he felt nothing but love for her. Noah wouldn't lie to himself. He'd been falling in love with this brave, beautiful woman since he first laid eyes on her.

Licking that sensitized flesh behind her ear, raining light kisses down the length of her throat, sliding his fingers lightly across her delicate collarbones, made her moan with need. He liked that low, husky sound slipping from between her lips. If Noah had had any doubts about how well they fit one another, he didn't now. His confidence grew and he gently eased Dair down to the mattress, helping her to lie on her back and get comfortable. That sleek, dark hair only emphasized her high cheekbones and those wide, lust-filled eyes. He liked that she was aroused, relaxed, and reaching out for him.

Allowing Dair to orchestrate what she wanted from him, Noah was fine with her taking the driver's seat tonight. There would be times in the future when they would share or he would initiate, instead. Right now, he wanted this first time to be wonderful for Dair, wanted her looking forward to the next time they loved one another. As he knelt between her legs, easing them apart, hands beneath her knees to support the movement, he felt her utterly surrender to him. It made him feel proud and strong as she relinquished any anxiety left in her, welcoming him into her arms.

As he leaned over her, seeking her mouth, kissing

her hungrily, she matched the pressure and consumed him with her body, arching up against his, brushing against his erection. Noah groaned, the white-hot heat surging through him as he claimed her, their mouths clashing against one another. He became lost in her woman's fragrance, the scent of her hair, the strands tickling his jaw as he deepened that long, wet kiss between them. As he pressed himself against her damp entrance, she lifted her hips, receiving him, wanting him as much as he wanted her. Noah felt how small and tight she was, despite her lush fluids welcoming him. Dair hadn't had sex in a long time, and he brutally controlled himself for her sake. This was about giving her pleasure first.

As he left her mouth, her breath was as ragged as his was. He framed her face, holding her in place, gently moving in and out of her, accustoming her body to his. Her heat felt so good wrapping around him, squeezing him, making him grit his teeth, his nostrils flaring as he controlled his hip movements with hers.

He gazed down into her lustrous, dark eyes, saw the arousal there, the same burning need shared between them. She was wild, responsive, and he nearly forgot about her injured knees, her body was so supple, teasing and pulling him ever deeper into her. His mind was dissolving, his need making him grunt as she lifted her hips, bringing him fully into her. Noah lost his direction, the fire of her body, the sweet, hot fluids surrounding him, and instinctively, he leaned down, tugging one of those hard nipples into his mouth. Dair cried out, but it was raw pleasure he felt as her body bucked wildly beneath his. She was no tame filly, that was for sure, and it encouraged him to release some of his control, sliding his hand beneath her hips, lifting her so he could plunge fully into her.

The rocking motion made her sob his name, her nails digging deep into his damp, bunched shoulders as he held and moved with her. Dair's little cries, caught in her exposed throat, urged him on, loosened his control until Noah felt them melting. Euphoria and hunger merged as he felt them becoming one. As her body tightened around him, he heard her cry out, felt those hot fluids suddenly embracing him, knowing she had orgasmed. Above all, despite what he wanted, Noah held her hips, nudging himself as deep as he could go into her sweet, tight body, giving her all the pleasure she could want.

And then, Dair turned the tables on him after she'd rested a moment from the orgasm that had consumed her like wildfire. She gripped his narrow hips, thrusting her hips against him, forcing him to instantly release his control. The woman was strong! Noah had no time to think. His body reacted and in seconds, a bolt of heat tore down his spine, erupting through his entire body, spilling himself deeply into her. His eyes shuttered closed, and his lips pulled away from his teeth. He was frozen above her, those hips of hers cajoling every last vestige out of him, until he collapsed upon her damp body.

Chapter Eighteen

May 24

The late May sun warmed Dair as she rode one of her training horses, Lulu, a brightly colored Appaloosa mare with a white rump blanket with huge black splotches across it. Next to her was Noah on Ghost, the gray quarter horse gelding. They were moving from one fence post to another, checking the five-strand barbed wire between them. She was glad to have her fleece sheepskin vest over her pink flannel shirt, leather gloves on to keep her fingers warm. Today she was taking out some of her training horses to acquaint them with ranch work, riding into different areas, from lush grass to pine-tree groves and wide puddles of water here and there.

Closing her eyes, she held her face up to the rising eastern sunlight pouring across the morning landscape of the wide Wind River Valley. The soft, lulling rhythm of the horse between her legs, having Noah's boot occasionally touching her own as they rode side by side, made her heart sing.

"Such a sun girl," Noah teased, grinning and catching her gaze as she tipped her head in his direction, opening her eyes.

"Hey, first day in almost a month we've seen real sun," she grumped, feeling her body go hot all over again. She reached out, touching his gloved hand for a moment, drowning in the warmth of his clear gray gaze.

"Glad you decided to come along and keep me company," he said, looking around. The land was a slight swell covered with blades of green grass that were poking up everywhere. There had been a late May blizzard a week ago, but the days were warming to the fifties, and most of the snow had melted.

"I can help you," Dair said pointedly.

"That's true. That new limb is doing wonders for your mobility," Noah agreed.

Patting her left leg, Dair said, "I'm silently thanking that stud for beating up my other one. This one is light-years better. I could never have afforded it if Dr. Radke hadn't put me into that company's ongoing testing program." And because of the new, superior prosthesis, when she walked, the sole of the foot actually curved to the condition of whatever terrain she was walking upon. Before, her foot was flat and there was no suppleness in it, making it harder for her to keep her balance. Dair was always compensating, and it put a constant strain on her back and hips. If not for Noah giving her wonderful back, hip, and thigh massages, Dair knew she'd have been seeing their local chiropractor for weekly adjustments before she got this revolutionary new prosthesis.

"Even a bad thing turned out to be a good thing," Noah agreed.

"I almost feel normal now," she confided, running her gloved hand down her left thigh. "This prosthesis is so incredible. My walking has improved. I'm not getting backaches or having my hips always go out of whack like they did before."

"In the long run, it's saved you money by not having to go to a chiropractor."

"I like your massages, though." Her eyes sparkled as she watched that delicious mouth of his curve slightly, pride in his glance.

"I like touching you anytime I can get my hands on you."

Laughing, Dair felt an incredible lightness bubbling within her. It had started the first night Noah had made love with her. And although they didn't love each other every night, because they woke up tired the next morning, she looked forward to the weekends when the pace was different. It wasn't less hectic, but they could love one another more than once.

Breakfast was always something she looked forward to with him. The weekends were theirs, and she was so glad that Shay and Reese made that rule for all of them. Although, now it was Saturday, and here they were, out riding fence and repairing it when necessary; but they were doing it together. She knew Kira and Garret had ridden off in a southerly direction, doing fence repair as well. They had to get the fences in good shape or cattlemen would not lease their rich pastures. Cattle had an affinity for pushing on and destroying fences, and it took year-round attention and constant repair to keep them strong.

She reached down, patting Lulu's short, thick bay neck. The mare's ears flicked back and forth, indicating she liked being stroked. "How many leases has Reese gotten so far?"

"Four," Noah said. "We've got four pastures where we've repaired the fence all around. He said that's going to help the ranch's bottom line. Before Crawford took the ranch down, there were a lot more leases. That was good money the Bar C made from June through September. Four is better than none."

"There's a long ways to go." She pointed ahead. "Does that post look like it's leaning, Noah?"

"Yeah," he grumbled. "Gonna have to be replaced."

As they rode up to it, they pulled the horses to a halt. Noah got out his iPhone and went to his app where he could put down the GPS location, the type of post it was, and whether or not it would have to be completely replaced. While he did that, Dair allowed the reins to drop to Lulu's neck and the horse quickly started eating the nutritious green grass. The sun felt so good. There were blue jays nearby, as well as a number of robins out in the pasture looking for worms. The Salt River Range to the east of her was still fully clothed in white snow. Only the lower slopes showed their green mantle of pine trees. It was a beautiful, quiet morning.

"There," Noah said, tucking the device into his vest pocket. "Another one cataloged."

"I just love what we do," she whispered, giving him a soft look. "Ranch work suits us completely." Both of them were outdoors people and preferred being in fresh air instead of inside. She saw him give her a lustful look and boyish grin.

"Didn't you get your fill last night?" She laughed, gathering up the reins on Lulu. Her whole body flared to life beneath that hot look he gave her.

"I'll never get enough of you," Noah told her lightly, urging Ghost forward.

They rode in companionable silence for a while and then Noah asked, "Are you happy living with me?"

She snorted. "Of course I am. Where did that question come from, Mabry?"

He grinned a little, resting his left hand on his thigh. "Just thinking, is all."

Raising a brow, she watched his profile and his mouth curving a little more. "Okay," she said, "what's going on? You're hedging, Noah." Living with him the last several months, their intimacy growing stronger with every passing day, Dair knew him much better. But then, Noah never tried to hide anything from her, either, which she appreciated. She was the one who hid things, and he was always digging them out of her, in a nice way. He was teaching her to be as forthcoming with him as he was with her. And she knew something was going on because she'd never seen him tease her like this before.

"Can't fool you, can I?" He chuckled.

"No. Are we going to drive over to your parents' home for a visit? Sunday dinner or something?" She truly enjoyed Noah's mom and dad. He had taken her home to meet them in early April. Dair had been nervous, but they'd immediately put her at ease. She was fairly sure that Noah had told them she was an amputee, because they didn't stare at her left leg hidden within the trousers she'd worn for the occasion. In fact, nothing was said, which was fine by her. She really hated being treated as an amputee.

"No, but if you want to, we can go maybe next weekend," he murmured. "I just thought later, near lunchtime, we'd ride down there." He pointed to a large circle of pines that stood a couple miles from where they rode. "Would you like to spread a blanket, sit and eat our peanut butter sandwiches?"

"Sure." The grove of pines grew next to a small stream that meandered throughout the many Bar C pastures. It was a natural watering trough for the leased cattle. She saw a glint in Noah's eyes, still sensing something was up. It was obvious he had a secret. There was an expression in his eyes she couldn't quite decipher.

Dair had taken her vest off, laying it aside on the bright turquoise wool blanket that Noah had spread out on the pine needles for them earlier. They sat near the grove of pines, enjoying the rays of the sun while their horses munched contentedly on nearby grass. They had taken off the horses' bridles, hanging them over the saddle horns, leaving their nylon halters in place. Both wore a pair of sheepskin-lined hobbles on their lower front legs. It allowed the horses to graze, but not run away. Dair had been getting Lulu used to the hobbles and she seemed to be fine, inching along as she grazed, with Ghost keeping her company nearby.

Noah had taken off his Stetson and leather gloves, setting them aside and stretching out near her, propped up on one elbow. They'd eaten their sandwiches, had some delicious brownies that Kira had made for everyone a few days earlier, and drank hot coffee from their thermos.

"Lie opposite me?" he asked, tugging at her hand, getting her attention. Today, Dair wore long, thick braids. He liked her shining black hair loose, but for ranch work, this was a wiser choice. He saw a smile lurk at the corners of her mouth as she lay down parallel to him, also propped up on an elbow, facing him. Reaching over, she caressed his recently shaven face.

"Okay, fess up, Mabry. I can see you've got something up your sleeve. What is it?"

"Ever the curious cougar that you are," he teased, leaning forward, sliding his hand behind her nape, drawing Dair against his mouth. She was warm, open, and he inhaled her scent, part sweet woman and part pine scent that surrounded them. As he drew away, he drowned in her gold-brown eyes that were filled with what he was sure was love for him. Oh, they'd never broached the topic yet. Noah had deliberately kept their relationship open-ended, with no demands. Dair had blossomed in those months after they'd agreed to love one another on that special night. He saw the laughter in her eyes as they parted.

"I like being called your cougar," she said throatily.

"Well, you are one, for sure," Noah agreed. He captured her hand beneath his, wrapping his fingers around hers. "I want to talk with you about something . . . about us."

"Sure."

"I was thinking," he began slowly, holding her gaze, "that maybe we should take our relationship to the next level, if it feels right to you."

Tilting her head, Dair asked, "Are there steps to this?"

He chuckled. "Well, my parents, who aren't from our generation, would tell you that there are very clear steps to take."

Frowning, she said, "Steps to what?"

"In my parents' world? They would never have lived together. They would have courted one another over time. And eventually, when they fell in love, Dad would ask Mom to become engaged to him. In our world? We live together, sometimes for years, and never get engaged."

"Or married," Dair agreed, nodding.

"I was wondering how you felt about such things? Are you happy with what we have?" He held her warming gaze, seeing her become less playful and more serious.

"I've never been happier, Noah. You know that." She curved her fingers more into his. "Is something wrong? Are you not happy?"

Hearing the worry in her tone, he said, "I've never been happier, either. I like what we have."

"There's a 'but' to this, Noah. What is it?" she pressed.

He laughed a little bashfully. "I wanted to tell you something when we weren't in the throes of our mutual passion." He saw her smile, her eyes alight with mischief. His heart opened wide, absorbing her playful smile. He lifted her hand and brought it to his lips, kissing the back of her flesh. "I'm in love with you, Dair." There. It was out. *Finally.* Noah had been holding on to those words for so long, fearful that it wasn't time yet. And maybe it wasn't the right time now, either, but if he didn't share it with Dair, it was going to kill him.

He watched her carefully for any hint of displeasure. Her lips softened and he saw a tenderness come to her expression. Girding himself, he knew this conversation wasn't easy for either of them, but it was one they needed to have.

"What we share? Is that love, Noah?"

"It is from where I stand. I know you didn't come out of a household where there was real love, so you couldn't have known what it was. And I can't imagine how that has impacted you in relationships after you left home."

Shaking her head, she whispered, "It's confused me.

But in April? When we went over to spend the weekend with your parents?"

"Yes?"

"I got to see two people who really do love one another." She slowly sat up, but kept her left limb straightened out. "I was mentally comparing my parents to yours, and how different they acted and reacted with one another."

"We have a good relationship, like my parents do, Dair."

"I know that." She pressed her hand against her heart. "I've been wanting to share with you how much it meant to me to be around your family. I love your mom's laughter and I love your dad's teasing her." She gave him a warm look. "Just like you tease me."

"The apple never falls far from the tree," Noah agreed. "I like to hear you laugh, too, Dair. You're always so serious, and I know why, but getting to see you smile, absorb your laughter, for me is a gift I couldn't buy."

She wove an unseen pattern in the soft wool blanket with her fingertip. "You're right about me not knowing what love really is, Noah. The guys I drew to me after I left home were not like my father, but they weren't very sensitive toward me. All they wanted was sex. They didn't want a relationship like I wanted. I made that mistake twice before I learned. The guys I attracted in the military were somewhat better, but nothing like what you and I share right now." She tilted her head, holding his narrowed gray eyes. "Watching Reese and Shay, Garret and Kira, and now your mom and dad? I realized what I hold in my heart for you is love. I honestly didn't know what love meant, Noah. But I do now." Dair reached out, caressing his jaw, watching that longing leap to his eyes as he held hers. "I do love you, too. I was just afraid to talk to you about it because I wasn't sure. I didn't want to upset what we had by bumbling in with what I thought was love. Do you understand?"

He caught her hand, kissing her fingers. "Yeah, that's totally understandable. But I see it in your eyes, in the way you respond to me when we love one another. The signs were there, and that's why I wanted to talk with you about it. I wanted to make sure we were on the same page together."

She sighed. "Thanks for bringing it up. It's so funny, Noah. I've been in combat and life-and-death situations, and never flinched or pulled back from a mission. But for the last month? I've been feeling this warm, wonderful feeling in my heart, and I so badly wanted to share it with you, but I was afraid."

"What were you afraid of?"

"That . . . I don't know . . . maybe you weren't feeling the same thing that I was. That I could screw things up and cause us to break up if I mentioned it?" She saw his eyes grow somber, and he squeezed her hand, as if to reassure her.

"That would never happen, Dair. I'm not about to get rid of you. I want you to stay with me, be an important part of my life, share my laughter and my sad moments."

"I feel the same," she admitted, her voice low and rife with feelings. "I should have brought it up."

Shaking his head, Noah rasped, "Not this time, but in the future? Do bring up to me how you're feeling, Dair. That's what a healthy relationship is all about: talking, sharing, and sorting things out. I often saw my parents sit down and hash things out between them. They never got angry, but they talked. Each side had their issues, and I learned early on that compromise was important for both of them. Sometimes my dad gave in to my mom's needs or concerns. And sometimes, my mom gave in to my dad's. It wasn't about being a winner or loser. They weren't keeping score, either. It was about them trying to navigate through life as a team."

"I'm seeing that with us," she murmured, leaning over, kissing him, and drinking in his strong mouth grazing her own. Dair could feel him controlling himself for her sake. As she parted from his mouth, she drowned in the turbulent gray of his eyes, seeing love in them for her alone. It made her feel incredibly confident and strong. All her feelings were genuine. Even better, Noah shared them with her. "I'm so glad you brought this up."

"From now on," he said, cupping her jaw, kissing her lips lightly, "you have a place at our table, Dair. You can bring up any and everything that's bothering you, that's making you happy, or anything else. I want to always know what you're thinking and feeling."

"Okay," she said, easing away from him. "It's just so different than how I grew up."

"I understand. It's that toxic pattern Libby was telling us about at that Friday night meeting."

"She's so good at reducing stuff like this to something simple that I can understand and grasp. That's what triggered me to seriously look at my feelings for you and how different they were from my parents' way of treating one another."

"We'll have struggles and challenges, Dair, but we can tackle them together as a team. That gives us more strength. and we can lean on one another during times like that. We don't have to fight life alone anymore. And having someone who has your back? It gives us strength and purpose."

Dair let his low, deep words flow through her. "Well, the only thing bad in our life is Ray Crawford."

Releasing her hand, Noah sat up and then helped her up. "He's our collective wound, as Libby calls it."

Snorting softly, Dair watched him rise to his feet. He held out his hand to her and she took it, slowly and carefully getting to her feet. Only when she was steady did he release her hand. It didn't bother Dair that he was always circumspect about her prosthesis. He never made her feel like an amputee; rather, it was his sensitivity toward her particular situation that overlaid how he worked and played around her. "That trial isn't until next March, Noah. I wish it could be tomorrow," she said, leaning down and picking up the small blanket after he'd put the other items into his saddlebags. She shook it out and then rolled it up. Noah took it and walked over to Ghost. She followed, unwrapping the halter lead from around the saddle horn on Lulu, bringing her head up so she could bridle the Appaloosa. She felt like shouting out her joy. She'd never been as happy as she was right now.

Noah moved his hand across Dair's damp back, leaning over her after making love with her earlier. He eased her thick, dark hair aside, kissing her nape, hearing the happy sounds in her throat as he lightly lavished that erotic spot. Drawing her long, firm body against his, he rested his head on her right shoulder, holding her close, his heart ballooning with a fierce love for her. Dair was exhausted from three orgasms, her arms beneath the pillow, her face partially covered with black strands of her mussed hair. Lunar rays flooded around the open drapes. Dair loved the moon's milky radiance that flowed silently across the bed where they lay.

Kissing the damp, warm flesh along her shoulder, he rasped, "I love you, Dair." He heard a soft sound escape her lips and smiled a little, knowing she was exhausted. So was he, but his heart was wild with joy because today's talk at lunch had been crucial to both of them. Noah realized it more than Dair, but that was all right. There would be times in the future when she'd be far ahead of him regarding something going on in their lives. He inhaled her sweet scent, her hair cool and silky against his cheek. Ranging his hand slowly down her rib cage to her flared hip and curved, strong thigh, he absorbed every particle of her into himself.

Noah had not entertained falling in love anytime soon. It just hadn't been a part of his life focus. Shay had given him a chance to earn his keep, gave him a roof over his head, three square meals a day, and let him know he was important to her, to the ranch and to the world. As he smoothed his hand over Dair's butt and hip, he smiled to himself. From the moment he'd seen her, he realized later that he'd fallen hard and completely for her. It was as if he'd finally met his lifelong mate. And he hadn't realized just how lonely he was until Dair walked into his life.

Easing from across her, he sat up and pulled open a drawer on the bed stand. He felt Dair stir and sit up.

"What are you doing?" she asked, pushing her hair away from her shoulder.

Chuckling, he said, "There's that curious cougar coming out in you." He shut the drawer and sat up, resting against the headboard. Dair was sitting there looking like a sated cat after a big dinner. "Come here?" He held out his hand to her.

Scooting next to him, his arm going around her shoulders, Dair sighed and rested her cheek against his shoulder. "What do you have in your hand, Mabry?"

A rumble moved through his chest. "Hold out your palm."

Dair did.

"This is something I've been planning on giving to you when the time was right," he rasped, kissing her brow. "Open it."

Dair took the small white satin box. It wasn't a ring box, so it had her mystified as she eased it open. Inside was a dainty heart with small, pink, faceted stones around it, suspended on a unique, link-like necklace. "This is beautiful," she breathed, easing it out of the box, holding it up between them. Even in the moonlight, Dair could see the pink stones sparkling as the heart slowly moved between her fingers.

Noah took the necklace and patiently unclasped it. "Well, I wanted something to tell you that I love you. And seeing that we're wranglers and we're working with thousand-pound horses or doing all kinds of hard, physical work, I didn't want to buy you a ring." He slid a look toward Dair, watching her lustrous eyes widening. "I wanted to give this to you as a token of my love, Dair. You can wear it around your neck and it will remain beneath your shirt. The necklace is white gold and the links are super strong without being heavy to wear." He ran his fingers along the delicate chain. "That way, it won't get broken as you do your normal, everyday athletic work." He smiled a little, watching her expression turn tender, seeing the love shining in her eyes for him. "Do you like it?"

"It's beautiful, Noah . . ." She choked up, staring at it. "What are the gemstones in it?"

"I talked with Maud about it. She knows a lot about gems in general. She said I should get something that had a good hardness to it. But pink diamonds were a little out of my price range. She suggested faceted pink tourmaline, instead. They come from a mine in Brazil. Do you like them?"

"Oh," she breathed, smiling at him, "I love them!" And she threw her arms around him, hugging him fiercely, choking out, "And I love you, too! Thank you . . ."

Noah laughed out of relief at her sudden, unexpected spontaneity. More and more, the past two months, Dair was allowing herself to be more vulnerable, and Noah loved her for becoming that way around him, allowing her innocent side to finally express itself. "I guess you do like it," he said, and turned, meeting and molding her soft, warm lips beneath his mouth. Her kiss was that of an eager, overwhelmed puppy, and they broke the kiss, both of them laughing, brows resting against one another.

"I never expected this," Dair confessed as she sat up, facing him a bit more. "Will you put it on me, Noah?" She lifted her hair and leaned forward so he could do it.

There was such pleasure in doing exactly that. The heart hung below her collarbones and above her breasts. Maud had counseled him to go with a longer length because that way it would be more protected. He fiddled with the clasp, which was strong and large, so that it could be easily opened and closed. "There," he murmured, satisfied as she released that black hair of hers. "It looks beautiful on you, Dair." He saw how happy she was, picking up the heart in her fingers, turning it, watching the moonlight dance through the facets. There was no question she liked it. And he loved her.

"This had to be expensive, Noah," she said, frowning, holding his gaze.

"I saved for it," he murmured. Money was always tight, and Dair knew it. Not wanting her to worry, he said,

"The jeweler in Wind River gave me a good deal, so wipe that frown off your brow, okay? He knows Maud and Steve Whitcomb, and I'd told him they'd sent me to him. It was nice of him to give me a price I could afford, because I had no idea the cost involved when I drove over to see him."

"Well," Dair whispered, smiling into his eyes, "I will cherish this forever, Noah. This means everything to me."

He moved his hand down her arm. "And I cherish you, Dair." His voice lowered with feeling. "I can't conceive of my life without you in it. You're a part of me. You own my heart."

She pressed his hand against her chest, tears springing to her eyes. "You spoil me rotten, Noah." Sniffing, she said, "And I've never felt before like I do about you. I wake up happy and I go to bed happy. I don't think it gets any better than that."

"No, it doesn't." He smoothed some strands across her shoulder, seeing how golden her eyes had become. Over time, he discovered that when she was happy, a lot of the brown color receded. When she was worried or upset, the gold receded. He was glad to make that discovery about Dair, because it served him well to know when to ask her if something was bothering her. They had a long way to go with one another, because Dair still struggled so often trying to be open with him.

Over time, Noah knew she would break that unhealthy pattern from childhood. She was learning how to honestly live in a relationship with a man for the first time in her life. It was a challenge, but it was one he more than felt up to surmounting with Dair. And because they truly did love one another, Noah knew she would eventually break that imprisoning pattern and they could soar together. He quietly dreamed of the day when he would ask Dair to marry him. That was in the future, but he was a long-range planner by nature. Even in his dreams, he saw them married, with three beautiful children. Dair had never had a loving family, but she would have one with him.

And her name: Dair, was a variation of the word "dare." It was a good name for her because, through all the challenges that life had thrown her, she had dared to meet and overcome them. Noah saw a future filled with happiness for both of them. He would keep all of this to himself, but some day, when the time was right, he'd share it with Dair. And she would dare to take the next step with him: marriage. He knew she had that kind of quiet courage to do just that, because she'd overcome and triumphed over so much already.

Please turn the page for an exciting sneak peek at

LONE RIDER

by Lindsay McKenna

Coming to your favorite bookstores and e-tailers
in April 2018!

Lone Rider is a Harper's romance.
Get to know all the wonderful people of
Wind River Valley!

April 2

Tara Dalton wiped her hands down the sides of her jeans before pushing the doors open to Charlie Becker's Hay and Feed. She stomped her feet on a well-used bristly mat in front of the doors to knock off the slush from the last snow storm. The wind was sharp, the temperature below freezing, the sky turgid with spots of blue here and there. Her blond hair lifted from her shoulders, flying around her face. Making a frustrated sound, she pulled the hair away with her gloved hands.

Would Charlie have a possible job for her? Something she loved to do that would keep her in Wind River, her hometown in Wyoming? Her heart felt like it was contracting in her chest, anxiety threading through her as she pushed open the wooden doors.

She saw Charlie sitting behind his long, L-shaped counter, slowly counting his receipts at the end of the day. He closed at five p.m. Tara didn't want people from Wind River to see her coming into the store. Everyone knew her. And she didn't want what she had to ask of Charlie overheard by anyone else, if possible.

The cold wind pushed her into the warm, empty feed store.

"Oh, hi, Tara," Charlie greeted, smiling. "I heard through the grapevine that you'd come home. How are you doing?"

Forcing a weak smile, Tara said, "Hi, Charlie. Yes, I got home a week ago."

She loved the smell of fresh new leather, row upon row of saddles sitting in one part of the large farming and ranching store. The wooden floor squeaked and creaked beneath her hiking boots as she moved toward Charlie. The redbrick building was a hundred years old and had been owned by generations of Beckers.

Charlie was tall, almost six foot, skinny as a proverbial rail, with thick, silver hair. Face lined with sixty-five years of living, he had always been a kind person to everyone. He was one of the fixtures of this small town. Tara had always loved coming here with her father to get hay and grain for her horse when she was in her teens. That was a while ago, and happy times for the most part. Charlie always had colorful candy suckers in a bowl beneath the counter near the cash register. Every kid, from four to ninety, was offered one when they left the store. Plus, Pixie, his wife, a baker of great repute, was always dropping something off to the rear of the store where the coffee table was set up. Lots of people wandered in to have a cupcake or a cookie.

"Finished with the Marine Corps and done being a combat camerawoman?" he teased, setting aside his stack of receipts, giving her an intense, scrutinizing look.

"Yes, I'm done. I didn't re-up," she admitted.

"Have a seat. Coffee? I'd like to catch up with you, Tara. Usually, when your dad came in here, he'd tell me you were in Afghanistan, but since you worked in black ops, he didn't have much he could share."

Tara pulled out one of the two wooden stools that sat in front of the counter. "I'd love some coffee, Charlie. Thanks." She pulled her gloves off and removed her bright blue knit cap from her hair. Quickly, she smoothed the flyaway strands with her fingers and opened up her blue nylon down jacket. "I need some help," she admitted, watching him pour coffee from the coffee station.

"Figured as much." He handed her a cup. "Cream? Sugar?"

"No, black. Thanks." Taking a sip, Tara watched him sit down.

"So? How can I help you?"

"Well," Tara said in a low tone, "I need a job, Charlie."

His gray brows rose. "But, I thought you'd work at your parents' hardware store in town?"

Mouth flexing, Tara avoided his sharpened and concerned gaze. "No, that's not going to happen." She saw the sudden sadness come to his eyes. "I mean . . . I've got PTSD from my years in combat, Charlie. When I came home, all I did was keep my mom and dad up at night, waking them with my flashbacks and nightmares. They want to help me, but right now? I need to try and get my act together alone."

"But you're still seeing them? Keeping in touch?"

"Oh, for sure, Charlie. We love one another. There's no issues there. They know I'm looking for another job. Something, I hope, that will get me outside, give me a lot of physical work. I-I have a lot of constant anxiety. I'm super restless and the only thing that helps tone it down is a lot of exercise, moving around and staying active. Then, I feel better." She gave him a pleading look. "I don't want this getting around to anyone here in Wind River."

He reached forward, patting her hand near her cup. "No, I'm not the town gossip, Tara. Our conversations are strictly between us. So? You're looking for an outdoor kind of job?"

"Well," she said, "I was hoping you would have an opening?" She held her breath, praying that Charlie did need help.

"No, I'm sorry. I have two men I employ and they've been here for years, Tara. And I don't need another employee." He brightened. "But, I may have a lead on a ranch that is looking for a wrangler. And I know you grew up with horses at your ranch. Even though your dad started out as an attorney here in the county, and then became a judge, your family always had a small ranch to run. You're used to mending fences, changing out bad posts, riding and doing all the things that a wrangler does."

Nodding, Tara tried to not look devastated by the news. Her heart was set on working with Charlie. "That's all true. My dad has two wranglers who run the ranch while he works as a judge."

"Couldn't you stay at their ranch and work?"

Shaking her head, she said, "Dad's wranglers have been there since I left at eighteen for the Marine Corps, Charlie. He can't fire one of them and replace him with me. That wouldn't be right. Everyone needs a job. And both those wranglers have families and mouths to feed. No, I wouldn't do that to them."

Giving her a twinkling look, Charlie said, "And your parents raised you to be a kind, good person, Tara. There's hope here. You know Shaylene Crawford? You two grew up here in Wind River and went through school together."

"Sure, I know Shay. Why?"

"Well, you've been gone a long time, and maybe your parents haven't filled you in yet on all the goings-on here in Wind River Valley. Shay's dad, Ray, suffered a stroke at forty-nine. Shay had to get a hardship discharge from the Marine Corps and come home and take over the reins of the Bar C. Ray, as I'm sure you know, is an alcoholic. That, in part, caused his stroke at such a young age. It left him incapacitated and in a nursing home afterward. Shay is the legal owner of the ranch, which was passed down to her from her mother's side of the family."

"Oh, wow," Tara said, stunned. "I didn't know any of this!"

"Yes," Charlie said, grave. "Shay's been home nearly two years now, and she's taken a broken-down ranch and is slowly pushing it from the red to the black column, financially speaking. It was hemorrhaging red while you were gone. Ray lost all his grass pasture leases, which had given him a lot of working capital, due to his alcoholism. Shay walked into a disaster and was two months away from foreclosure at the hands of Marston, the local banker, when she took over for her father." Disgust filled Charlie's voice. "Marston was waiting for the Bar C to fail. He had a multimillion-dollar condo deal with a New York realtor who was gonna turn the ranch into nothing but condo rentals for tourists."

"Oh, no," Tara whispered, her eyes widening. "That's horrible!"

"Really. We like our tight little community. No one wants to see condos and realtors like that around. But we're a valley that is sliding into economic oblivion, too. So, from Marston's perspective, condos would bring fresh money into our valley, which we desperately need."

"I know everyone drives through here to get to the

Grand Tetons National Park near Jackson Hole," Tara grumbled. "Or drives fifty miles further north to reach Yellowstone National Park."

"Well, Maud and Steve Whitcomb, who own the largest ranch in the valley, are working to turn our economy around here in Lincoln County. They've got a lot of new projects underway to invite the tourists driving through to stay and play with us on their way to the Tetons or Yellowstone."

"That's good to hear, because we need jobs."

"Yep, and I'd like to make a call to Shay on your behalf. She's married now, you know? An hombre who's an ex-Marine Corps captain by the name of Reese Lockhart. Stand-up man. Together, they're working hard to bring the Bar C back to life and out of foreclosure jeopardy, but it's a fragile state they're in right now. Shay, when she took over running the Bar C, wanted to hire military vets like herself. She saw firsthand how vets with PTSD and wounds, either seen or unseen, need a hand up. All her wranglers, some men, some women, are vets. And they're all doing well."

"That's wonderful," Tara said softly. "I lost touch with Shay when we both went into the Corps. It's nice to hear she's married and happy."

"Well, her father is a huge burr under everyone's saddle over there at the Bar C. He's trying right now to get well enough to legally take her to court to sue her and get the ranch back." Charlie frowned. "It's a real bad scene, and something that's ongoing. They just put out a restraining order on Ray to stop him from ever stepping foot back on the Bar C again."

Tara knew a lot about the workings of the law because of her father. "That's pretty serious, a restraining order."

"Yes." Charlie sighed. "It is. Terrible, ongoing stress

for Shay, especially. That's her father. But that aside? I know they're looking for another military vet to fill an opening at the Bar C. Might you be interested in working over there?"

"Sure," she said quickly, hope suddenly filling her. "What do I need to do?"

"Well, Shay and Reese are coming into town tomorrow at noon to pick up a big order of grain for their horses." He grabbed his cell phone. "How about I call them? Tell them you're back and looking for work? Maybe they can have lunch with you at Kassie's Café in town. It would be a good way for you to catch up with Shay, talk with her and see if you're a fit for her ranch. Does that sound good?"

Did it ever! Tara tried to tamp down her wild hope that this sounded like the perfect job for her. "It sure does, Charlie."

"Just give me your phone number, okay? I'll call Shay right after I get done putting my receipts in my accounting book here. I'll let you know if it's a go or not. You're staying with your parents at their ranch, yes?"

"Yes," she said, barely able to tamp down her need for a job. "That would be wonderful, Charlie. Thanks so much." She reached out, gripping his long, work-worn hand, squeezing it warmly. "I appreciate your help."

Giving her a wink, he said, "The people of our valley are tighter than thieves and we always try to support one another where and when we can. I'll give you a call in about an hour. I'm pretty sure Shay will be more than open to having you apply for that wrangler job at the Bar C, so keep your hopes up."

* * *

Tara hugged Shay hello when they met just inside the door of Kassie's Café. The place was filling up fast with lunch patrons.

"It is so good to see you again!" Shay said, grinning happily. "I'd just heard from Garret, who works for us, that you were back in town. I've been meaning to call you, but I didn't have your cell number." She gave her a silly look, releasing her hands. "And stupid me? I should have thought and called your mom and dad at your ranch. I knew you'd be there."

Tara smiled and gestured to a table in the back near the kitchen. "Don't worry, you are just a little busy out at the Bar C, from what Charlie said. Come on, let's sit down in a quieter corner."

Shay pulled off her bright red wool jacket, tucking it over her arm. Everyone knew everyone else. Kassie's was the town's center, not the city hall or sheriff's office down the street. She said hello to many of the patrons as she passed near their tables, smiling.

Tara tried to appear relaxed, but she was anything but. Sitting with her back to the wall, she pulled out the other chair that was nearest the wall. Assuming that Shay had probably seen combat, neither of them would be comfortable with their backs to doors or windows. Shay gave her a grateful look.

"You know we're the same when it comes to being exposed," Shay said, gesturing toward the plate-glass window. She sat down after hanging her jacket over the back of her chair.

Placing her down jacket aside, Tara said, "Are we that obvious?" and she laughed a little.

A waitress came over, offering glasses of water and the menu. Tara thanked her.

Shay gripped her hand. "It's so good to see you again, Tara! We lost touch with one another. I gave a yelp of happiness when Garret came in to fix our Sunday afternoon dinner for everyone. He's ex–black ops, so he's always got his ear to the ground when he comes into town. I couldn't believe it! You were in for twenty in the Corps. What happened?"

"Let's just say, because I'm black ops, too, that I couldn't take it anymore." Tara wasn't going to lie to Shay, because if she got the job, she wanted to earn it fair and square. Setting the menu down, she said, "Where's your husband? Reese? Charlie said you are happily married."

"Oh, I am! Reese is just wonderful! He's over at Charlie's helping to load our truck with about fifteen hundred pounds of grain sacks. He and Harper, one of our wranglers, will then drive it back to our ranch."

"But, I thought he'd be here for lunch," Tara said. Or did Shay make decisions such as hiring? She saw the gleam in Shay's eyes.

"I packed Reese and Harper a lunch this morning. They'll have beef sandwiches and chips on the way home. No worries."

"I was hoping to meet him."

Shay pulled out her cell phone and showed a photo of Reese to her. "He's a real hero and I know you'll like him, too."

"What a good-looking guy," Tara said sincerely, handing her back the cell phone. "Remember when we were in the fifth grade? We'd go ride horses together at your or my parents' ranch? And we'd wonder what kind of boy we'd fall in love with?"

"Oh, that! Gosh, yes, I remember those fun times. But we were so young, so starry-eyed, and we didn't really know anything of the world yet. I remember I wanted a Sir Galahad kind of guy and you wanted a King Arthur kind of guy."

Giggling, Tara nodded. "We were way too young and knew *nothing*!"

The waitress came over, they gave her their orders, and she poured coffee into the thick white ceramic mugs. Picking up the menus, she hurriedly left, the place packed with lunchtime patrons.

"You said you have PTSD?" Shay asked quietly.

"Yes. When I became a combat camerawoman in that MOS for the Corps, the captain of my unit asked if I wanted to work with special ops. I jumped at it because the Corps is still trying to figure out if women can handle combat or not."

Snorting, Shay said, "Yeah, I know. They are so Neanderthal. Women handle it as well as any male Marine does. No more, no less."

"Yes, that's true. But I couldn't re-up after going black ops. I'd had enough, emotionally speaking."

"I can't even begin to imagine what you saw through your lens," Shay said, giving her an understanding look. "But let's talk about something good."

"I'm more than ready for that."

"Good, because when Charlie called me, I was at my wit's end. I'd lain awake half the night, anxious and needing another wrangler. Reese told me not to worry, that the right person would show up." Her eyes sparkled with humor. "And then Charlie calls us, telling us about you."

A little relief trickled through Tara. She gripped the coffee mug a little less tensely between her hands. "He said he thought you needed another wrangler."

"Yes. And you need to know that we have two women vet wranglers we've already hired: Kira and Dair. They're doing a great job. They're just as good as any of the male vets we hired. Let me tell you what we need, Tara, and then you can tell me if it's a fit or not."

"Sure," she murmured, more hope in her tone.

"We need a full-time wrangler. But we also need our vets to have an outside source of income. For example, Kira is a translator and earns money doing Arabic-English translations. Garret is a heavy equipment operator. Harper is presently going to college to become a paramedic, and he takes care of our horse barn. We rent horses, stable other people's horses, as well as selling to the public. He's especially good with our broodmares. Reese has a CPA, and when he first came here, he was the ranch's accountant. He also took on jobs as an accountant for several businesses in Wind River. Noah was training horses before he went into the Army. Now, he has a huge training program, and Dair Wilson is his assistant trainer. Everyone contributes through their other skill sets, putting twenty percent of their earnings into the ranch kitty, because we don't charge rent to stay at one of our homes on the property. We pay the utilities, you don't. All you supply is food to eat."

"Gosh, that's an easy one for me, Shay. I'm a professional photographer. I already have a website, and I sell my pictures to stock-photos sites. I make a reasonable amount monthly, and I could contribute in that way."

"Sounds good to me. We'll pay you an hourly wage as a wrangler. We put ten percent of that into a savings account for you, so that you can build equity and someday be able to afford your own home, if you want. Or buy something you really want."

"I like that idea. But I saved a lot of my monthly paycheck when I was in the Corps. I have my money in the stock market because of my dad and his broker." She crossed her fingers. "So long as we don't have another crash like we did in 2008, I am pretty well off, economically speaking."

"Which is unlike everyone else who works here, including me and this ranch."

"I'm using some of it to build the website, plus it costs money to drive to places to take photos. I have to buy new equipment now that the Marine Corps no longer lets me use theirs." She smiled.

"We have four homes on the ranch, two bedrooms each. Two are filled with wranglers. The fourth one was where my father lived until we permanently kicked him off the property. We're in a legal battle with him because he wants to return to that house, saying it's his. I can't assign it to you under the circumstances." She opened her hands. "The only other house available is where Harper Sutton lives. He was a Navy combat medic."

"It wouldn't bother me to bunk in with him. We'll each have our own bedroom, I'm assuming. And we'll probably share cooking and cleaning duties?"

"Yes, everyone else does in the home they're assigned to. You two can work that out between you."

"What's Harper like?" Tara saw Shay's face melt.

"He's such a sweetie. He's quiet, gentle, and gets your trust immediately. He was the perfect medic."

"Especially if you're bleeding out," Tara said, smiling faintly. "Yes, I was with mostly Delta 18 combat medics on the team I was with. They are the best of the best."

"They sure are. But you know the medic type?"

"All quiet, like shadows, speak softly, get your trust even if you're hysterical because you're bleeding and you know you're dying."

"Yep. That's why Harper is so good with our broodmares and foals. He's got that special touch of a healer."

"He sounds nice."

"He is. But don't let his type B appearance fool you," Shay warned. "He was in black ops, too. He was always in the thick of danger and you know you have to be a type A to do that kind of job."

"No disagreement. The medics I ran with appeared to be type B's, but in reality? They were ball-busting type A's beneath that veneer. I suspect Harper is too?"

"Well," Shay said, as the waitress brought them their food, "I've yet to see his type A side, but I know it's there."

"If he's working with broodmares and foals, he can't show that aggressive side of himself. Horses wouldn't work with him."

"Right you are," Shay agreed. "Here's our lunch."

Midway through the lunch, Shay turned serious once more. "Why aren't you working on your parents' ranch?"

In as few words as she could, Tara told her what she'd told Charlie the day before. She saw Shay's features reflect understanding when she finished her explanation.

"But are Scott and Joanna okay with it?"

Shrugging, Tara offered, "Well, not at first, but the more I explained, the more they accepted my situation. It's not like I'm leaving town or anything. My mom was happy when I told her that every once in a while, I'd drop in for dinner and see how they are, plus we'll always have cell phones and emails. And I'll continue to help fill in for her at the hardware store when she needs me. They're okay with it now, but you know that civilians who haven't been in combat just can't understand where we're at. It's not their fault. They don't know."

"There are days, even now, when I feel like I'm going to tear out of my skin," Shay admitted between bites of her ham and Swiss cheese sandwich. "Fortunately, Reese does understand."

"Because he's a vet who's seen combat, too. So he knows. My parents are trying to understand, but they can only go so far to grasp it."

"You have to have lived it," Shay agreed grimly, "to know."

"Yeah." Tara sighed.

"You probably don't want to discuss this, but I have to bring it up. I remember when Cree Elson kidnapped you when you were sixteen."

Rolling her eyes, Tara said, "Believe me, I've never forgotten it. Do you know, Shay, I still get nightmares about that time? About him?" She shivered.

"I heard he's out of prison now and working in Jackson Hole doing odd jobs."

Stomach knotting, Tara said, "My dad told me when I got home."

"That's fifty miles away from us. But you know his mother, Roberta, still lives here, same place, same dumpy trailer on that fifty-acre ranch on the slope of the Salt River mountains. His three brothers and his sister—Hiram is 31 now, Kaen is 29, Cree is 27, and Elisha is 24—they all live at the southern end of the valley and they're all up to their hocks in the drug trade. While you were in the service, did your parents keep you updated on the Elson clan?"

Shaking her head, Tara muttered, "I told them I didn't want to know anything about that dysfunctional family. I wanted to leave them behind me once I left."

"Not much has changed except that your dad sent Hiram and Kaen to prison for three years apiece for drug smuggling," Shay told her. "They just got out a couple years ago, came home, and now they're back doing the same thing. Sheriff Sarah Carson has someone undercover trying to get into their ring to prove they're at it again. That toxic family has never changed.

They're just as violent and unpredictable as Cree is. Only he never got into selling drugs as much as using them."

Her hope withered. "One of the reasons I joined the Marine Corps was to get strong and be able to fight off a man like Elson. I never want to be a wimpy, helpless, freaked-out girl again like I was back at that age."

"I know. I joined the Corps to escape my alcoholic father. You ran away to leave that kidnapping behind you."

"We both ran," Tara admitted, frowning.

"Did you know Cree was out?"

"Only after I got home. I'm still in my PTSD soup, and he wasn't on my radar at all. I'm having enough trouble trying to appear normal to everyone."

"Well, if it makes you feel any better, Sarah Carson is the Lincoln County sheriff and she's already got the ear of the Tetons Sheriff's Department commander, Tom Franks, up in Jackson Hole. She knows Cree is dangerous and now that he's been released and served his time for kidnapping you, she keeps an eye on him. Sarah ran for sheriff after her dad retired from that position and the folks of the county happily voted her in. That should make you feel a little better."

"My dad has nothing but praise for Sarah. He says she's a fine law enforcement officer. Her dad, David, taught her how to be a law enforcement deputy from the time she was young. She grew up wanting to be one. I was glad to hear she's the sheriff. Everyone likes her. Well, I'll amend that: People who obey the law, love her. The people who don't, most likely hate her as much as they hated her father. And yes, it makes me feel better. When I got home, one of my worries was knowing Cree was around. That he could come and get even with me."

"Yes, I remember he told you in court that he was

going to get even with you for putting him in prison. It's an Elson twisted gene: They always seek revenge and want to get even with the person or group who threw them in prison. Nothing's changed. They're still that way."

"That was another reason why I didn't want to stay at home, put my parents at risk, in case Cree was crazy enough to try it again."

Shay nodded. "Well, don't worry about the Bar C. We're all vets. We're all licensed to carry a concealed weapon. And we all know how to use a pistol if it came down to that."

"What about Harper?"

"Oh, he knows how to use a weapon, no worries. We all carry weapons, but they are in locked safes in each home when we're not out on ranch property. There's a target range we use on the ranch, and we all go out every two weeks and practice."

"I would die if Cree came onto your property and hurt anyone," Tara admitted. "I've been wondering, since I found out Cree was nearby, if I should just leave Wyoming, disappear and go to another state a long ways from here. There's also the worry about his three brothers. I worry about what they might do to us, to my family, if Cree is still obsessed with me or wants revenge."

Reaching out, Shay gripped her hand. "Don't you dare run again, Tara. Your family has been here for generations. No one has the right to chase you off with threats. And I feel confident that if he did try, he'd get a very unpleasant welcome if he set foot on the Bar C. And the other three brothers are always around, but so far, we haven't had any run-ins with them. No, I want you to stay and I would love to have you as one of our wranglers. Please say you'll take the job?"

Also available from Lindsay McKenna:
Her new military series,
Delos!

Nowhere to Hide
Tangled Pursuit
Forged in Fire
Broken Dreams
Secret Dream
Unbound Pursuit
Secrets
Snowflake's Gift
Never Enough
Dream of Me
Trapped
Taking a Chance
The Hidden Heart

Available from your favorite e-tailer.

For more information,
please go to
www.LindsayMcKenna.com.